Praise for Catherine Bybee

Wife by Wednesday

"A fun and sizzling romance, great characters that trade verbal spars like fist punches, and the dream of your own royal wedding!"

—Sizzling Hot Book Reviews, 5 Stars

"A good holiday, fireside or bedtime story."

—Manic Reviews, 4½ Stars

"A great story that I hope is the start of a new series."

—The Romance Studio, 4½ Hearts

Married by Monday

"If I hadn't already added Ms. Catherine Bybee to my list of favorite authors, after reading this book I would have been compelled to. This is a book *nobody* should miss, because the magic it contains is awesome."

—Booked Up Reviews, 5 Stars

"Ms. Bybee writes authentic situations and expresses the good and the bad in such an equal way . . . Keeps the reader on the edge of her seat."

—Reading Between the Wines, 5 Stars

"*Married by Monday* was a refreshing read and one I couldn't possibly put down."

—The Romance Studio, 4½ Hearts

Fiancé by Friday

"Bybee knows exactly how to keep readers happy . . . A thrilling pursuit and enough passion to stuff in your back pocket to last for the next few lifetimes . . . The hero and heroine come to life with each flip of the page and will linger long after readers cross the finish line."

—*RT Book Reviews*, 4½ Stars, Top Pick (Hot)

"A tale full of danger and sexual tension . . . the intriguing characters add emotional depth, ensuring readers will race to the perfectly fitting finish."

—*Publishers Weekly*

"Suspense, survival, and chemistry mix in this scintillating read."

—*Booklist*

"Hot romance, a mystery assassin, British royalty, and an alpha Marine . . . this story has it all!"

—*Harlequin Junkie*

Single by Saturday

"Captures readers' hearts and keeps them glued to the pages until the fascinating finish . . . romance lovers will feel the sparks fly . . . almost instantaneously."

—*RT Book Reviews*, 4½ Stars, Top Pick

"[A] wonderfully exciting plot, lots of desire, and some sassy attitude thrown in for good measure!"

—*Harlequin Junkie*

Taken by Tuesday

"[Bybee] knows exactly how to get bookworms sucked into the perfect storyline; then she casts her spell upon them so they don't escape until they reach the 'Holy Cow!' ending."

—*RT Book Reviews*, 4½ Stars, Top Pick

Seduced by Sunday

"You simply can't miss [this novel]. It contains everything a romance reader loves—clever dialogue, three-dimensional characters, and just the right amount of steam to go with that heartwarming love story."

—Brenda Novak, *New York Times* bestselling author

"Bybee hits the mark . . . providing readers with a smart, sophisticated romance between a spirited heroine and a prim hero . . . Passionate and intelligent characters [are] at the heart of this entertaining read."

—*Publishers Weekly*

Treasured by Thursday

"The Weekday Brides never disappoint and this final installment is by far Bybee's best work to date."

—*RT Book Reviews*, 4½ Stars, Top Pick

"An exquisitely written and complex story brimming with pride, passion, and pulse-pounding danger . . . Readers will gladly make time to savor this winning finale to a wonderful series."

—*Publishers Weekly*, Starred Review

"Bybee concludes her popular Weekday Brides series in a gratifying way with a passionate, troubled couple who may find a happy future if they can just survive and then learn to trust each other. A compelling and entertaining mix of sexy, complicated romance and menacing suspense."

—*Kirkus Reviews*

Not Quite Dating

"It's refreshing to read about a man who isn't afraid to fall in love . . . [Jack and Jessie] fit together as a couple and as a family."

—*RT Book Reviews*, 3 Stars (Hot)

"*Not Quite Dating* offers a sweet and satisfying Cinderella fantasy that will keep you smiling long after you've finished reading."

—Kathy Altman, *USA Today*, *Happy Ever After* blog

"The perfect rags to riches romance . . . The dialogue is inventive and witty, the characters are well drawn out. The storyline is superb and really shines . . . I highly recommend this standout romance! Catherine Bybee is an automatic buy for me."

—*Harlequin Junkie*, 4½ Hearts

Not Quite Enough

"Bybee's gift for creating unforgettable romances cannot be ignored. The third book in the Not Quite series will sweep readers away to a paradise, and they will be intrigued by the thrilling story that accompanies their literary vacation."

—*RT Book Reviews*, 4½ Stars, Top Pick

Not Quite Forever

"Full of classic Bybee humor, steamy romance, and enough plot twists and turns to keep readers entertained all the way to the very last page."

—Tracy Brogan, bestselling author of the Bell Harbor series

"Magnetic . . . The love scenes are sizzling and the multi-dimensional characters make this a page-turner. Readers will look for earlier installments and eagerly anticipate new ones."

—*Publishers Weekly*

Not Quite Perfect

"This novel flows extremely well and readers will find themselves consuming the witty dialogue and strong imagery in one sitting."

—*RT Book Reviews*

"Don't let the title fool you. *Not Quite Perfect* [is] actually the perfect story to sweep you away and take you on a pleasant adventure. So sit back, relax, maybe pour a glass of wine, and let Catherine Bybee entertain you with Glen and Mary's playful East Coast–West Coast romance. You won't regret it for a moment."

—*Harlequin Junkie*, 4½ Stars

Not Quite Crazy

"This fast-paced story features credible characters whose appealing relationship is built upon friendship, mutual respect, and sizzling chemistry."

—*Publishers Weekly*

"The plot is filled with twists and turns, but instead of feeling like a never-ending roller coaster, the story maintains a quiet flow. The slow buildup of a romance allows readers to get to know the main characters as individuals and makes the romantic element more organic."

—*RT Book Reviews*

Doing It Over

"The romance between fiercely independent Melanie and charming Wyatt heats up even as outsiders threaten to derail their newfound happiness. This novel will hook readers with its warm, inviting characters and the promise for similar future installments."

—*Publishers Weekly*

"This brand-new trilogy, Most Likely To, based on yearbook superlatives, kicks off with a novel that will encourage you to root for the incredibly likable Melanie. Her friends are hilarious and readers will swoon over Wyatt, who is charming and strong. Even Melanie's daughter, Hope, is a hoot! This romance is jam-packed with animated characters, and Bybee displays her creative writing talent wonderfully."

—*RT Book Reviews*, 4 Stars

"With a dialogue full of energy and depth, and a twisting storyline that captured my attention, I would say that *Doing It Over* was a great way to start off a new series. (And look at that gorgeous book cover!) I can't wait to visit River Bend again and see who else gets to find their HEA."

—*Harlequin Junkie*, 4½ Stars

Staying For Good

"Bybee's skillfully crafted second Most Likely To contemporary (after *Doing It Over*) brings together former sweethearts who have not forgotten each other in the eleven years since high school. A cast of multidimensional characters brings the story to life and promises enticing future installments."

—*Publishers Weekly*

"Romance fans will be sure to cheer on former high school sweethearts Zoe and Luke right away in *Staying For Good.* Just wait until you see what passion, laughter, reconciliations, and mischief (can you say Vegas?) awaits readers this time around. Highly recommended."

—*Harlequin Junkie*, 4½ Stars

Making It Right

"Intense suspense heightens the scorching romance at the heart of Bybee's outstanding third Most Likely To contemporary (after *Staying For Good*). Sizzling sensual scenes are coupled with scary suspense in this winning novel."

—*Publishers Weekly*, Starred Review

Fool Me Once

"A marvelous portrait of friendship among women who have been bonded by fire."

—*Library Journal*, Best of the Year 2017

"Bybee still delivers a story that her die-hard readers will enjoy."

—*Publishers Weekly*

Half Empty

"Wade and Trina here in *Half Empty* just might be one of my favorite couples Catherine Bybee has gifted us fans with so far. Captivating, engaging, lively and dreamy, I simply could not get enough of this book."

—*Harlequin Junkie*, 5 Stars

"Part rock star romance, part romantic thriller, I really enjoyed this book."

—*Romance Reader*

Faking Forever

"A charming contemporary with surprising depth . . . Bybee perfectly portrays a woman trying to hold out for Mr. Right despite the pressures of time. A pitch-perfect plot and a cast of sympathetic and lovable supporting characters make this book one to add to the keeper shelf."

—*Publishers Weekly*

"Catherine Bybee can do no wrong as far as I'm concerned . . . Passionate, sultry, and filled with genuine emotions that ran the gamut, *Faking Forever* was a journey of self-discovery and of a love that was truly meant to be. Highly recommended."

—*Harlequin Junkie*

Say It Again

"Steamy, fast-paced, and consistently surprising, with a large cast of feisty supporting characters, this suspenseful roller-coaster ride will keep both series fans and new readers on the edge of their seats."

—*Publishers Weekly*

My Way to You

"A fascinating novel that aptly balances disastrous circumstances."

—*Kirkus Reviews*

"*My Way to You* is an unforgettable book fueled by Catherine Bybee's own life, along with the dynamic cast she created that will capture your heart."

—*Harlequin Junkie*

Home to Me

"Bybee skillfully avoids both melodrama and melancholy by grounding her characters in genuine emotion . . . This is Bybee in top form."

—*Publishers Weekly,* Starred Review

Everything Changes

"This sweet, sexy book is just the escapism many people are looking for right now."

—*Kirkus Reviews*

Be Your Everything

OTHER TITLES BY CATHERINE BYBEE

Contemporary Romance

Weekday Brides Series

Wife by Wednesday
Married by Monday
Fiancé by Friday
Single by Saturday
Taken by Tuesday
Seduced by Sunday
Treasured by Thursday

Not Quite Series

Not Quite Dating
Not Quite Mine
Not Quite Enough
Not Quite Forever
Not Quite Perfect
Not Quite Crazy

Most Likely To Series

Doing It Over
Staying For Good
Making It Right

First Wives Series

Fool Me Once

Half Empty

Chasing Shadows

Faking Forever

Say It Again

Creek Canyon Series

My Way to You

Home to Me

Everything Changes

Richter Series

Changing the Rules

A Thin Disguise

An Unexpected Distraction

The D'Angelos Series

When It Falls Apart

Paranormal Romance

MacCoinnich Time Travels

Binding Vows

Silent Vows

Redeeming Vows
Highland Shifter
Highland Protector

The Ritter Werewolves Series

Before the Moon Rises
Embracing the Wolf

Novellas

Soul Mate
Possessive

Erotica

Kilt Worthy
Kilt-A-Licious

Be Your Everything

CATHERINE BYBEE

This is a work of fiction. Names, characters, organizations, places, events, and incidents are either products of the author's imagination or are used fictitiously. Otherwise, any resemblance to actual persons, living or dead, is purely coincidental.

Published by Montlake, Seattle

www.apub.com

ISBN-13: 9781542034883 (paperback)
ISBN-13: 9781542034890 (digital)

Cover design by Caroline Teagle Johnson
Cover images: © Yasuhiro Nakajima / EyeEm, © sarayut Thaneerat, © Carlina Teteris, © maple's photographs / Getty Images; © Nina Buesing / plainpicture

Printed in the United States of America

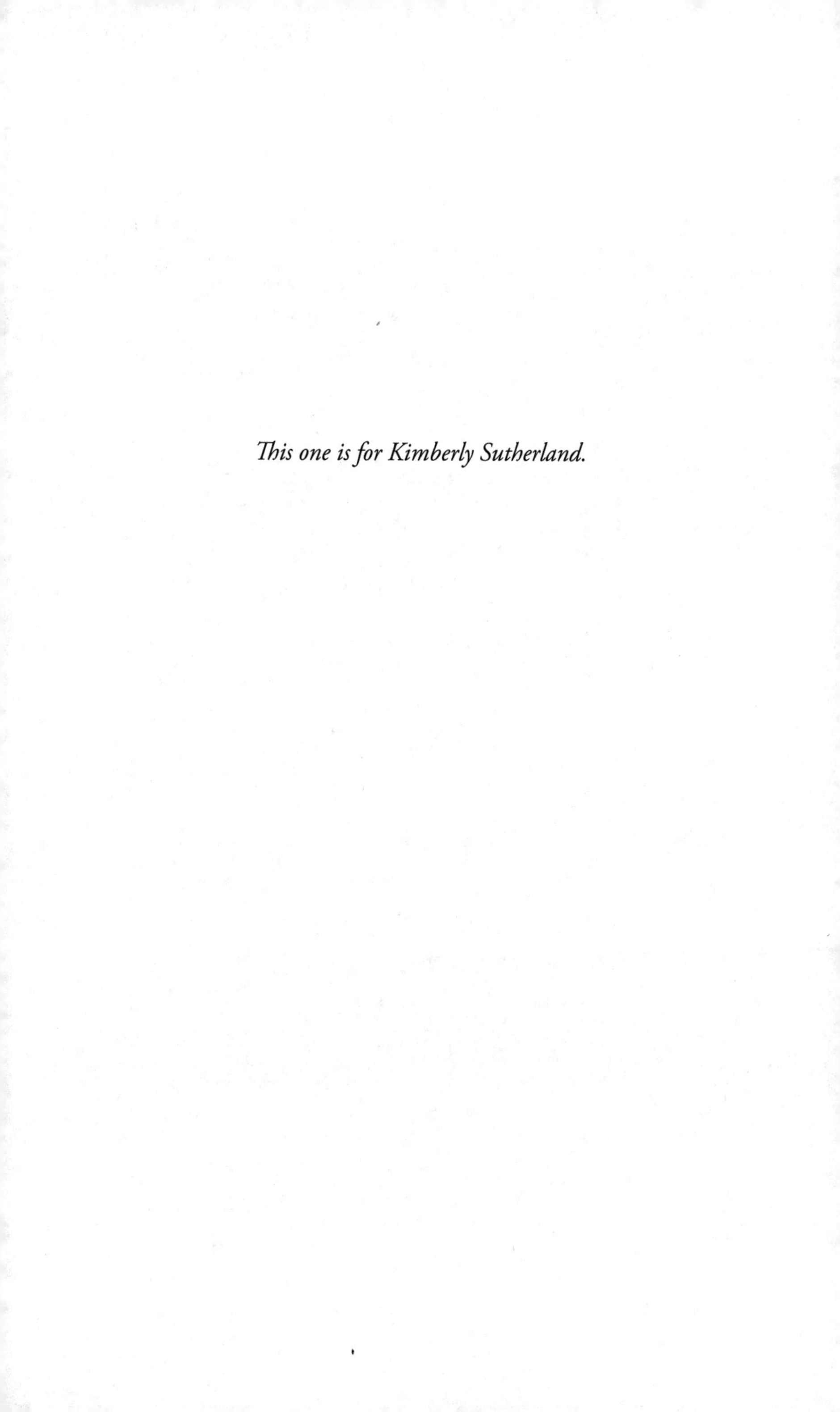

This one is for Kimberly Sutherland.

CHAPTER ONE

"Go! I don't want to see any of you back here until Monday."

Chloe stood outside the back door of their home in Little Italy, surrounded by both her brothers and her soon-to-be sister-in-law. They all had small suitcases at their feet as the Uber van pulled up to take them to the airport.

Mari, their mother, had a hand on Francesca's shoulder as they saw the bachelor/bachelorette party off.

"Mama, are you absolutely certain?" Luca, the husband-to-be, her over-worried oldest brother, couldn't stop the concern that crossed his face any more than he could the love he had in his eyes for the woman at his side.

He and Brooke were the real deal. Head over heels, all in . . . completely lost in each other.

Chloe couldn't be happier for them.

They needed Vegas. Boy, did they need two nights in Vegas.

"I ran this restaurant before you were born and after with all three of you jumping around. I have it, Luca. Go. Just don't get married. Wait until you come back for that."

"What about babies?" Gio, the middle child and smart-ass in the family, asked.

"That you can do," Mari said with a wink.

Brooke knelt to Franny's level and gave the eight-year-old a kiss. "Listen to your *nonna*."

There were hugs and waves as Giovanni, or Gio, as he was most often called, shoved all the suitcases into the back of the van.

Gio took the front seat as the rest of them climbed into the back.

"I can't believe you talked me into this," Luca said to his brother. "Busiest time of the year."

"It is not. That's in the summer," Chloe argued. It was early December. The family restaurant was fully staffed and ran like a well-oiled machine, even with three of their employees out at the same time. "It's going to be nothing but family and friends, celebrations and ceremonies from here on out. This is the last chance for you two to let loose until it's all over," Chloe reminded them.

"You mean until after Christmas," Gio said.

"Right." They weren't taking their honeymoon until after Christmas. After they returned shortly after the New Year, it would be Chloe's turn to get out of town. Her long-awaited tickets to Bali were burning a hole in her pocket.

This was her last opportunity to cut loose until it was all over as well.

Chloe watched their family home disappear from sight. It was a four-story building with the family restaurant on the bottom floor. The second story was the family home where they'd all grown up, and the third floor was where Luca, Brooke, and Franny now lived. On the very top was what used to be guest quarters but now was the bachelor pad that Gio took over. Secretly, Chloe was hoping Gio would find Mrs. Right and move on himself so she could occupy the upstairs apartment as her own space. She loved her mother, but living with her was getting old. As an Italian, Chloe wasn't going anywhere until she was married, that's just the way things were done in her culture.

"Franny is going to be okay, right?" Brooke asked Luca as they settled in for the short ride to the airport.

Chloe rolled her eyes.

Francesca, Luca's daughter from his first unfortunate marriage, was probably already elbow-deep in gelato and milking Mari for all the attention and goodies a *nonna* could give her.

"She'll be fine," Luca said, kissing Brooke's forehead.

The ride to the airport took less than ten minutes, a perk when you lived in San Diego and everything was close.

Getting through security and waiting in the airport would take longer than the actual flight to Vegas, but it beat a long drive across the California desert any day of the week.

"Thanks again for inviting Mayson to join you guys," Brooke said to Gio and Luca.

"He's a friend of yours. He's a friend of ours."

"Besides, we need even numbers," Chloe added. As she said that, she saw Salena waving them over to her side before they entered the TSA line.

"Vegas, baby!" Salena all but yelled for everyone to hear.

Chloe tossed her arms around one of her dearest friends for a hug. They'd known each other before braces and periods. As ride-or-die friends went, Salena was someone Chloe could count on to be there.

"We could have picked you up," Gio said.

Salena, who lived in Little Italy as well, shrugged. "It's okay. I had Joey take me."

"Joey? Do I know Joey?"

She waved a hand. "Flavor of the month."

Gio narrowed his eyes. "You're worse than me."

"No one is worse than you," Chloe and Salena said in unison.

The three of them fell in line behind Luca and Brooke, who were arm in arm and whispering in each other's ears.

"They do know that we have separate rooms, right?" Chloe asked her brother.

"Yes."

"I don't think that's going to matter," Salena added.

"Divide and conquer. Once everyone arrives, we have dinner, pull straws on who is in charge for the night, and go to our separate clubs." Gio lowered his voice. "We'll give them tomorrow afternoon to knock it out."

Chloe laughed. "We may never see them again."

Salena nudged Chloe's shoulder as they inched their way up the line. "Is Dante flying directly from Italy?"

Just hearing Dante's name had Chloe standing taller. Gio's best friend, and the one boy that had always been "off-limits" for oh so many reasons, was the cause of many sleepless nights.

The man only grew more beautiful with every year that passed.

And he knew it.

And the women knew it.

All the women!

"He's already in the States. New York. He'll be in Vegas about an hour after we land."

Salena nudged Chloe again with a grin once Gio turned around.

Stop. Chloe mouthed the word without sound.

Once they moved through security, they found their gate for the forty-five-minute wait to board the plane.

Salena and Chloe sat with their luggage while the others went to find coffee and waters for the flight.

"Are you prepared for a weekend with Dante?" Salena asked once they were alone.

Chloe shook her head. "Listen to you. It was a high school crush."

Salena laughed. "I'm pretty sure it started in fifth grade and never ended."

"He's lived in Italy for the better part of five years."

"And every time he comes home, you forget how to speak."

"That's not true."

Salena glared.

Okay, it was a little bit true. "I did better last year." It helped that she stayed out of his orbit that time around and he was only home for a month.

"How long is he staying this time?"

"No idea," Chloe said. Her cell phone pinged, grabbing her attention.

She opened her messages inside a dating app she'd been on for a few weeks.

"Who is that?" Salena asked, looking over her shoulder.

Chloe glanced at the image on her screen, the one she'd swiped right on. He was thirty, no kids. Worked somewhere in La Jolla. "His name is Eric. We've been texting for a few days."

"He's cute."

"I thought so."

His text came through, asking what she was doing. She started typing.

"Have you met him yet?"

Chloe shook her head, finished her message about the bachelorette party in Vegas.

"Are you going to?"

Three dots indicated he was typing.

"Only if he asks." As progressive as she was, she found it necessary for the man to take the first steps.

"You know . . . if you stack the deck with dates while Dante is in town, it might be easier to be around the man."

Salena had a point.

Chloe's phone buzzed.

How about meeting for coffee when you get back? Tuesday enough time for you to sleep off the hangover?

Chloe showed the message to Salena.

"Say yes."

Her friend was right. Chloe needed all the help she could get when Dante was home. If her attention was elsewhere, maybe he'd lose his appeal.

She agreed to coffee with Eric on Tuesday and told him she'd get in touch when she returned.

"I have a feeling this weekend is going to be one for the record books," Salena said as she watched more passengers arrive for their flight.

"It's likely the one and only time I'll be in Vegas with both my brothers."

"Considering how they've helicoptered you since your papa passed, that's not a bad thing."

She'd been seventeen when their father died. Luca became the head of the family while he had a one-year-old and a failing marriage. What a crappy couple of years that had been. Now, things were looking up. For all of them.

She'd finished her college classes and earned her business degree. But instead of working for someone else, she wanted to do something on her own. She blamed her family for that. Yes, she waited tables at their restaurant and, honestly, liked the job. But what she loved more than anything was teaching yoga. Her trip to Bali was supposed to happen the year the world shut down, and it was only now that time and world health were giving her the opportunity to go. She knew, somehow, that the trip was going to guide her to whatever her path was going to be. Maybe she'd start her own studio or her own online channel. Brooke had a boatload of knowledge about marketing and was on board with helping her start-up. Financially, Chloe had banked nearly everything she'd earned from the first day she started working and was more ready than most to begin her future.

Her father, in all his wisdom, had taken out a life insurance policy that their mother had divided and put into investment plans for each of them. Luca immediately put everything in his name to his daughter. Giovanni was itching to invest in a vineyard. The resident sommelier wanted to spend time in Tuscany as much as she wanted to spend time in Bali. So, while they did pull shifts waiting tables, doing what had to be done to make the family restaurant run, it wasn't their lifelong ambition. Well, Luca was the chef, and that was his life's choice . . . and she and Gio were thankful for it.

"They promised not to act like big brothers in Vegas," Chloe said.

"Yeah well, they aren't going to the same strip clubs we are."

The image of her brothers holding a hand over her eyes made her smile. "Thank God for that."

~

The Venetian Las Vegas was one of those hotels where every room was a suite. Put two of them together and everyone had their own bed with plenty of room.

Two rooms for the women, two for the men.

On different floors. Although Luca wanted to argue that arrangement when they were checking in.

"Oh, no. If we're out late, you are not going to pull that older-brother card on us," Chloe started in at the reception desk.

"How late do you plan on being out?" Luca asked.

"The real question is how early in the morning will we be walking in," Salena informed him.

Gio patted his brother's shoulder. "They're all talk."

Brooke waved her phone in the air. "Carmen just landed."

Carmen was Brooke's best friend, and maid of honor, from Seattle.

"When is Mayson arriving?"

"Not until three."

"We should be good and buzzed by then," Gio pointed out.

The receptionist handed them their keys and they headed toward the elevators.

They passed the casino, and even at eleven in the morning, the people sitting in front of the slot machines appeared as if they'd been there all night.

"Do you gamble?" Salena asked Brooke.

"I don't mind giving it a whirl, but I don't see dropping a paycheck chasing odds that are stacked against me."

Gio nudged his brother. "I take it you didn't tell her about your little addiction."

Brooke snapped her attention toward the two of them.

Luca pushed him away, punched his shoulder. "He's kidding."

Chloe laughed, pressed their floor when they got on the elevators.

Gio pressed two floors higher.

Luca moaned.

"Dinner at six thirty, downstairs at the steakhouse," Gio reminded Chloe.

"We'll be there."

A few moments later Chloe grabbed Brooke's free hand and dragged her out of the small space. "C'mon. Time to have fun."

They laughed as they made their way to their rooms. Inside, they opened the first of the two doors. The welcome package they'd requested—complete with chilled champagne and a basket of fruit—was in the living room portion of one of the suites.

The door between the rooms was open, and in the other room was another bottle of bubbly and a basket of cheese, crackers, and cold meats.

"Salena and I will take this room and you and Carmen take the other," Chloe suggested.

"Sounds good to me," Brooke said as she pushed through and rolled her suitcase to the second room.

"This is beautiful."

The view from the massive windows looking out over the Vegas Strip was something to marvel at.

"I wonder if it's even brighter at night with Christmas lights?" Salena asked.

"Probably." Chloe turned to her friend and handed her the champagne. "Let's get this party started."

"Wow. This bathroom is huge!" Brooke's voice called from the other room.

"Glad you like it."

The sound of the cork popping out of the bottle filled the room. "Hey yo!"

Brooke bounced back in, a smile on her face. "I heard that."

Salena poured the wine and Chloe made a toast. "To your last single weekend in Vegas."

"You make it sound like we're going out to find random men to hook up with."

"Not hook up with, but look up at," Chloe countered.

"Thunder Down Under." Salena lifted her glass high.

"Magic Mike," Chloe said.

They drank the bubbly wine and turned to the food. "Pacing, food, and hydration," Brooke added.

That was the plan.

Only by the time Carmen arrived, less than an hour later, the first bottle of champagne was gone and the second was open.

~

Dante Mancuso walked through the Vegas casino with a suitcase the size of a smart car. To anyone looking, they'd think he was moving in and not there for a weekend bachelor party.

He bypassed the reception desk, already aware of the room he was in, and headed toward the elevators.

Music met his ears as he approached the door to the suite. He smiled, anticipating his friends.

It had been too long.

He knocked twice. "Open up, you drunk bastards."

The door swung open wide. "About time." Gio stood there, a huge smile on his face.

God, it was great to see him.

They hugged, long and hard. Strong pats on the back. "You look good."

"You do, too."

He stepped in the room, dragging his suitcase behind.

"Jesus, Dante, what do you have in there, a body?"

"Shut up. I was going to ship it from Italy, but this made more sense."

Gio stood back, lifted his voice to the room beyond the door connecting the two. "Luca, Dante is here."

Luca walked around the corner, put the glass in his hand down. "Damn, look at you."

They hugged. "Doing it again, huh?"

"Doing it right this time," Luca told him.

"I can't wait to meet her."

Luca stepped back. "We can go to their room now and I can introduce you."

Gio stepped between the two of them. "Oh, no. We just got here. They're probably tits-up in fingernail polish and facial lotion. Dinner is soon enough." Gio patted Luca's chest.

"Who is with the bachelorettes?" Dante asked, fishing for information.

"Chloe and Salena. And Carmen, who you haven't met," Gio told him.

The guest list brought an instant smile to his face. "Salena, huh? That's gonna spell trouble."

"Brooke and Carmen will keep the younger girls in check," Luca told him.

Dante patted his friend on the back. "If that's what you want to believe, old man." Luca earned the title by being the oldest and cemented it by being Mr. Responsibility from the day his father passed. "You look happy."

Luca sighed. "I love her."

"And Franny?"

"She loves her, too."

Dante shrugged out of his coat. "What are we drinking?"

"Whiskey."

"Perfect."

CHAPTER TWO

Chloe wore red. The hip-hugging dress stopped midthigh and enhanced her barely-there breasts. All the yoga she practiced shaped her butt in ways many women dreamed of, but it also slimmed down the rest of her to where it took dresses like this one to make her feel like a woman.

The three-inch heels helped, too.

Her olive skin and Italian heritage gave her a glow, even in the dead of winter. Her thick black hair had some bounce that the stylist put a little extra in at the salon.

Even though the night was about Brooke . . . she wasn't trying to be noticed. Not by anyone but Luca.

Chloe, on the other hand, wanted at least one person to see her.

See her and ruin his vision for anyone else who walked his way.

Hadn't she been trying to do that her entire life?

Yeah, she wanted Dante to notice, and then she wanted to smile and turn away.

Because no matter how she flipped that coin over in her hand, it would never happen. Nor should it. He was a player that rivaled Gio, in two countries. He treated her as if she were his sister, even down to teasing her when she went through puberty. As if two brothers weren't enough to deal with at the time, Dante was right there with them, asking if they made training bras for seventeen-year-olds.

Yeah. She would show up tonight in her *eat-your-heart-out* dress, followed by tomorrow night's *little black dress* to end all little black dresses, and make sure Dante saw her as the woman she was and not the lanky little girl he grew up beside.

Salena rounded the corner of the bathroom and blew out a whistle. "Whoa. You do realize it's forty degrees outside, right?"

Chloe smiled at her friend through the reflection in the mirror. "I have a long coat." She swiped her lips with the perfect shade of red lipstick. "Besides, the restaurant and the clubs won't be cold."

"You two ready in there?" Carmen called from the other room.

"Yup." Chloe dropped her lipstick in her bag and flipped her hair over her shoulder.

Brooke and Carmen both wore pantsuits. Brooke wore white and Carmen was in black.

"You can tell who is married in this group," Salena offered.

Carmen waved a thumb between Brooke and herself. "We're both from the Pacific Northwest. We understand cold weather. You two obviously don't."

Salena's dress had a little more to it, the material thicker, with long sleeves, but it was still short and revealing.

"Our ride is picking us up at eight to take us to the club. We're sticking with vodka tonight, right?" Chloe asked.

"Yes," Brooke said.

"I'm in charge of Brooke," Carmen pointed out. She'd already agreed to be the somewhat-sober responsible player for the bride.

"Oh, shoot, I almost forgot something." Carmen ran back into their room and returned a few seconds later. In her hands was a white and silver sash she handed to Brooke. *Bride To Be* was spelled out in sparkly thread.

"Really?" Brooke said with a grin.

"It's perfect."

"You have to wear it."

Carmen helped her put it on, then took a picture.

Chloe slipped into her trench coat and checked her purse for the essentials. Tip money, lipstick . . . a condom. Although she had no intention of using that, a girl was always prepared.

They wormed their way through the growing Saturday crowds. The casino floor was already hopping. Some people were dressed up, but most were dressed down in jeans and sweatshirts, even in a high-end hotel like theirs.

The four of them turned heads as they walked by. Each step brought Chloe's chin a little higher as she ignored the thump of her heart against her ribs as they moved into the massive indoor piazza that held the restaurants of the Venetian.

They approached the hostess of the steakhouse and Chloe took charge. "We're with the D'Angelo party."

"This way."

Chloe turned to Brooke and let her take the lead.

She heard his laugh before she saw his face.

The round table was in the back of the still-empty room.

The four men were spaced out, every other chair. Dante's back was to them as they walked in.

Luca saw them first and he all but jumped to his feet. *"Cara!"*

His expression stopped whatever they were talking about as they all turned to watch them walk in.

Her brothers cleaned up well. Dress jackets and nice shirts . . . slacks. Mayson wore a thick turtleneck and had a jacket on the back of his chair.

Then there was Dante . . .

He'd been living in Italy and it showed. My God, he looked like he'd stepped from the pages of a men's fashion magazine out of Milan. A tailored jacket that could have been leather, but she'd have to touch it to be sure. Not the shiny kind, but soft. The dark gray, nearly black shirt under that opened enough to show the sex appeal of his throat. Broad shoulders that filled it all out. Strong jaw with a perfectly manicured short beard and mustache that was more than a five-o'clock shadow but nothing close to the lumberjack variety. And if that wasn't enough, the man's eyes locked you down with one look. Some would say they were brown, but Chloe always thought they resembled golden honey. When he caught you in his stare it was impossible to breathe.

All this Chloe took in as she watched Brooke and Luca hug and kiss as if they hadn't seen each other in days instead of hours.

At Chloe's side, she heard Carmen greeting Gio and Mayson.

"You must be Dante," Brooke said once she broke away from Luca's embrace.

"Your bride is beautiful," he said to Luca in Italian.

"*Grazie*," Brooke said, smiling.

"You speak Italian."

"No, but I understood that."

Instead of a handshake, which wouldn't have gone over in this group, Dante hugged Brooke as if he knew her, and kissed both of her cheeks. "Congratulations."

"Thank you," Brooke said. She turned to her left. "My friend Carmen."

Dante's gaze zeroed in on Carmen, he reached for her hand and kissed the back of it. "You have stunning friends."

"Oh, my . . ." If Carmen could pant, she'd be in a puddle of saliva.

"She's married, Dante," Chloe found herself saying with an eye roll.

That's when he turned his honey-colored eyes her way. The sly smile on his face drifted to a thin line and he narrowed his gaze. "The voice I recognize, but the face . . ."

"Give it up, Dante," Gio warned.

Salena moved in. "What about me? Do I ring a bell?"

He kissed both her cheeks. "My God, Salena. How is it you're not married yet?"

"Yeah, yeah."

"I mean it."

She moved to the other side of the table and placed her purse in an empty seat.

Disappointment seeped in, as it did when Dante was around. He flirted with everyone but her. Chloe smiled anyway and started to shrug out of her coat.

"Let me."

Dante's low voice was at her ear.

She pulled one arm out, then the other . . . and felt his hands on her arms as he moved the coat away.

Then she heard it . . . a little something that said he noticed. It was a cross between a woosh and *Jesus* . . . or maybe a knock of air out of the lungs.

"Damn, Chloe, could you spare a little material for that dress?" Gio chided.

"If I wanted your opinion, I would have asked for it." She looked over her shoulder, smiled at Dante. "Thank you."

"It's good to see you," he said, finally.

"Welcome home."

He took a deep breath, as if it cost him to do so, before pulling out a chair for her to sit.

Then, as if he couldn't get away fast enough, he moved around the table and sat between Brooke and Carmen.

Salena caught her eyes and offered a soft, sad nod.

All her effort and Chloe didn't get so much as a hug.

"Where are you ladies headed after dinner?" The question sounded innocent enough coming from Dante's lips.

Carmen didn't fall for it. "Oh no you don't. Joint general location for a bachelorette party doesn't mean a full itinerary is going to be handed out with maps and descriptions. We do the girl stuff. You do the boy stuff, and we'll meet in the middle."

Dante looked across the table at Luca. "I tried."

The worry that fell on Luca's face had most of the table laughing.

"Brooke is pretty resourceful, Luca. I wouldn't worry," Mayson assured him.

"Thank you, Mayson," Brooke said.

Chloe found her brother's concern endearing, even if he wasn't going to get any information out of them.

She glanced up to find Dante's gaze on her, and for a moment, he stared directly into her eyes. Air pulled into her lungs in tiny bits as she lifted the corners of her mouth ever so slightly.

". . . don't you think, Dante?"

The sound of his name pulled her out of the moment as his eyes shifted to the person who had just said his name. "I'm sorry?" He hadn't caught what was said either.

And that made the smile on Chloe's lips even wider.

"Are we drinking wine?" Gio asked.

A chorus of "Vodka" came from the female voices at the table as the waiter arrived with the menus.

~

He couldn't sit next to her or he'd touch her.

He didn't dare hug her in front of the others or someone would notice how impossible it would be for him to let go.

But damn it to hell, she had to be wearing that impossible dress, and even sitting across the table, as far as he could, Dante couldn't keep his eyes from falling on Chloe every few minutes. Seconds.

This was bad.

His body was waving him on, suggesting it wasn't an awful thought in the least, but his head reminded him why he kept his distance all these years.

A very long distance.

She had one drink with dinner, and not enough dinner.

"Saving the real drinking for the club," she'd said.

Dante knew Chloe could drink. He'd seen her in action a couple of times. But that was at home, where she didn't have far to go to fall asleep in her own bed and her family was there to take care of her.

This was Vegas.

He was sure there would be plenty of men willing to "take care of her," especially dressed as she was.

Hot.

Sexy. So damn . . .

He shook his head as if he could scratch off the word *sexy* that he'd attached to Chloe's name and face at the same time.

As their dinner wrapped up, his nerves sputtered.

"Well, ladies," Carmen started. "The driver will be here in twenty minutes. We might want to make our way to the front of the hotel soon."

"I'm going to freshen up first," Chloe said, pushing her chair back.

Salena followed suit. "I'll go with you."

Dante chimed in. "I could use the little boys' room." He didn't, really . . . he just wanted an opportunity to talk with Chloe.

The three of them made their way around the tables in the restaurant to the location of the restrooms.

"Are you sticking around past the holidays this time, or leaving again right after?" Salena asked him.

Dante glanced at Chloe as he answered. "I'm going to be here for a while."

"Really? What changed?" Chloe asked.

"That's a long conversation. Maybe when we're home."

They located the hallway to the restrooms, and Dante found his hand reaching out to touch Chloe's shoulder. "Can I talk to you for a second?" he asked.

She hesitated; surprise crossed her brow.

"I'll meet you in there," Salena said as she proceeded without her.

He guided her away from the hall, and they stepped into a quieter corner. "Chloe." Saying her name made him smile.

"Yes?"

He took a deep breath. "Before you say no, hear me out."

She closed her lips and stayed silent.

"Let me put you on Friend Finder."

Her breath came out in a rush, along with a roll of her eyes.

He squeezed his fingers, the ones still holding on to her. "You can put me on, too. No one else has to know. This way, you ladies can go, have a great time—"

"We're going to do that anyway."

"Right, but it's Vegas." As Dante's gaze moved down her frame, his breath caught. "And you're dressed to fucking kill."

When his eyes reached hers again, there was a smile on her face and heat in her cheeks. There was a look, the one he'd caught more than once from her that was not at all sisterly or family-friendly. A look he always ignored for both their sakes.

"Luca won't let himself have a good time if he's worried." Which was probably true, but he tossed that in there knowing that Chloe would want her oldest sibling to let loose.

He could see her thinking.

Dante softened his hold on her and lowered his fingers to her elbow. "Please. It's just information. You'll know where we are all night, can see if we're headed your way."

Her eyes shot to his.

"Which we won't do! Emergencies only. I promise," he quickly added.

"If I see you coming and it's not an emergency, I'll stop sharing and we'll move to another location. There is more than one male strip club in this town."

Yes!

He blew out a breath.

Chloe turned toward the hallway and Dante pressed his hand to the small of her back.

A man walked past and looked her over. Dante found his other hand coming up to her hip with possessiveness, as if he had the right to touch her.

The man walked by and looked the other way.

Only at the door to the restroom did Dante let her go. "Meet you out here."

Then, because using the bathroom had been an excuse, he simply stood to the side and waited.

As he did, he lifted his hands in front of him and saw a slight shake.

"Whoa."

Chloe and Salena emerged a few minutes later.

Fresh lipstick and mischievous smiles.

"After you."

He took up position behind them.

When did Chloe's ass become so . . .

Dante swallowed hard and forced his eyes somewhere else.

Back at the table, everyone was standing and gathering their things.

Luca held Brooke, was speaking only to her.

Dante took the opportunity to help Chloe with her coat.

She turned to him, a little closer than he liked with this many people around.

"I sent a friend request. You have ten minutes to do the same or I delete it."

"Grazie, bella." He winked, stepped back.

"Have fun," Mayson called out.

"Not too much fun," Luca countered.

The women filed away from the table.

Salena turned toward them. "What happens in Vegas . . . Ciao!"

Luca moaned.

Dante reached for his phone, found Chloe's invitation to follow, and accepted. Then followed through with letting her keep tabs on him.

"Okay, gentlemen. It's time to get my brother less than stable on his feet to forget about what his bride is doing tonight."

"I don't know."

Gio pulled Luca away from the table.

Dante and Mayson followed.

"Would you feel better if I told you I have tabs on the ladies?" Dante asked.

Luca turned on a dime. "You what?"

Dante raised a hand. "Chloe and I have a pact. GPS. Emergency only."

Gio patted Dante on the back. "I knew I could count on you."

Luca nodded a few times, continued to walk out of the restaurant. "All right, then. Yeah." He clapped his hands together. "Where should we start?"

CHAPTER THREE

Salena slid back to their table, her hair tossed in so many directions you'd think she'd just had sex in the hallway. "Oh my God, that was awesome."

"Do we want to know?" Carmen asked.

They'd moved from the Magic Mike show to a smaller club where they had a much more intimate show at their fingertips.

"Rafael's lap dance was better than my last naked experience with my ex." She pulled a business card from her bra and waved it in the air. "I might have to call him later."

Chloe snapped the paper from her hands. "And start the antibiotics in the morning? Please. If he has these in his pocket, he gives them out every night."

Salena rolled her eyes as if it didn't matter.

As dizzy from the alcohol as Chloe was, she wasn't about to let her friend hook up with a male stripper from Vegas.

The owner of the Bellagio, maybe, a stripper, no.

She found herself pondering the logic of her thoughts and finding them deeply flawed.

The music was loud, and the tables filled with women in groups like theirs who were just as tipsy, heading toward hammered.

The men working the club circulated from table to table, smiling, sitting on a lap, offering a dance or a little corner private lap dance like Salena had just dropped forty bucks on.

Chloe reached for her drink, found it nearly empty, and frowned. "Who is sucking down my cocktails?"

Brooke started laughing.

Chloe waved a finger her way and reached for the bottle they'd ordered for the table and mixed herself another one. When she did, she filled Brooke's glass.

Carmen quickly picked it up and put half of the contents into hers. "We can't have anyone tossing their cookies on the way back to the hotel."

Salena grabbed a bottle of water and lifted it in the air. "Water! Water is key."

Rafael walked by, winked at Salena. "Bridal party?"

As if the "Bride" sash wasn't a big enough clue.

"Yes, and I do believe our bride hasn't had a lap dance yet," Carmen pointed out as she reached for her purse.

Brooke immediately lost her grin. "Oh . . . I don't think—"

"That's right, don't think. Bachelorette party is a permission slip."

Brooke lifted a hand and covered her eyes. But she was smiling.

Rafael turned his south-of-the-border charm over to Brooke's side of the table. "Shall we head to the back?"

"No!" she all but shouted.

Not that the man needed a dark corner to make a woman blush.

For ten minutes he slid his body all around her, his tight butt and sculpted torso up close and very personal without being completely inappropriate.

Salena signaled for Chloe to lean closer.

"It was better in the back."

She had questions, ones that would have to wait.

Once he was done, he whispered something in Brooke's ear, took the money Carmen was paying him, winked, and walked away.

"Oh my God." Brooke was blushing.

Salena lifted her drink in the air. "We need to do this more often."

A woman at the other table leaned over and clicked her glass to Salena's. "I agree."

The announcer walked onstage, and the lights dimmed. "Okay, ladies, I hope you're ready to save a horse and ride the cowboys tonight."

A cheer went up.

Chloe grabbed her purse and yelled over the noise. "I have to use the bathroom."

Without any takers to join her, she found her wobbly feet and moved her way slowly through the crowd of women to the back of the club.

The one thing that was nice about the strip club environment was that the men in the joint were employees and not patrons trying to pick the ladies up. As far as going to the bathroom alone in Vegas went, this was probably the safest place to do so.

Once there, she found a stall and took the opportunity to look at her phone. The first thing she checked was Dante's location.

The men had moved to a second strip club, this one a little closer, but not close enough to suggest they were following them.

She considered sending a text asking if the ladies offered private lap dances, too. But thought that might push the fire a bit much if her brother managed to squeeze information out of Dante.

Instead, she put her phone back in her purse to save the battery.

Back in the club, the rodeo was in full swing and the women were tossing money on the stage as every item of clothing came off the cowboys.

Carmen pointed to the darkest cowboy in the club with a smile. "Now that's who I want a lap dance from."

For the next hour Carmen slipped to the back of the room, came back smiling. Salena found Rafael again and returned with what looked like a hickey on her neck.

And the bottle of vodka was getting dangerously low.

Salena, slurring her words, pointed a finger Chloe's way. "You're not leaving tonight without a lap dance."

It wasn't that she was opposed, it was that none of the men in the room really did it for her.

"You pick or I will," her friend threatened.

Her head was swimming, and since she knew her friend would spend her money on Rafael, and that felt like a bad idea, Chloe pointed to a guy who had put on a kilt.

Who didn't like a kilt?

"Outlander action. Okay!" Brooke laughed.

She was hammered.

Carmen had been feeding the bride water constantly, but Brooke was not feeling any pain.

None of them were, if Chloe was honest with herself.

Salena waved Outlander over and pointed a thumb toward the back.

"Oh, no."

"Oh, yes. You're not the one getting married next week," Salena told her.

Left without an excuse, Chloe took the man's hand and let him lead her to the back of the house, where other women were getting private lap dances. While it all looked innocent enough, there were a couple of women who weren't giggling.

Which was exactly what Chloe started to do once the man suggested she sit down on a bench.

"Is this your first time?" he all but yelled in her ear. The music was so loud it was hard to hear your own voice.

"Isn't it obvious?"

He smiled before he started.

Chloe wasn't sure what to do, so she left her hands on the bench and looked to her right, where she saw the woman touching the dancer's leg.

Yeah, she didn't want to do that.

He was a good-looking man. Mr. Scotsman. A little older than some of the dancers in the club.

Leaning closer, his lips to her ear. "You're nervous."

"I'm drunk," she said without humility. "This was my friend's idea."

The lady across from them lifted her leg, and someone from the club walked behind the dancer and tapped his shoulder.

Even with Chloe's double vision, she noticed the dancer push the patron's leg down.

"Oh, boy."

"Try and relax," Mr. Scotsman suggested.

Chloe took a deep breath, liked the look of the man's bare chest in front of her. He had to work out a lot.

"You spend a lot of time at the gym," she said.

He kept dancing, his body close and brushing against hers.

"Yeah. An hour and a half every day."

"Every day?"

"Sundays off."

Chloe smiled. Each time they spoke it was practically yelling.

"You must be exhausted."

He leaned his head to the side, shimmied close, and put his ear to her lips.

"You must be exhausted. Workouts and then this all night long."

He moved his body over hers like a snake yet didn't touch. "I sleep in."

I bet you do.

When their time was up, Chloe all but jumped from the bench, a little more sober than when she'd sat down and yet ready for another drink.

The stage show was over and some of the crowd was thinning.

Back at the table, Carmen was chatting with a woman from another party, Salena had made her way to the bar and was talking with dancers, and Brooke was MIA.

"Where is the main attraction?" she asked Carmen.

"Bathroom."

As the party went on around them and a few more minutes passed, Chloe decided to check on the bride.

She found her standing in the bathroom, leaning against the wall. Her face was a little whiter than normal.

"Hey. Are you okay?"

Deadpan, she said, "I'm wasted."

Chloe started to chuckle until they were both laughing.

"Are you feeling sick?"

Brooke squeezed her eyes shut, shook her head, then nodded.

"We should call it a night."

"But you're having such a good time."

"This night is about you." Chloe wasn't about to tell her that visions of Dante did a good job of dimming the lights of every man on the stage that night. Even Mr. Bodybuilding Scotsman who tried hard but didn't work for her.

"You sure?" Brooke looked as if she was letting her down.

"I'm fine."

They walked back into the noise of the club, another act onstage.

Carmen sat up the second she saw them. "Everything okay?"

"She's not feeling great."

"It's late. You wanna go?"

Brooke made a pouting face.

"It's okay."

"Where's Salena?" Chloe asked.

Carmen pointed a thumb to the back. "Rafael lap dance number four."

"Okay, no. I'm fine." Brooke made a grand gesture of sitting down.

"Please. I don't want to tell you how much of that bottle you drank tonight. Let's get you back to the hotel." Carmen picked up her purse and reached for Brooke's.

"I'll go get Salena."

"No! She's having a great time," Brooke insisted.

Carmen stood. "Fine. We'll divide and conquer. I'll get you back to the hotel, you two follow behind," she said to Chloe.

"We can do that."

Carmen held on to Brooke as they made their way out of the club, Brooke's step less than steady.

Which, as Chloe saw it, was as it should be on the woman's last weekend of singlehood.

Left at the table alone, Chloe turned her attention to the show and cheered along with the other women in the club as the performers did their thing.

She finished her drink, considered another, then looked at her watch.

Where the hell was Salena?

Right about the time when Chloe was about to search for her, Salena stumbled back.

"Don't judge me."

Chloe couldn't help but laugh.

"Carmen took Brooke back to the hotel."

Salena's eyes focused. "Is everything okay?"

"Too much vodka."

"She was putting them back tonight."

"You're one to talk."

Salena shook her head. "I'm more drunk on the scene. Rafael wants to take me back to his place."

Chloe lost her smile.

"He's a nice guy. In med school."

"What?"

"Okay, nursing school, or whatever. This job pays the rent."

"Salena . . ."

"I know, I know. I'll use a condom. Jesus. It's Vegas. I'm young."

Chloe didn't like it.

"Give me your phone."

Without a choice, Chloe reached in her purse and gave Salena her phone.

"This is his number, his address. You have me on Friend Finder."

"Salena . . ."

"This is a bad idea. You're drunk."

"I started drinking water two hours ago while you bitches were sucking down the vodka. I'm fine. You know where he works. It's a weekend in Vegas."

Chloe looked up, saw Rafael smiling from across the room.

She waved him over at the same time she dialed his number.

He reached in his back pocket, put his phone to his ear. "I'm Italian. I have friends."

He smiled, lifted the phone in the air, then disconnected the call.

Salena leaned over, kissed Chloe's cheek.

Then, in Italian, she told her not to wait up.

With that, Salena grabbed her purse and coat and walked to the back of the club.

The buzz of the music rang in her ears as she looked around the room.

One of the waiters walked up to the table. "Can we get anything else for your party tonight?"

Chloe smiled, shook her head.

He handed her the bill.

That's when her stomach reached her throat.

"Excuse me. Did Carmen put a credit card on the table?"

The waiter looked at her. "Let me check."

Panic started to push into her veins.

She'd left only her ID and some cash in her purse. Everything else was at the hotel. They were all going to settle up for the expenses at the end of the weekend. The clubs were Carmen's deal.

The waiter returned, his expression apologetic. "Not sure how this happened, but no. Either we can't locate it or . . ."

Shit!

"No worries." She picked up her phone, poured what was left of the not-paid-for vodka into a glass, and tossed some ice into it.

Brooke's phone rang and rang until voice mail picked up.

This was not for her to figure out, and Chloe didn't have Carmen's phone number.

There was no way of knowing if they were back at the hotel yet.

Another look at the bill and she swallowed more liquor.

Never again.

She would never leave her wallet home again.

Her brothers.

Fuck!

She looked at her phone, pulled up Friend Finder.

She'd taken her brothers off the list for the weekend, but Dante showed up like a beacon of light in the dark.

He was back at the hotel.

Fuck!

Left without many choices, she called the man who might be able to keep this from her brothers. At least for the weekend.

She pressed his number and plugged her other ear to hear him.

He picked up on the second ring.

"Is she okay?"

"What?"

"Brooke, is she okay? She called Luca, said she was on her way back. It doesn't look like you've left yet."

Picturing what Dante was seeing, she huddled into her phone to try and muffle the noise around her. She would've left the table but was afraid the staff would think she was ducking out on the bill.

"She should be there any minute. They left a while ago."

"What?"

"Shhh. Please, Dante . . . Tell Luca she's almost there and walk out of the room."

"Chloe?"

"Just do it."

The receiver on his side of the phone was blocked, and a few seconds later she heard him again. His voice serious.

"What's going on?"

"Brooke should be there any minute. She and Carmen left a while ago."

"You're still at the strip club?"

Chloe looked around.

"I am."

"You and Salena?"

"Well . . . Salena is occupied."

"What?"

"Don't even pretend you don't know what that means or haven't done it before."

The words in Italian that came out of his mouth didn't translate well.

Chloe smiled.

"You're there alone."

"Yes, but that isn't the problem."

"How is that *not* a problem?"

"I can Uber my way back to the hotel. The problem is, Carmen was supposed to settle the bill. Only she didn't leave her card with them. My credit card is in my hotel room."

The next stream of Italian obscenities translated, but . . .

"Don't move. I'm on my way."

"You can just give a credit card over the phone—"

For a moment there was silence. "Don't. Move."

The line went dead.

CHAPTER FOUR

Dante had traveled to many places in the world where midnight still had crowds of people moving from one place to another.

But none like Vegas.

How was that?

The taxi ride to the strip club Chloe was stranded in wasn't a long one, but the traffic on the Vegas Strip did a great job of keeping him from getting to her quickly.

And like everyone else in Vegas, he was more than a little buzzed.

Yeah, the call had sobered him a bit, but he'd be lying if he said he was a hundred percent sober.

Mayson had texted to say that Brooke had in fact arrived at the hotel and, instead of crashing in her room, was cuddled next to Luca in his.

Gio was crashed on one of the beds in their room, and Mayson had left the lovebirds alone and was in the casino spending money he didn't have.

All was good there.

And Chloe was alone, in a male strip club without money or a sidekick.

When they pulled up at the club, Dante tossed cash at the driver and jumped out of the car.

The bouncer at the door stopped him.

"There's a cover charge."

Dante looked at him like he was crazy. "I have a friend in there. She forgot her wallet and needs to settle a bill."

The larger man stared at him as if he didn't understand a word of English.

"Twenty bucks."

Fishing out his wallet, Dante paid the man and then walked inside.

He walked around the dark corners until he found the main stage.

Ignoring the scene, he searched for Chloe.

She sat in the center, close to the stage.

Alone.

Empty glasses all around her.

Strangers were stuffing money in the G-strings the men were wearing.

He released a breath he didn't realize he was holding.

Safe.

She was safe.

Taking his time now, he walked up behind her and placed a hand on her shoulder.

Chloe jumped.

One look and she was on her feet and her arms were around him.

He pulled her close, not thinking . . . just doing.

She spoke to him in Italian, thanking him. Her lips were close to his ear and all he could do was hold on and breathe her in.

When she pulled away, he placed a hand on the side of her face and looked in her eyes.

There, he saw relief.

He looked down at the table, saw the bill, and picked it up.

As he walked to the bar, he noticed Chloe following, her purse and coat in hand.

He settled the bill, tipped as he would for himself, and grasped Chloe's hand to lead her away from the club.

Once they were far from the noise and closer to the front door, they could hear each other without yelling.

"Are you okay?" he asked.

"I am now."

They stopped at the door, and she set her bag down to put on her jacket.

Dante stepped forward to help her.

"Thank you."

"You're welcome."

"No. For everything. This was not supposed to happen."

"Best-laid plans . . ." Dante looked to the bouncer as soon as they were at the door. "We need a taxi."

"The only one getting *laid* tonight is Salena."

"I'm going to kill her," he said, half joking.

"Leave her alone. She's fine. I'm tracking her."

"She left you stranded," he pointed out.

"I would have been fine if Carmen had left her credit card. I'm not sure how that even happened."

The taxi pulled up, and Dante opened the door for her.

"I'll be giving everyone hell in the morning."

Chloe stopped mid-scoot. "No, you won't. This is between you and me. If you say anything it will ruin the weekend for Brooke, and this is in no way her fault."

"It isn't. It's Carmen and Salena's."

Chloe moved over, giving him room in the back seat.

"The Venetian," he told the driver.

"No. I'm not done."

"What?"

"Buy me a drink."

Dante looked at her like she was crazy. "Didn't I just buy all of them?"

She rolled her eyes. "I'll pay you back for those. I'm way too amped up after sitting there without any money all that time. The Bellagio," she said.

The driver looked through the rearview mirror, caught Dante's eyes.

He nodded and the man left the strip club parking lot.

Chloe lowered her head on the back seat. "That sucked."

"I can't believe you left without any money."

"I had money. Lap dances require cash."

Dante looked at her. "And how many of those did you need tonight?"

She smiled, rolled her head to the side. "Wouldn't you like to know."

Yeah, actually . . . he would.

"How was your night?"

It was his turn to settle into his seat. "It was okay."

"Ah-huh . . . two clubs? The first one wasn't enough?"

So she had kept tabs. "I could say the same for you girls."

"The first one was a big show. This place was a party. Brooke had a great time."

"We made sure Luca had a good time."

"Lap dances?"

Dante pictured what they'd done during the night, kept his lips sealed. "What happens in Vegas . . ."

"I'll take that as a yes."

The driver dropped them off in front of the fountain at the Bellagio, where music filled the air and the water danced.

Dante stood beside Chloe and watched her more than the show.

Her eyes lit up with excitement as the music heightened and the water reached for the star-filled night. Even at the end of the night, she was the most beautiful woman in the room. Or the sidewalk, as the case was in Vegas.

When she shivered, he took the liberty of placing his arm over her shoulders. "You're freezing."

"I am."

He pulled her toward the entrance of the hotel, amazed that she managed with the high heels. "I'm not sure how you ladies manage in those shoes."

Chloe started laughing as they walked into the casino. "When did I become a lady in your eyes?"

That was a minefield question. "Have you looked in the mirror lately?"

She rolled her eyes and headed straight to the closest bar. "You barely said hello to me when I walked into the restaurant tonight. Hugged everyone *but* me."

Oh, boy. "I have a good reason for that."

She stopped midstep, looked over her shoulder.

Silence stretched between them.

"What are you drinking?" He chickened out.

She shook her head and focused on the room in front of them. Seeing an open table, she pointed. "Vodka martini, two olives. I need the salt."

He took the reprieve and headed to the bar.

There, he looked at his phone, saw that Gio had checked in.

Not seeing any harm in telling the truth, he sent his friend a quick message saying he was chaperoning Chloe since they both had more energy than the rest of them. Then, because he wasn't going to share her with any of them, he put his phone away, with no intention of looking at it again for the rest of the night.

It took him twenty minutes to get them their drinks.

By the time he made his way to her, a man was sitting beside Chloe, leaning on the table and looking entirely too comfortable.

"Hello?" Dante made himself known.

Chloe had a perfect smile as she lifted a hand Dante's way. "See. I told you I was with someone."

Mr. Poacher turned his eyes on Dante and sighed in disappointment. He lifted both hands in the air as he stood. "I had to try," he said to both of them. With a nod, he said to Dante directly, "You're a lucky man." And he walked away.

Dante placed their drinks down and then shrugged out of his coat. "Who was your new friend?"

"Cash."

He hesitated. "You're kidding."

Chloe shook her head and laughed. "That's what he told me."

Looking at her sitting there, her coat on the back of her chair, the killer dress that fit her like a glove and left any heterosexual man's mouth watering . . . how could Dante blame the man.

"Are you disappointed that he left?"

She reached for her drink, leaned forward. "That depends."

Something playful passed over her eyes. Or maybe that was the previous drinks in the evening.

"Depends on?"

She lifted the glass to her lips, sipped. "If you're going to treat me like a baby sister all night or if you're going to own up to some of the bombshells you've been dropping since you arrived."

Dante's eyes took a slow dance down her frame, just about as slow as they could, to the impossible shoes she wore on her feet, back up her crossed legs that were exposed to midthigh . . . all the parts in the middle he wanted to experience in every way possible.

Yeah, his days of seeing Chloe D'Angelo as a baby sister were long gone. Had been for a while and were blasted out of the water long before she showed up in the impossible dress she wore now.

His eyes met hers. "You will always be Gio's younger sister. And that respect will forever be given."

Her brow furrowed.

Dante let a corner of his mouth lift. "But you're not *my* sister."

"What the hell does that mean?"

He lifted his glass. "I don't know, Chloe. Shit. Look at you."

She looked down at herself, lifted her dress away from her skin enough so she managed a personal peep show. "I remember when you teased me the first time I wore a bra."

Laughing, he took a drink, looked her over again. "I can't tease you now, you're not wearing one."

"Perks of a B cup."

He had no problem with that.

"And when I started high school, you told everyone I liked girls."

"Hey, I had a pact with your brothers. Keep the boys away."

She picked at the olive and sipped her drink. "Ha. I have news for you. The guys thought that shit was hot."

"What?" Wait . . . it kinda was.

"Salena and I played that up our junior year. Dated anyone I wanted."

"You're kidding." He was in college by then and already feeling the need to move away from the place he'd grown up.

"I had to do something with the legacy you guys left me with. If Salena and I are still single by our ten-year reunion, we're going to tell people we were secretly married but it didn't work out."

"I don't think you have to worry about that." The thought combated the liquor he was pouring in. Chloe had it much too together to be single forever.

"What? Being single? Finding the right person is impossible. Dating sucks."

He lifted his drink. "We can agree to that."

She touched her glass to his, they drank.

The buzz he'd collected earlier in the evening was quickly returning.

"It can't be as bad for you," she insisted.

"Why is that?"

"Oh, please. You walk in the room and women's ovaries start dropping eggs like hens on a full moon."

Dante tossed his head back and laughed so hard he felt tears in his eyes.

A waitress walked by. "You doing okay over here?"

He looked at their drinks, ordered another round.

"I promise you, it's not that easy," he said when they were alone again.

"Has to be better than Little Italy, where everyone still thinks you might go both ways."

That almost made him feel guilty. "Italian men are more common in Italy."

She pointed a finger in his face. "I've been to Italy. This . . . this isn't on every corner."

He snatched her finger, turned her hand her way. "Neither is this."

The singer finished her song and the audience clapped, breaking their conversation.

The next song was louder and had him pushing his chair closer to Chloe so they could continue to talk. He couldn't remember the last time he'd talked so openly with a woman.

From nowhere, Chloe started laughing.

The sound of it brought a smile to his face. "What?"

"I can't believe we drove up a three-hundred-dollar bar bill at a strip club and I couldn't pay it."

"I'm going to hold that over you for a long time."

"Don't I know it."

Their second round came. "Do you want to open a tab?"

Dante looked at Chloe and they both started laughing.

He reached for his wallet.

~

The dice flew to the other end of the table and those around it cheered.

Chloe had no idea what was happening, but the people surrounding her and Dante were very happy with how she tossed the dice.

She had no idea what time it was.

They'd had two drinks at the blues bar and made their way to the casino.

Dante stopped them at a craps table and the drinks kept coming.

His chips kept stacking up.

"C'mon, *bella*. Do it again."

"I don't know what I'm doing," she said to him in Italian.

"Trust me. You're doing fine," he replied.

She tossed the dice again.

Cheers went up.

Dante pulled her into his arms with the hug he hadn't given her earlier.

"The lady is on a roll."

Dante took half of the chips the dealer had just given him off the table and rubbed Chloe's shoulders. "It's all gravy, *cara*."

That sounded good.

Twice more, luck was on her side, and then the dice turned.

Dante took his chips from the table and told her to open her purse.

Her evening bag didn't hold them all, but his pockets did the rest.

"We did good?"

His hand rested around her waist like it belonged there. And frankly, she'd gotten used to it since he'd slid it there over and over all night.

Even as many drinks in as she was, she was aware of that.

"We should go."

She rolled her head from one side to the other. "Let's walk a bit. I need to sober up or I'm going to regret this in the morning."

"Anything you say, *bella*."

The frigid temperatures outside hit her hard. "What time is it?"

"One thirty."

"What? I thought it was later." Only there were still people everywhere.

"Prime time in Vegas."

"Shouldn't we cash this stuff out?"

"Tomorrow."

Once they reached the Strip, the lights and energy had them both smiling. "I don't remember the last time I had this much fun."

Dante looked at her. "Me either."

She walked in front of him a few feet, turned to walk backward. "You know why?"

"Why's that?" He was smiling.

"Because I don't have to pretend with you. I mean . . ." Vodka was giving her all truth serum. And with any luck, she wouldn't remember in the morning, or it wouldn't be in vain. But Chloe didn't feel the need to hold back. "Okay, total truth." She tried to focus on him, knew he was as buzzed as she was.

"Total truth," he replied.

She undid the tie of her coat and exposed her dress to him. "I wore this for you."

His feet faltered.

"You did not."

Chloe walked straight to him, pushed a finger in his chest. "And you didn't even hug me." Her hand fell away with a whole lot of drama.

He blinked, twice.

She twisted on her heel, felt his hand on her elbow keep her steady.

"It's okay, though. You made up for earlier." Damn, it was cold.

A group of men walking by whistled. "Right?" She was laughing.

Dante moved around her, stopped, and tied her jacket belt around her waist.

"I couldn't," he said.

"Couldn't what?"

"Hold you."

She stopped in the middle of the street.

"What?"

He placed his hand on the side of her face, stepped closer. "Jesus, Chloe. If Gio or Luca saw the way I look at you . . . really look at you, they'd gut me."

Dante came into focus, his eyes drifted to her lips. "How do you look at me?"

He closed his eyes, and when they opened, they glanced over her head and he started to laugh.

Damn . . . for a minute there, she thought he was going to kiss her.

He took her shoulders in his hands and turned her around.

That's when she saw what he did.

They were standing in front of a tiny Vegas wedding chapel.

"I look at you like a man looks at a woman he's taken here first."

She started laughing. "You're not a virgin."

His chin came to rest on her shoulder. "No," he said in her ear with a chuckle.

"I'm not a virgin," she said.

When he was silent, she started laughing harder.

Dante turned her around to face him.

He stopped laughing, his hand found the back of her head.

The world stopped, came into focus.

"I have a really good bad idea," he told her.

Her breath caught in her chest as Dante's lips fell on hers.

CHAPTER FIVE

An axe sat in the center of Chloe's skull.

The entire Nevada desert had drifted into her open mouth while she slept, and her heart was beating to a Metallica song that she didn't know the words to.

When she moved, her stomach reached up to her throat and said, *Oh no you don't, bitch!*

So she didn't.

Nevada.

Vegas.

Strip club.

Dante.

So many memories crashed in at once, Chloe wasn't sure which ones to process first.

Instead of trying to do any of that, she kept her eyes closed and willed her stomach to behave.

That last drink . . .

When was that last drink?

The Bellagio? The craps table . . . or was there another one later?

Something happened later . . .

A noise woke her in what felt like a few minutes later, but the light in the room had shifted.

"Holy shit!"

The words startled Chloe from the half sleep she was in.

Her body came upright.

Her head regretted the sudden movement.

"You look worse than me."

Salena.

Chloe moaned. "Leave me to die in peace."

Her friend laughed and walked farther in the room. "It's almost noon."

"I don't care." She rolled to her side and her stomach rolled twice.

With no choice but to run, Chloe made it to the bathroom to purge what little was in her stomach that the evening didn't want to digest. Regret came up in painful gulps of air. When it was all done, she felt better for it.

Looking at her hands as they rested on the toilet seat, she saw something that had the night slamming back at her in vivid colors.

There, on her left hand, her ring finger, was a white band that hadn't been there when she'd left the hotel the night before.

Dante!

"You okay in there?"

She started to breathe faster. "Fine. I'm fine."

"Do you want some coffee?"

Chloe pushed herself off the floor and gazed at herself in the mirror. She looked like hell. Makeup everywhere but where it was supposed to be. Her dress still on, but twisted and . . . She closed her eyes, tried to remember everything.

So many holes.

"No."

She pulled at the zipper in the back of her dress. "I need to shower."

Her dress slid to the floor and with it some assurance that nothing intimate had happened.

No, Dante wouldn't have.

Yet her left hand suggested they'd done something a little bigger than a toss in the Vegas hay.

No, no . . .

The hot water helped bring a few details into focus.

Dante had kissed her.

She was so caught up in the fact that he was doing it, she had a hard time remembering the details. Then he was pulling her into the chapel.

They were laughing and she thought he was joking.

The guy running the place was half-asleep.

Chloe pushed her face under the spray of the water.

What the hell did they do?

As the water dripped down her frame, her eyes were glued to her hand. Or more importantly, the ring on her hand.

She had to talk to Dante. STAT.

Yes, she wanted the man to notice her. Maybe flirt with her, suggest a romantic dinner, but a drunken wedding chapel in Vegas at two in the morning? Had it been two in the morning?

Steam started to fill the bathroom, prompting Chloe to make use of her time in the shower.

While her stomach felt marginally better once she was out from under the water, her head was a complete mess.

Realizing the ring would prompt a thousand questions, ones she could not answer, she removed it and started to slide it onto her other hand. That's when she noticed the green ring around her finger. "Damn it."

Much as she scrubbed, the green didn't erase.

Once Chloe was back in the room, Salena took her place. The night's drama still needing to be washed from her skin as well.

Only her friend looked happy with what had taken place, whereas Chloe was in a state of panic. "Do you have any idea where everyone is?" Chloe asked.

"I was about to ask you the same thing."

She grabbed a bathrobe from the closet, replaced the towel she had wrapped around her, and then knocked on the adjoining door to the connecting room. When there wasn't an answer, she opened the door.

It was empty.

She found her purse and her phone. There was only five percent charge left on the thing. The first thing she looked up was Dante's location.

He was in the hotel.

As she shuffled around the room in search of the charger for her phone, she dialed his number and put the phone to her ear.

It rang five times and then went to voice mail.

"I'm not a hundred percent sure what the hell happened last night . . ." She looked at the green ring around her finger. "But we have to talk . . . in private." And she hung up.

She plugged her phone in, tossed it on the bed, and turned to sit.

This all had to be a crazy dream.

~

One look in Dante's eyes and she knew it was more than a dream.

It was a nightmare.

Salena and Chloe met up with the rest of the group as they waited for Brooke and Luca to return from the fake gondola ride through the man-made Vegas-style Venetian canals throughout the hotel.

"A photo opportunity" was how Carmen had spun the idea.

Or so Chloe was told when she showed up to the party.

"What happened to you last night?"

The hair on Chloe's neck went up, but Carmen's question was pointed to Salena.

Salena, with a cat-ate-the-canary smile, said, "What happens in Vegas . . ."

Mayson and Gio laughed.

Chloe's eyes met Dante's.

Those eyes. The ones she'd thought about a hell of a lot over the years. They had this gold ring, almost amber look that almost shocked you the first time you saw them. Only she'd grown up with them, so they didn't knock her back the way they did other women. And when he turned on the charm . . . again, that's when the ovaries-start-dropping-eggs thing happened.

Right now those eyes looked deep into hers as if to say . . . "It happened in Vegas." Only she couldn't tell if he was scared, confused, or just as unknowing as she was. Yet there was something else. What that was, she couldn't name.

". . . and you. I'm not sure what time you crawled into bed, but you were loud." Carmen pegged Chloe with a stare.

Swallowing hard, Chloe shook out of Dante's trance. "I was?"

Gio lost his grin. "Wait. What happened with you?"

"Relax, Gio. She was with me." Dante looked between them.

Gio released a breath.

"I made sure she got to her room before I left."

So, he did remember more of the night than she did.

Now the question was . . . how much more.

"Here they come." Mayson pointed to the fake canal and gondola floating their way.

Carmen moved forward with her phone in hand and started snapping pictures.

As everyone stood, Chloe waited in the back of the group to catch Dante.

"We need to talk." And as if she needed an exclamation point to her suggestion, she removed her left hand from the pocket of the coat she was wearing and showed him the remnants of the green film on her finger from the cheap ring.

His eyes narrowed. "It was fake?"

She slapped his arm. "Are you joking right now?"

"You don't remember anything?" he asked.

"Yes. I remember."

He sighed.

"I remember how drunk we were. Somewhere between tossing dice and—"

"Hey! You two joining us or what?" Salena called from a few yards away.

Dante's shoulders shot up, gaze moved toward the group. "Coming."

They started walking.

"We. Need. To. Talk." Chloe felt her heart skipping beats with every word and every breath as they took the last position with their family and friends.

"Give me a few minutes."

She faked a smile his way.

"Now that everyone is vertical, should we hit a casino? Bloody Marys with brunch? Mimosas?"

Chloe's stomach flipped just thinking of it.

Salena lit up. "All the above."

"I'm starving," Brooke announced.

"You haven't eaten?" Chloe asked.

"Hours ago. Probably about the time you were getting in," Luca said accusingly.

Salena slid in to the rescue. "Hey . . . it's Vegas."

"I suggest brunch close by and some casino hopping. Maybe Fremont Street tonight," Gio said. "Unless you ladies want to hit the clubs a second night in a row."

Brooke shook her head. "I think I'm good there."

Salena shrugged.

"Oh, please, you have a stripper on speed dial," Chloe said, outing her friend.

Salena smacked her arm.

Carmen laughed.

"We have a plan, then."

The thought of sitting in a restaurant . . . food. "I don't think I can eat," Chloe announced.

Salena started to laugh. "Considering how you looked this morning, I'm not surprised."

"I'm not feeling it either," Dante agreed. He turned to Chloe. "Hey . . . last night we passed that place, thought of a great wedding gift for Luca and Brooke . . . remember?"

Chloe looked at him as if he were crazy. "No."

His eyes opened wider. "Remember, it was next to that wedding chapel?"

Chloe's stomach rolled. "Right."

Dante turned to the rest of them. "Tell you what. We'll meet up with you after you eat."

"You sure?" Brooke asked.

Chloe's head wasn't in full gear. It took that long for her to realize Dante was giving them time away from the group. "Positive. My head is killing me, and my stomach isn't going to accept anything anytime soon."

Gio pointed her way. "Hair of the dog, sis."

She shook her head.

Dante took her arm. "I got her. Let me know where you end up," he said.

Then, just like an onion, they peeled away from the group.

As soon as the others were out of sight, Chloe stopped, turned to Dante, and pulled the ring she'd woken up with on her finger from her pocket.

"What the hell is this?"

~

Dante grasped her elbow and pulled her through the crowd until they were outside the hotel and the cool air was helping clear his head.

"We were pretty drunk last night."

Chloe stopped mid-sidewalk and stared him down.

Her chest was rising and falling rapidly. Her eyes, a little deeper set than the night before, and admittedly bloodshot, didn't so much as blink. "We got married."

Her words were a statement.

Which was a relief. It said she remembered . . . at least some of it.

"We did."

What started out as heavy breathing started to turn into hyperventilating.

Chloe raised both her hands to her face, covering her eyes.

Her purse fell from her shoulder and swung like a pendulum on her arm.

"Oh, God."

He moved forward, pulled her into his arms.

She shrugged him away at his first touch. "Don't. Just don't."

"Chloe . . ."

"An indiscretion, a one-night stand, a fling . . . but marriage?" She nearly screamed the last word.

Dante looked around them to see if he recognized anyone watching them.

Everyone was a stranger, and thankfully, they just walked by.

He switched to Italian. "There was no fling."

She ran a hand through her hair. "I could have lived with a fling." In two steps she was up and in his space. Lifted her chin and nearly touched his. "A fling I've wanted with you from the day boys stopped being icky." She thrust her left hand in his face, pointed to the green hue on her ring finger. "But saying 'I do' to a man who had to be drunk to get me there is not my fairy tale."

"Of course it's not." He knew that when he was holding her hand and promising his future to her. But that didn't stop him. "But we did do this."

"We need to *undo* this."

"I don't think it's that easy."

She grabbed his hand and pulled him toward the circular drive. "We have to try."

Chloe was right. He knew she was right.

Adult, sober logic that had slapped him upside the head the moment he'd opened his eyes that morning was looking him in the face now, and he told the valet to get them a cab.

"Where to?" the cabbie asked.

"There's a wedding chapel . . ."

The cabbie laughed. "On every corner in this town. You want Elvis to do the deed, drive-through Denny's . . . what?"

Dante shook his head. "I think it was by the Bellagio."

The cabbie put the car in gear.

Chloe spoke in Italian. "Do you remember the place?"

"I will when I see it."

Her hands clenched her coat, but at least her breath had stopped coming out in short spurts.

He wanted to pull her hand into his, calm her nerves that were obviously dangling on her fingertips.

Dante took a chance and covered her hand with his. "We'll figure this out."

Only as they drove by the first chapel, the driver slowed down. "Is it this one?"

He couldn't tell for sure.

Dante looked at Chloe for some kind of recognition.

She shrugged.

"Let us out here." He paid the driver as they exited the cab.

"Congrats, man. She's beautiful."

He heard Chloe cuss in Italian.

Dante thanked the driver anyway and stepped aside. He had to jog to catch up to her as she marched to the front doors. "Is this even the place?"

He looked up, saw the cross. "The outside is fuzzy to me."

She rolled her eyes and swung the doors open.

Once inside, he looked around and knew immediately it wasn't the right location.

The place was pink. As if someone vomited the color everywhere.

"This doesn't feel right," Chloe said.

A woman walked out from behind a corner. "Can I help you?"

Dante stepped forward. "Perhaps." He let his smile do what it often did to the opposite sex. "Last night, we'd been drinking quite a bit."

The woman was smiling. "That happens here."

"Right." He looked at Chloe, who was looking around the small space, with its tiny white chairs and pink and white tulle framing the altar. "We stepped into a chapel like this one. Perhaps you can tell us where others are on the Strip that look similar to yours?"

The proprietor looked between the two of them, her smile unwavering. "I'm sure I can meet whatever needs you have."

Dante shook his head. "You misunderstand. We, ah . . ." He looked at Chloe.

Where he was missing the words to say what needed to be said, Chloe found them. "Apparently we got married last night, and today we need to get unmarried."

"Ah!" The woman sighed and folded her hands in front of her. "Now I understand. How much did you have to drink last night?"

"Enough." Chloe rolled her eyes.

"Does it matter?" Dante asked.

The woman grinned. "What are your names? I'll check our registry."

"It wasn't here," Chloe spoke up. "There was white and gold. Not pink."

The woman was walking toward an office anyway. "So, you weren't as intoxicated as you think."

"We were both pretty—"

"I'm sure you were. I only ask for my own policy. If a couple comes in late at night, after the party, so to speak, and it appears they're both intoxicated and making a regrettable decision, I will hold off on sending in the legal paperwork for a couple of days."

Chloe blew out a breath.

Dante's back stiffened.

"That's my policy. Not everyone on the Strip does the same thing."

"Why?"

The woman smiled. "My job is to marry people. Not divorce them."

"And if it was a mistake?" Chloe asked.

"That's for the courts to figure out. An annulment." The woman flipped open the registry. "What are your names?"

Dante told her.

"You didn't get married here."

Chloe sighed. "How many chapels are on the Strip?"

"Plenty. But most are in the hotels."

"It was on the Strip," they both said in unison.

"There is one north of here a couple of blocks and another south. Unless you think you walked farther."

Dante smiled. "Thank you."

"You're welcome."

They walked toward the door.

"For what it's worth," the lady called after them. "I think you make a lovely couple."

~

Two hours later they were at the scene of the marriage crime, looking at the registry with both their names in the book.

Chloe's feet hurt, her head was pounding more than it had when she'd woken that morning, and her heart was speeding at the rate of an overworked basketball player looking for a better contract.

The white chapel had gold accents and wasn't nearly as gaudy as the other they'd walked into earlier.

But it wasn't a church with a priest and with family . . .

It wasn't right.

The people running the place that afternoon were not the same people who had been there the night before.

"Congratulations," the minister on duty said when he realized they were looking for confirmation that they had in fact married the night before.

Chloe found laughter escaping her vocal cords without a request from her brain.

Dante slid a hand around her waist and spoke to the man.

All she could do was stare at the tiny chapel and try and recall every detail of the night before.

"We might be having a little next-day remorse," Dante explained.

"I'm sorry?"

The gold cherub that sat to the side of the cross at the front of the altar had this look on its face that was half smile, half sneer. Almost like it knew that the people who were there were making a mistake.

"We'd been drinking last night . . ."

Could a cherub cast a spell?

Through the daze that Chloe found herself in, she felt Dante lead her away from the register and into a small office, where the man in charge was looking at the notes from the previous evening's minister.

The damn cherub watched her as they walked through the small chapel.

She felt reality coming back as they moved into a room with lower ceilings and office supplies.

"Please, have a seat."

Dante moved his chair closer to hers and grasped her hand.

"Here you are." The man speaking—Chloe couldn't remember his name for the life of her—smiled as he spoke and read his colleague's notes. "'Dante Mancuso and Chloe D'Angelo arrived at 1:40. While they had both been drinking, they both assured me they had known each other since childhood and have always wanted the other in their life forever. The couple did not have a marriage certificate and agreed to the emergency call and fee.'" The minister stopped reading and looked up. "You must have been very determined. We almost never call in a favor from our contact at the county clerk's office."

Chloe remembered the wait and how surreal it felt to have Dante holding her hand as they waited for someone to come with a legal form.

As the memory poured in, the reality of their situation settled in her chest.

The minister continued reading: "'Once the proper paperwork was complete, the ceremony was performed in usual fashion. The documentation was signed by myself, my clerk, and the bride and groom and dropped in the mail at the post office.'"

Chloe squeezed Dante's hand. "What does that mean?"

The deep blue eyes of the man speaking stared at her, then Dante, then back at her. "It means you're married."

"There's no way to stop it?" she asked.

He shook his head. "Short of breaking into the post office and retrieving the documents before they open on Monday, no. Which is a felony, I believe. Nevada will acknowledge your marriage as valid."

Nervous laughter erupted.

Dante stood, dragged her to her feet. "Thank you, Reverend."

"I'm not . . ." The man paused, changed what he wanted to say. "You're welcome."

There was a disconnect in her body. She was walking back through the chapel. Her head was on top of her body, looking at the gold and laughing cherub. She lifted a hand to the thing in an Italian gesture of *fuck off.*

Outside, the Vegas sun met with the cold of a high-desert winter and slapped her face. "What do we do now?"

"Bust into the post office?"

Chloe glared at him.

Dante pulled her to a photo spot provided by the chapel and sat them down. He took her hands in his.

If she were keeping score, he'd touched her more in the last couple of hours than he had in their entire lives.

It didn't matter.

"We're going to fix this."

Chloe couldn't help it.

She laughed.

A slow, manic laugh that anyone watching would think was coming from someone a bit less mentally stable than the other guy.

"Chloe. We *can* fix this."

"We're married."

His eyes met hers. "Apparently."

"I'm Mrs. Mancuso."

A corner of his mouth lifted.

Her eyes snapped to his and that smile dropped like the stock market after a three-year high.

"We can fix this . . . ," he said again.

"An annulment."

His head started to nod. "Right."

"How do we do that?"

"I don't know. But I'll figure it out," he said, his voice softened.

"We can't tell anyone, Dante."

He looked away. "I know."

"This is Luca and Brooke's time."

"I know that, too."

Her hand was still in his.

She squeezed it, forced him to look at her. "We're going to be okay?"

Dante reached over, pulled her in, his lips close to her ears. "One day we'll tell this story to our grandchildren."

Chloe sucked in a breath through her nose.

All she took in was the scent of the moment.

Dante, who was still fresh from his morning shower, with a unique fragrance that was part him and maybe an aftershave or cologne he'd been using forever. The mix of cold Vegas air and desert flowers that were blooming nearby filled her lungs.

All of it mixed together with day-after regrets of a nature she never saw coming.

CHAPTER SIX

Downtown Fremont Street was filled with hot lights and old-town Vegas charm.

Chloe had eaten by dinner, but liquor was something she'd sworn off until the Second Coming.

Or until there wasn't a desirable male within twenty miles.

She pulled on an old slot machine without thought.

Salena leaned over. "You okay?"

"What?"

"You haven't been right all day."

Chloe's eyes moved toward Dante. Saw him laughing at something Gio was saying from another part of the casino. "I'm fine. Tired."

Salena narrowed her eyes.

"You know . . ." Salena pulled the handle on the machine. "You and Dante haven't said a word to each other all night."

The nervous laugh that had been hovering all night erupted.

Salena's gaze snapped to Chloe.

Sucking her lips in, Chloe stopped her giggles. "We said enough last night."

Salena lost interest in the slots and turned toward her. "I knew it. Something happened."

"No."

"Don't even pretend. I've known you since grade school."

"Nothing happened." The lie escaped her lips without pause.

"Liar."

Chloe felt the pause before the gasp and knew that was her downfall. "Nothing," she insisted.

Salena rolled her eyes and signaled to the woman wearing less than a bikini for another vodka tonic. "If you were drinking, I'd know exactly what happened last night."

Good reason to stay sober.

Chloe looked over her shoulder, saw Dante tipping a cup to his lips. "Don't let someone take my spot."

With that, she left her perch and made her way across the casino floor.

"Hey, sis," Gio greeted her.

"Having fun?" she asked.

"More tonight than watching over that guy last night." He pointed toward their brother, who was hanging off Brooke. She was pulling on the arm of a slot machine and laughing.

Chloe's heart warmed, looking at the two of them. "They're good together."

"The best."

"Meant to be," Dante said.

Chloe couldn't help but look Dante's way. Her eyes drifted to his drink. "I can't believe you have the stomach for liquor after last night."

"What can I say?" He shrugged. "I doubt I'll be back in Vegas anytime soon."

"The next bachelor party," Gio said.

Dante lifted his glass to his lips and then seemed to have second thoughts when his gaze met Chloe's. "That requires someone else getting married."

Her stomach twisted.

Gio laughed. "We all know that isn't you," he said, smacking Dante on his shoulder.

He surged forward slightly with the playful slap. "You never know."

Chloe narrowed her eyes.

"Oh? Is there someone in Italy you haven't told us about?" Gio asked.

An instant image of Dante holding another woman made Chloe's already-uneasy stomach want to lurch.

She tilted her head to the side and watched Dante through his silence. "Give it up, Dante . . . who is she?"

His eyes snapped to hers and locked.

The ever-ready smile on his lips fell into a flat line.

Chloe swallowed . . . hard.

"You know me," he said, his voice void of emotion. "Someone on every shore."

"Some things never change." Gio swung his arm over Dante's shoulders and broke the spell.

"Hey, guys?" Carmen called from several feet away. "Group photo time."

Luca and Brooke were walking toward a giant Christmas tree in the center of the casino.

"Let's start with the wedding party," Carmen suggested, taking the lead in composing the best photo.

Mayson and Salena stepped away as they took up positions.

They lined up as a wedding party does. Chloe and Carmen stood to Brooke's side while Gio and Dante took up the space beside Luca.

After a couple of shots, Mayson switched it up. "Boy, girl."

Chloe took a deep breath as Dante walked her way. Carmen and Gio were the best man and maid of honor, which put her with the man she'd been avoiding all night.

He smiled as he placed an arm around her waist.

She flinched and the smile on his face wavered. "I won't bite," he whispered.

Chloe felt her breath start to thicken, her lungs had a hard time pulling in air with him so close.

Mayson waved his hands together. "Closer."

Dante stood behind her and placed both of his arms around her, his lips close to her ear. "Think of it as our wedding picture."

Without thinking, she nudged her elbow into his side.

He laughed.

"Smile," Mayson directed.

The flash of the camera had her pulling out of Dante's orbit.

"Wait, a couple more."

"What are you, a closet photographer?" Chloe asked.

He moved in, snapped another picture. "Yup." And another . . . and another.

When he was finished, he snagged an employee to get a few shots of all of them.

Chloe took the reprieve to distance herself from her husband.

She squeezed her eyes shut.

Good God.

He was her husband.

~

Dante wasn't sure what was worse. Chloe yelling at him or her complete silence.

Silence, he decided.

The plane ride back to San Diego was quick. Their conversation limited to what had to be said.

Most of the time she wouldn't even look at him.

Salena, on the other hand, looked between the two of them often.

If there was one thing he knew about Salena, it was that the woman couldn't keep a secret. There was no way Chloe leaked their little indiscretion.

He ran a hand through his hair. *Little indiscretion.* Who was he kidding?

They'd both jumped in the water without seeing how deep it was first, and now what?

An annulment?

Easy enough.

Once the wedding festivities were behind them, he'd find out exactly what they needed to do. After all, it was his crazy idea to get married in the first place.

The memory of Chloe's smile as she recited her vows had visited him the night before and woke him at dawn.

As the plane landed on the short runway of San Diego's airport, Gio patted Dante's back. "Welcome home."

"Good to be back."

Mayson and Carmen had taken direct flights back to their homes, with the promise of seeing them all again at the end of the week for the wedding.

"I missed Franny," Brooke said to Luca as they piled into an Uber.

"I did, too."

Salena laughed as she pushed into the seat with Luca and Brooke.

Gio took the front seat, leaving Dante little choice but to sit beside Chloe in the smaller back seat of the van.

She scooted over far enough that they didn't touch.

"You're not taking her on your honeymoon," Chloe said as the driver closed the sliding door of the van.

"Was that an option?" Dante asked.

"Franny asked and these bozos hesitated," Chloe told him.

Dante reached forward and placed a hand on Luca's shoulder. "You have the rest of your life for family vacations. Enjoy your bride for a week. We'll make sure Franny is so busy she won't notice you're gone."

Luca turned in his seat. "So, you're not rushing back to Italy?"

Without realizing he did it, Dante looked at Chloe, took a breath. "No."

"When are you returning?" Gio asked from the front seat.

Chloe finally looked him in the eye.

He could melt in the depth of her soulful gaze. "I don't know."

"Business is good, though, right?" Gio turned around in his seat.

Dante felt Chloe's foot kick his shin, breaking his stare. "My partner is running things while I'm gone. Winter is slow."

"It will be nice to have you around for a while," Salena said.

The driver turned the corner to the street they'd all grown up on.

He took it all in.

Nothing had changed. Yes, some of the restaurants had new owners. And the street itself had less parking and more outside seating and entertainment. But it was the same.

They dropped him off first, even though he was only a handful of blocks from the D'Angelos'.

Gio jumped out of the van.

When the others started to follow suit, Dante stopped them. "I'll come by later. No need for goodbyes."

Luca smiled. "I'm glad you're here."

"I'm happy to put a face to all the stories," Brooke said.

He winked at Luca's bride and turned to Chloe.

Without thought, he leaned in and kissed the side of her cheek. At the same time, he placed a hand on her knee and squeezed.

Then he escaped the van and heard his mother calling his name and saw her running down the steps of his childhood home.

~

Chloe held it together until the moment her bedroom door closed behind her.

Her purse fell from her hand, and she shoved her suitcase aside and slid to the floor.

Never in her life had she felt the weight of the world on her as she did since she'd woken up the day before with a fake ring on her finger and a cavern of regret sitting in the middle of her chest.

How had this happened?

She'd been caught in the moment.

High on Dante's kiss. He'd kissed her.

Something she'd dreamed of . . . hoped for, for as long as she could remember.

As the day cleared the memories of the night before, she realized she wasn't completely without fault in all of this.

He'd taken her hand and laughed as he dragged her into the chapel.

"You're drunk," she said to him accusingly.

"But we've known each other forever. We're perfect."

She'd thought he was joking. That he'd run out of the gold-and-white venue as fast as they'd run in.

Only he hadn't.

Halfway through the short ceremony, with both of them laughing, she'd thought that it wasn't real. That maybe he'd put the minister up to a prank.

Then the words *husband* and *wife* were said, and Dante was kissing her again.

Chloe covered her face with her hands as her shoulders started to shake.

CHAPTER SEVEN

The days following Vegas were a blur.

Most of the wedding planning was long behind them, but as the bridesmaid in closest physical proximity to the bride, Chloe was in charge of making sure all of Brooke's needs were being met.

Brooke's dress had undergone last-minute alterations and was hanging in Chloe's room so Luca didn't see it.

Every time Chloe looked at it, the white lace laughed at her.

Never in her life did she imagine she'd be the one to get married in a red *come-screw-me* dress in Vegas.

Family started to show up days before the actual event.

Gio temporarily moved back to his old room next door to Chloe's, giving the upstairs apartment to their grandfather, who'd made the trip from Italy along with his sister.

In addition to everything wedding, the Christmas season was in full swing. Little Italy overflowed with tourists enjoying Southern California's weather, which vacillated between requiring short sleeves and cotton pants one day and light sweaters or jackets the next.

Never did one have to don snow boots and thermal underwear, unless they visited the slopes.

The restaurant, thankfully, was packed every night.

Luca often handled all of the operations of the kitchen and the management of the family business. Along with their mother, of course, but Luca drove the day-to-day needs of the place.

Gio and Chloe made a pact early in the wedding planning that they would step up to give Luca room to enjoy the process of his marriage to Brooke, so this was where they were focused.

Thankfully, Luca had trained the staff through the years, and they ran a well-oiled team that did the job when Luca or their mother wasn't behind the spatula. They could help, but it wasn't in them to take charge in the kitchen.

In short, things were running well even if Chloe's personal stress level was pinging in the red.

There was no earthly way anyone could guess what had happened between her and Dante in Vegas, but that didn't stop her from wondering if there was some kind of neon sign over her head that everyone could see and she couldn't. One that said, "I have a huge secret that everyone would be screaming about if they knew."

The tightness in her chest reminded her of when she'd lost her virginity. The feeling that people could tell what she'd done just by looking at her was something she didn't shake for months.

"You okay?" Misha, one of the servers, asked behind her.

Chloe jumped, spilling the salt over the counter where she was refilling the shakers.

"Fine."

"Really? Because you've been standing there looking at the wall for ten minutes."

Chloe quickly twisted the cap back on the tiny glass bottle in her hand and moved to the next. "I have a lot on my mind."

"I bet. Hard to believe the big day is almost here."

With a smile, Chloe let Misha believe what she needed to. "I know."

"I still can't believe your family is closing the restaurant on a Saturday and invited all of us."

Misha wasn't Italian, and she was new to the staff. She wasn't familiar with how things were done at D'Angelo's. "There is nothing more important than family. And our staff is part of that."

"It almost makes me wish I could be a career waitress."

Misha was in college studying accounting. Waiting tables was a way to pay the bills while she earned her education.

Chloe smiled at the girl as a presence behind her demanded her attention.

Dante.

He entered the restaurant and removed sunglasses from his face. The man filled out a pair of jeans, wore a simple leather jacket and a smile that reached his honey-colored eyes.

Her shoulders straightened and her breath caught. Every neuron in her body fired as it always had.

She closed her eyes and attempted to slap down her attraction.

When she opened them back up, the hostess, who didn't know him, was in his space.

Chloe could just imagine what was being said.

"Who is that?" Misha asked, her voice carrying a breathy air to it that it hadn't a moment before.

"Rosa's son."

Misha nodded a few times. "Damn . . . he is . . . damn."

"Yeah. He knows it, too."

The hostess pointed to the back of the restaurant where Chloe was standing.

"I have to check on something," she said before leaving Misha's side and ducking into the kitchen.

Chloe's shift was over, her tables already turned, and there was absolutely no need for her to be around. Yet she didn't want to look like she was running away the moment Dante showed his face, so she sat at the mouth of the kitchen, looking for something to do to make her look busy.

Anything to keep her out of Dante's orbit.

"How is the lunch special moving today?" she asked the chef in charge.

"Not bad," Tony told her as he tossed an order into the window for one of the servers.

She moved to the far end of the kitchen. "When it slows down, box up three orders for me."

Tony's lips fell in a thin line. "The homeless never need a soup kitchen when you're in charge."

"It's Christmas, Tony, where's your spirit?"

"What was your excuse last month? Or the one before that?"

The same argument, different day.

"There you are."

Chloe looked up, found Dante staring at her from the entrance to the kitchen.

"Hey." She acted surprised. "Were we expecting you?"

A waiter passed, tapped Dante on his shoulder with a smile and a quick hello.

Chloe straightened up, ready for whatever Dante tossed her way.

"Do you have a minute?" he asked.

She looked around as if he were interrupting her life. "I'll be back," she told Tony.

One fortifying breath later, she exited the kitchen and met Dante in the hall that separated the restaurant from the stairs to the upper levels of the building where their family lived.

"You've been avoiding me," he said under his breath once they were alone.

"I have not."

"I've texted you twice."

She glanced over her shoulder. "Phones these days . . ."

Dante moved in front of her, making it impossible for her to miss the spicy scent of him. The memory of him leaning in and touching his lips to hers.

Squeezing her eyes shut, she took a step back.

"If you continue like this, people will think there's something going on."

"You're kidding yourself. You never looked my way twice, ignoring me now won't raise any suspicion."

Leaning back on his heels, Dante sucked in a breath. "We need to talk. And not here."

"And not now," she added. Her phone buzzed in her pocket, giving her the distraction she needed.

"I called the courthouse in Veg—"

Chloe was up in his face, stopping his words. "Not here."

His smile fell on her like a wave on the sand. It covered her entire body in a breath. "Then where?"

Her phone buzzed again.

"Let's get through this week like nothing has changed."

He scoffed.

"I mean it, Dante. The rehearsal, the wedding . . . reception. We'll talk once Luca and Brooke are away on their honeymoon."

He nodded a few times. "I can do that."

"Good." Chloe removed her phone from her pocket, saw the text. "Damn it."

"What?"

"I'm late."

"For what?"

Eric. "My date." She'd pushed off coffee with Eric by a day, and yet he was still willing to meet her. She texted him, telling him she was running behind and she was on her way.

Chloe felt the silence more than she heard it. Looking up, she took in the lack of emotion on Dante's face. "What?"

"You have a date?"

Was that accusation in his tone? "Yes," she said without apology. "Believe it or not, I had a life before you came in and—" She looked around them, left what she wanted to add to his imagination.

Dante took a giant step forward, his breath mingling with hers. "You're married," he told her as if she didn't know.

Chloe pushed against him, matched his hushed tone. "Am I? Was there a priest or a man who clicked a few times on the internet and decided he was worthy of making that happen?"

His nose flared, but it wasn't until she felt his hand touch her waist that she flinched and stepped back. "You'll have to excuse me," she said as she ducked to his side and walked away.

On her way out, she grabbed the bags with the extra lunch specials Tony packaged up, all the while aware that Dante watched her exit.

~

Outside, the streets were filled with holiday tourists and locals enjoying what Little Italy had to offer.

The cooler air put a bounce in Chloe's step as she zigzagged through the crowd to the coffee shop where she was meeting Eric.

She saw Charlie sitting on his perch, a cardboard sign in his lap asking for money, and slowed her step. "Hey, Charlie."

"Chloe." The local homeless knew her.

She handed him all three bags. "Can you do me a favor and make sure these get to people who need them?"

He put his nose to the bag. "Happy to."

"Ciao," she said as she left his side.

Chloe all but jogged to the coffee shop, where she was late for a simple meet and greet.

She pushed through the door, the bell slamming against the glass as she entered. A quick scan and she noticed the man behind the pictures.

Why was her heart beating so fast?

She waved and found herself looking over her shoulder.

Dante wasn't there. Why would he be?

Looking back at Eric, she smiled.

Coffee.

That's all this was.

"Hi," she said, taking a seat across the table. "I'm sorry I'm late. I got caught up at work." Eric looked like his photograph. Kind smile, blue eyes, light blond hair.

He rose when she walked up to the table. "I thought I was being stood up."

"Oh, gosh, no. It's a busy week for me, but I said I'd come."

"Your brother's wedding?"

She smiled. "You remembered."

"You mentioned a bachelorette party in Vegas."

Her gut twisted. "Right."

"Ciao, Chloe," Armando, the owner of the coffee shop, greeted her.

She accepted Armando's kiss to her cheek and exchanged a few words in Italian. "This is my new friend, Eric."

"A friend of Chloe is a friend of ours, welcome."

"Thank you," Eric said.

Once Armando walked away, Chloe took a deep breath and settled into her seat.

"You know the owner?"

She nodded. "Yup."

He looked her up and down. "Did you run here from your job?"

Chloe pointed a thumb outside the door. "Just down the street. This is my neighborhood."

Eric sat back in his seat. "Smart. Home turf. Make sure there are people around you in case the coffee date is a psycho."

"You've been there, I take it?"

"More times than I care to admit."

"People never really are who they say they are on these apps," Chloe said.

Eric's smile reached his eyes. He leaned forward and crossed his arm over the other. "I'm guessing you're a double-shot expresso."

She shook her head. "A simple cappuccino is enough for me today."

Eric stood and started toward the counter where they took the orders. "Let me take care of that."

The thing about online dating . . . you know within ten minutes if the guy has a snowball's chance in hell for a shot at a second date.

Eric showed up. That's a first point.

He looked like his picture. Point number two.

He paid for their coffee and didn't try and duck out of the expected thirty-minute meet and greet after five minutes.

"You still live with your mom?" he asked, clarifying when she'd mentioned she lived above the family restaurant just down the street.

"I do. I know it's not an American custom, but Italian girls often live with their families until they get married." Saying the word *married* aloud made her look at her left hand. Thankfully, the green hue on her ring finger had worn off as quickly as it had smudged on.

"I guess that works as long as you get along with your family."

"Family is everything," she told him.

"Some families." He took a sip of his black coffee.

"You don't get along with yours?"

"It's complicated."

"Your way of saying you don't want to talk about it."

Eric shrugged.

"I won't pry. What about you? Do you live alone? Roommates?"

He smiled, sipped his coffee. "Two."

"San Diego is pretty expensive."

"True. You grew up here?"

She thought that was obvious. "Yeah. You?"

He shook his head. "Bay Area. Came here for college and stayed." He had five years on her, so that made sense.

"The weather is hard to beat."

"Everything beats San Francisco's weather and traffic."

The bell chimed on the coffee shop door, drawing her attention away from Eric.

Her glance had her doing a double take.

Dante . . .

And he'd dragged Gio with him. "Oh, shit."

Eric turned in his seat. "What is it?"

"I'm sorry in advance." Her eyes collided with Dante, who quickly diverted his attention to her date.

"Sorry about what?"

"My brother and his best friend just walked in the door."

The confession had Eric looking again.

With Eric's back turned, Chloe glared Dante's way with a shake of her head.

"Is that a problem?"

"Could be embarrassing." At that moment, Gio looked over at the two of them and acted surprised.

Gio and Dante walked to their table. "Hey, Chloe." Gio greeted her first. "I thought you were working the lunch shift."

"I did."

"Huh." Gio turned his attention to Eric. He extended a hand. "I'm Giovanni. Chloe's older brother."

Eric stood, shook hands. "I'm Eric."

When it was Dante's turn, Eric extended his hand and waited a beat before Dante took it. Although Dante didn't offer his name.

"You are?" Eric asked.

Chloe saw Dante's jaw twitch before he gave up his name.

That's when Chloe realized that they hadn't stopped shaking hands.

White-knuckled hands.

She stood and nudged Dante's shoulder. "Okay, you guys have done the protective brother thing, now go away."

Her words had Dante releasing Eric's hand and stepping back.

"We just came for coffee. I had no idea you were here," Gio said.

The look on her brother's face suggested he was telling the truth.

Dante didn't look as innocent.

"I'll see you at home."

They turned to leave.

"A pleasure to meet you," Eric managed as he sat back down.

"It's always good to see who Chloe is spending her time with," Gio said.

"Go away!" Chloe warned.

Gio laughed.

Dante frowned.

Only after the door closed behind them did she take a deep breath.

"Wow . . . that was—"

"I know. I'm super sorry."

Eric looked at his watch. "It's okay. If I had a sister that looked like you, I'd be protective, too."

"Should I take that as a compliment?"

Eric smiled and placed his hand on her arm. "Absolutely."

Chloe picked up her coffee, and the movement dislodged Eric's touch. Unable to help herself, she glanced over her shoulder to see if Dante or Gio lingered outside, watching.

"You seem distracted."

She sighed, let her shoulders fall. "I have a lot going on. I'm sorry."

Eric shook his head, took a final sip of his coffee, and set the cup down. "No, no. You said you had a half an hour. I get it."

"And my family ate into our time."

He looked her in the eye and smiled. "I still spent time with you."

Damn . . .

Eric stood, pushed one arm into his jacket, then the other. "Maybe we can do it again after the wedding?"

Her thoughts went to Dante . . .

"Or not," he started.

Chloe shook her head. "No. Yes. I'd like that. I-ah . . . sorry. The wedding, then it's Christmas. Maybe after would be best."

"You sure?"

No. "Yes."

Eric looked around the coffee shop, then back to her. "I'll call you."

"Okay."

With nothing more, Eric walked away.

When she was alone, she placed her head in both hands and realized she was trembling.

CHAPTER EIGHT

"Do you want to tell me what is going on with you?"

Dante snapped out of his thoughts and into his beer before he looked over at Giovanni and attempted to blow off his friend's concern.

"I don't know—"

"Don't even start with that bullshit. We've known each other too long. Who is she?"

Dante ran a hand over his face, scratched at the hair on his chin.

"I knew it was a woman."

"You're wrong."

"The hell I am. Cough it up."

Dante hid behind his glass, shook Chloe and Eric from his brain. "It's being back here," he said. "Every time I think it will be different."

"That's your mistake."

"I know."

"How is business?" Gio asked.

Dante and his partner chartered boats for pleasure out of Positano. A venture he fell into with a friendship and now couldn't imagine living without. "Slow this time of year, easy for Marco to manage on his own."

"Marco would tell you that even if the phone was ringing off the hook."

"True. 'Family over the business' is the rule he lives by."

Gio took him in over the rim of his glass. "And what's the rule you live by?"

Dante couldn't stop the image of Chloe from entering his brain any more than he could stop his next breath from coming. "Family."

"Yet you live thousands of miles away," Gio pointed out.

He'd considered coming home, finding a balance between Italy and San Diego. And now there was Chloe. But instead of saying any of that to his best friend, Dante took a swig of his beer.

"How is your mama doing? Really doing?" Gio asked.

Dante offered half a smile at the two women walking by the bar he and Gio were seated at without so much as a double take. "She doesn't complain. Accommodating, makes all the excuses. About Anna . . . my father."

Gio was quiet for a few moments. "She's lonely."

"I'm going to confront Anna after the wedding."

Anna was his sister, and unlike many of the unmarried Italian daughters in Little Italy, Anna lived on her own with a friend, Jackie. A girl that was a friend, but more than a friend. And everyone knew it. No one cared. Even Rosa, their mother, was ready to accept what was and would always be.

Anna had attempted to tell their mother once about her sexual preference shortly after their father had left, but their mother wouldn't let her finish.

Dante encouraged Anna to give their mother time and circle back to the conversation.

That never happened. And once Dante left to find their father, Anna couldn't keep up the facade. She moved in with her girlfriend.

"Your mother wants more than her daughter in her life. She misses you."

Dante set his beer down. "I know. She tells me every day."

"And your father."

"My father's an asshole."

"Do you know where he is now?" Gio asked.

Dante's father hadn't lived in the same home as his mother in over seven years. Five years before, Dante had left to drag the sorry ass of the man home. Only when he caught up with him, in a town outside of Naples, Italy, it was apparent his dad wanted nothing to do with returning to the States. He wouldn't divorce his wife or stop providing for her, but he wasn't going to "play house" in San Diego any longer.

It gutted Dante. He was barely out of high school, a couple of years into college, and his father up and left without so much as a goodbye. Dante had come to realize, in the last year or so, that his father's physical abandonment of all of them was written on the wall from day one. He'd always been gone, even when he was in the room. Looking back, Dante would have been surprised if the man had remained faithful to his mother during the time that he lived with her. He knew damn well the man wasn't faithful now.

"Yes," Dante said, answering Gio's question. "But who knows if he's still there. He skips around a lot. Probably to avoid me."

"Maybe he's afraid your mother will get sick of this and finally divorce him. Moving around stops anyone from serving him papers."

"My mother doesn't have it in her." Sadly, that was the truth. His mother lived in a world of delusion.

"She'd be better off," Gio said.

"I know it."

Her husband was on a "business trip" and would eventually return—that's how she'd spin the tale when someone new asked. Anyone who knew her didn't bother with questions.

And Anna was an independent woman that lived with her girlfriend.

When it came to Dante . . . he would settle down and move back to Little Italy to raise a family of his own one day soon.

Yup, Rosa told everyone what she wanted to believe was the truth so often, Dante truly believed that she'd convinced herself that her thoughts were facts.

He chased the condensation on his glass and thought of how Chloe played with the stem of a wineglass when she didn't think anyone was looking.

"Did I lose you again?" Gio asked.

Dante pushed his beer aside. "Yeah." He shook his head. "What did you think of that Eric guy?"

"Eric guy?" Gio looked confused at first. "Oh, you mean Chloe's date."

"Yeah."

Gio shrugged. "Okay, I guess. Not from around here. Why?"

Instead of answering, Dante asked, "Does she date a lot?"

"Probably. It isn't like she goes out of her way to tell Luca or me. We hear about it if she stays local. Someone says something about the guy eventually."

"You hear about a lot, then?"

Gio narrowed his gaze. "What are you getting at?"

Dante lifted the beer he had no intention of finishing. "I didn't like how that Eric guy was looking at her."

"Really? I didn't notice anything off."

Dante just didn't like the Eric guy looking at her at all.

"Like he couldn't be trusted." Total bullshit. But putting doubt in Gio's head felt like the right thing to do.

Shitty for Chloe, but right for Dante.

"I wouldn't worry. Chloe's a pretty good judge of character. Selective."

"How so?"

Gio tilted his beer back. "She doesn't bring a lot of guys around."

"That doesn't necessarily mean anything."

"C'mon. It's a small enough town. We'd hear about it if she was involved with someone without telling us. Besides, she's not good at keeping her love life a secret. It's made it really hard for Luca and me to stay out of punching matches with a couple of familiar faces."

The hair on Dante's neck stood tall.

A feeling he wasn't familiar with. "Who?"

"Doesn't matter. Ancient history. Not the point anyway. Chloe's an open book. If she's involved with someone, we know about it. She either gets super quiet and acts like nothing is happening and spends all the time on her phone texting said nonexistent man, or she clamors on endlessly about him. There is no in-between."

What did that do for their little-big secret?

"And if she's drinking . . . complete truth serum," Gio added.

Dante looked at his beer. "How much drinking?"

"Around the third glass of wine. Unless she's dieting—"

"Dieting? That's ridiculous." Chloe's body had always been perfection.

"Don't get me started. Anyway. If she's not eating, the second glass of wine gets her talking. If this Eric guy was someone, you would have heard all about him with as much drinking as we did in Vegas."

"She didn't mention him." They were too busy getting married.

Dante sighed.

Gio leaned forward. "You all right?"

Dante pushed his glass farther away and reached for his wallet. "I'm tired. Not feeling this tonight."

"It's going to be a busy week."

He stood, dropped a couple of bills on the bar. "The rehearsal is at four tomorrow, right?"

"Yup."

"If you need any help with anything, you know where I am." Dante patted Gio on the shoulder.

"You got it."

Dante walked out of the bar and onto the main street of Little Italy, where the holiday spirit was strung from every light post and corner. Christmas trees, lights, and garlands adorned almost everything. The evening air was crisp but far from bitter cold.

The main piazza's fountain trickled, and a street performer entertained the shoppers with a single guitar and Christmas carols.

He looked for a familiar face and was surprised to come up empty.

Yes, the square was mainly filled with visitors and tourists, but that didn't mean the locals didn't also come out to enjoy a drink or a gelato, even on a cool night.

But Dante didn't recognize anyone.

Not that he was in the mood to socialize.

If he wanted to do that, he would have stayed at the bar with Gio.

He walked past the busy restaurants and shops and up a quieter side street to his childhood home.

Every time he returned, the place felt as if it had shrunk.

There were three bedrooms, his being the smallest since his sister was older than him.

Her bedroom had changed, mainly because his mother had rented the room out. Ironically, to Luca's first wife before they were married, and again the previous spring when she returned briefly. Dante's room, however, remained the same. Although every time he came home, he packed another box and either gave useful things to Goodwill or found a corner in the garage to stash his childhood memories. He was grateful to have a home to come back to, but he didn't expect his mother to keep his bedroom ready for him should she want or need to rent the space.

Dante let himself in the front door and was greeted with the smell of his mother's cooking.

Sure enough, he found her in the kitchen.

"What are you doing?" He kissed her cheek.

"I thought you might be hungry."

"It's after nine."

"They eat later in Italy."

No arguing with that. He looked at the lasagna cooling on the counter. "You don't have to do all this."

"Have and want are two different things. Now sit and I'll get you a plate."

"You made the meal, you don't have to serve it."

His mother shook her head. "Too independent. Can't I do this for my only son?"

He didn't argue, he simply went about dishing himself a portion of lasagna and moved into the dining area.

"Are you on a diet?" Rosa asked with her gaze on his plate.

"I need to keep it trim for the ladies."

"Ladies . . . huh. Where are they? You never speak of anyone in Italy."

"You don't want to hear about my love life, Mama."

She sat to his side, folded her hands on top of the table. "I want to know my son is happy. When I was your age, your father and I had already married and you were on the way."

Pointing out that they were now living estranged lives, still married but on different continents, probably wasn't the best course for the conversation. Instead, Dante changed the subject. "You're not eating?"

Rosa patted her hip. "The doctor says I need to lose some weight."

"So, give it all to me then, eh?"

She smiled and watched as he dug in.

The first forkful of the cheesy pasta goodness brought back a truckload of memories. Sunday dinners, birthdays, and gatherings. As many times as he'd attempted to capture the essence of his mother's recipe, he couldn't do it. The dozens of restaurants in many corners of Italy . . . none did the trick. "It has to be a spice," he said between bites.

"Family secret."

"I'm family."

Rosa laughed. "When you get married, I'll tell your wife."

"That's a reason to get married right there."

His mother warmed to that idea. "You know, there will be plenty of single, beautiful women at Luca and Brooke's wedding on Saturday."

He pointed his fork at her. "Don't go playing matchmaker."

"I wouldn't dream of it."

"Yes, you would." He took another bite, reminded himself to peek at her spice drawer in the kitchen when she wasn't looking.

"I can't help but wish my son finds love closer to home."

He reached a hand across to hers. "I know, Mama."

"I think Brooke is perfect for Luca. And so good with Francesca. You know, she and Chloe have become very good friends."

Chloe's name had him hesitating to bring another bite to his mouth. "Is that so?"

"Oh, yes. Mari tells me they practice yoga all the time together. Tell each other secrets. Almost like sisters."

Dante took the bite, chewed slowly. "Huh."

"They even have girls' night on the town, just them. I don't think that ever happened with Luca's first wife."

While Rosa rattled on, Dante's head swirled with what secrets Chloe shared with Brooke.

No way she would share *their* secret.

". . . family, don't you think?"

"What?" Dante had no idea what his mother had asked.

"I said, it must be wonderful to have such a connection with a new family."

"Yes. Yes. The D'Angelos always make everyone feel like they belong."

"Very true. Mari is a sister to me."

"And Gio and Luca my brothers."

His mother smiled at him. "And Chloe?"

Dante sucked in a breath and slowly nodded. "Yes." But not a sister. God no.

He pictured Anna and Chloe. Hugging his sister was filled with love and joy. Holding Chloe made his blood boil.

"They are all family," he said instead.

For twenty minutes, Dante finished his meal and listened to his mother talk about anyone and everyone in the neighborhood that he spent time with when he lived there. And when he found an opportunity to duck out of the conversation and off to his room, he did.

He shot a text message to Chloe the moment he closed the door behind him.

Are you awake?

Dante toed off his shoes and moved to the edge of his bed.

Three tiny dots flashed on his screen and his heart started to pound.

Yes.

He smiled.

Then he thought of Eric and lost that smile. Are you alone?

No tiny dots.

Nothing.

Chloe?

He found himself moving his right leg up and down as he waited for her answer.

No answer must mean she wasn't.

All he wanted to do was caution her against having that extra drink that got her talking, and here he'd stumbled on her doing something else.

What was she doing?

Dante dropped the phone on his bed and put his head in his hands. "Get a grip."

His phone rang and he jumped.

A very old photo of Chloe filled his screen.

He answered in a rush. "Who are you with?" He squeezed his eyes shut and wanted to kick himself.

"What is your problem?" She sounded mad.

He sighed, and some of the tension in his shoulders left with his breath. "I don't know."

Chloe released a slight laugh. "Well, at least you're honest."

"Are you . . ." No, he couldn't ask if she was alone again. It wasn't his business. It was, legally, maybe. Not really. "Can you talk?"

"I can talk."

Maybe she was alone. The thought made him feel a hundred pounds lighter. Or maybe a hundred and eighty pounds, or an Eric size lighter. "I, ah . . . was out with Gio earlier tonight. We got to talking about things."

"What things?"

"You know . . . things. Like how many drinks it takes to start telling the truth."

"Gio has to nearly pass out to get to that point. And that almost never happens," Chloe said.

"Right. But we weren't talking about him. We were talking about you."

"Why were you doing that?"

Dante leaned back on the bed and stared at the ceiling. "I don't know. You just came up. Anyway, he said two to three drinks is all it takes to have you singing like a canary. I thought maybe we needed to have a strategy for the next few days to get through the wedding."

"To keep me from telling everyone about Vegas."

"Right."

"Because you think I'd do that?"

That sounded like an accusation. "I don't think you'd *want* to do that."

"But you think I would."

This wasn't going the way he wanted it to. "Chloe . . . I haven't stopped thinking about Vegas since Vegas. And the person that I would normally talk to about something this enormous would cut off my left nut if he knew—"

"Gio."

"Yeah, or Luca, for that matter. And you're a girl."

Chloe started laughing. "You noticed."

"This isn't funny."

"Actually, it's hysterical how you're worried that I'm the one that's going to tip someone off when you're the one stalking me in coffee shops, talking me up with my brother, and calling me late at night and asking me who I'm with. The person you need to check is staring at you in the mirror."

"You're saying that you can go on as normal and not say a word to anyone?"

"I'm doing fine so far."

Dante sat up on the bed, switched the phone to his other ear. "And after a few drinks?"

"Who says I'll be drinking much at the wedding?"

"It's a wedding. We're Italian. You not drinking will look suspicious."

"If you're that worried, you're the groomsman to my bridesmaid. It won't look unusual for the two of us to be seen together. Stick close and be sure and fill my glass with club soda."

That wouldn't be a hardship. "I'd . . . that would be . . . I'd like that."

"Fine."

He was pretty sure that wasn't fine, but he was taking her word at face value.

"And, Dante?" She paused. "If you follow me into a coffee shop again, you won't have to worry about Gio removing your left nut."

Why did the thought of her hand on his left nut, even if it was a threat, make him warm all over?

He chuckled.

"That was not me flirting," Chloe scolded.

"Sorry."

"I'll see you tomorrow."

Dante smiled into the phone. "Sleep well, *bella*."

He wasn't sure if she growled or hummed.

He liked to think it was a hum before she disconnected the call.

Either way, he flopped back on the bed, much more ready to crawl into it knowing Chloe was alone in hers and he was the last man she spoke with before falling asleep.

Or so he hoped.

CHAPTER NINE

Thursday's rehearsal dinner was a breeze.

Chloe stuck to her word, drank very little, and let Dante sit by her side throughout the evening. If anyone noticed he was clingy, no one said a word.

Friday was spent at the spa, filled with manicures, pedicures, and facials. The wedding party distracted Brooke from any and all things stressful.

"I keep thinking I've forgotten something huge," Brooke said, sitting in her reclining chair with a technician at her feet and another filing her nails.

"The only thing you've forgotten is that we all did this last week, and doing this twice is overkill," Carmen told her.

"Trust me, I've checked the list three times over. My mama has checked it more than me. We're good. Relax and enjoy the rest of your time as a single woman." Chloe closed her eyes and tried hard not to think about the fact that she no longer spoke from the single side of the fence.

"Marion is coming in the morning, right?" Brooke asked.

"Your hairdresser is coming. I spoke with her yesterday. We're all going to be beautiful."

"The cake—"

"And the flowers and the tiny gifts for all the guests . . . everything. Do you know what Luca is stressing over right now?" Chloe asked.

"What?"

"*Nothing.* Absolutely nothing."

Carmen started laughing. "He isn't getting his nails done."

"He's probably in the kitchen, helping with the lunch rush."

The owner of the salon walked over with the bottle of champagne to refill their glasses. "Ladies?"

"Yes, please," Carmen said.

Chloe shook her head. "Give mine to Brooke."

Brooke narrowed her gaze. "That's not like you."

Dante's hit wasn't off the mark when it came to her loose tongue and alcohol. "It's all been less attractive since Vegas," she told them both.

"That must have been one hell of a hangover." Carmen looked her up and down.

"You have no idea."

Brooke sipped her sparkling wine and put her glass aside. "As long as there isn't something you need to tell us about."

Chloe sat a little taller. "What do you mean?"

"I don't know. Everyone watches me to see if I'm drinking as if that's the pregnancy barometer."

"Oh my God, no. Is that what . . . please don't tell me that's what people are saying."

Brooke shook her head. "No. Not people. I just . . . I don't know, you've been a little quieter, and since—"

Chloe cut her off by lifting the glass of champagne that she'd been served when they walked into the salon and took a big swig. "I absolutely am *not* pregnant."

"Good." Brooke blew out a breath. "Bailing Luca out of jail before our honeymoon puts a damper on the whole thing."

"Wait, does Luca think I'm—"

"No. I know how he is, though. I feel sorry for any boys that come around when Franny starts dating. He's going to make it impossible for them."

"Trust me. I'm aware. I keep most of my dating life far away from our corner of San Diego."

"I bet. And since you haven't talked much about your dating life lately, I thought I'd bring it up. I know my marrying your brother might seem like I'd share everything with him. But I can and will keep anything you want to avoid telling him from him. You know that, right?"

Chloe instantly thought of Dante and knew that as far as secrets went, that one was too big not to share with her brother. And would in fact end with someone getting a bloody nose.

Worse, it would end friendships.

She faked a smile and lied through her teeth. "Rest assured, there is nothing to tell."

Brooke sipped her wine again. "Not even about Eric?"

Chloe rolled her eyes. "Shouldn't everyone be talking about you? Eric was a coffee date. That's it."

"Helloooo! I need to know about coffee dates."

"Helloooo!" Chloe mimicked. "You've been busy. And there is nothing to tell. It was coffee. Nothing remotely close to baby-making action."

"Will you see him again?"

"Maybe. Let's get you married first."

And start Chloe's divorce . . . no, *annulment* process.

Damn. When had her life become so complicated?

~

"You're beautiful."

Chloe and Carmen stood back as the photographer snapped pictures of Brooke as she took herself in for the first time once the veil had been attached to her head.

From the top of her head to the satin tip of her two-inch heels, Brooke was stunning.

Luca was going to melt.

"This is really happening." Brooke's eyes filled with unshed tears.

"Oh, God. Don't start that," Carmen warned. "Deep breath."

Chloe rushed forward and fanned Brooke's face as Brooke widened her eyes in an attempt to get ahold of her emotions. "I never thought I'd see this day."

"Every woman deserves the fairy tale." Carmen placed both hands on Brooke's shoulders. "Especially you."

"Hold it right there," the photographer told them.

The sentimental stuff was shoved aside for the pictures until there was a knock at the door before it creaked open. "It's only me." Chloe heard her mother's voice before she peeked behind the door.

Mari sucked in a breath and instantly started to tear up. "Oh, my dear. *Bellissima.*"

"Don't start that, Mama. You'll get everyone crying," Chloe warned.

"I can cry. It's what I do when my children get married."

Mari opened her arms and moved into Brooke's. "I'm so blessed that I can call you my own after today."

"Thank you, Mari."

"Mama. You must call me Mama from now to forever."

Oh, boy! Brooke's eyes swelled again.

Carmen reached for the tissues.

The photographer snapped more pictures than the paparazzi.

Another knock on the door and Franny came running in. Her flower girl dress was laced up in the silver color of the bridesmaid's dresses but fit for an eight-year-old.

Chloe put an end to the fun. "I believe the car is downstairs waiting. We don't want to be late or someone is going to get nervous."

They walked down the stairs of the family home and out into the restaurant that was completely empty. A sight almost never seen in the middle of the day.

In front of the building, beside the outdoor dining patio, a limousine waited for the wedding party.

The moment they stepped from the restaurant doors, the people in the streets stopped and gave them room. It wasn't as if they asked, it was just how it worked out.

Chloe made sure the doors to the restaurant were locked behind them and slid the key into the small clutch that held very little before moving beside Brooke to help get her into the car without, as much as possible, disturbing her dress.

As the limo took off, Franny bounced in her seat. "You're so pretty, Mama."

Hearing Franny call Brooke mama warmed everyone's heart. Considering Chloe's niece had been all but abandoned by her biological mother, it was a blessing she had Brooke in her life.

"Thanks, sweetheart."

"I'm going to have lots of bridesmaids at my wedding," Franny announced.

"Is that right?" Mari asked.

"Yes. And they will all be beautiful like Auntie Chloe and Carmen."

Chloe and Carmen smiled at each other.

"Just make sure you pick a dress the girls can use again," Chloe suggested.

"Unlike the one you picked," Brooke chided Carmen.

"Hey, it wasn't that bad."

Brooke frowned.

Carmen looked at her feet.

Chloe laughed.

"Taffeta," Brooke said as if that explained it all.

"My mother was the worst mother-of-the-bride ever."

Mari leaned forward and tapped Chloe's knee. "You won't have to worry about that with me."

Chloe swallowed.

Hard.

"I'm sure I won't."

"I should have eloped," Carmen said with a sigh.

Chloe coughed on her own saliva.

Her mother handed her a bottle of water that was in the door of the limo. "Are you okay?"

"Fine."

Carmen and Brooke talked about Carmen's wedding and the ill-fated dresses while Chloe attempted to keep color in her face.

She just needed to get through the ceremony, the reception . . . Christmas. And then the week that Luca and Brooke were gone for their honeymoon. Then she would be on a plane for her long-put-off trip to Bali, where she could sit on a beach, meditate in a temple, and tell complete strangers all about the mess she'd made of her life with one simple "I do." Maybe by the time she got back, Dante would have figured out how to get it to where they said, "I don't."

Or maybe she'd miss her flight back and stay in Bali until it was all over.

That didn't sound half-bad.

Not bad at all.

~

I've got this.

I've got this.

I've got this.

The mantra sang in Dante's brain as he stood beside his best friends and waited for the women to make their entrance.

I've got this.

Then the back door to the church opened and she stood there.

"Awh shit," he whispered under his breath.

Chloe wore silver, not white . . . and certainly not red as she had when they'd married.

Franny walked in first. Her dress bounced in her excitement as rose petals were tossed to the floor.

Dante was having a hard time concentrating on anything but Chloe. She took her time walking down the aisle, her smile radiant.

Flowers rested in her hands as she glanced from one side of the church to the other.

Here, in the church where they'd both had their first communion, there was a radiant air that surrounded her, an elegance Dante couldn't name.

This is where Chloe deserved to get married.

A real church with real flowers and a real husband.

Only when she was within a few feet of the altar did her eyes drift to the three of them. It seemed, at first, that she would avoid eye contact with him altogether.

That didn't happen.

When their eyes met, the air in his lungs literally didn't move.

I'm losing it.

She lifted a corner of her mouth as if she could sense her effect on him, before looking away to take the stairs and her position at the front of the church.

It was when Carmen moved next to Chloe and his view of her was partially blocked that it dawned on him that he'd been staring.

Thankfully, the music changed, and everyone in attendance rose to their feet to welcome the bride.

The moment Brooke and her father stepped into the doorway, Dante heard Luca's gasp.

Luca looked up at the rafters of the church and mouthed the words *thank you.*

Gio patted Luca's shoulder as he pulled himself together.

Brooke and her father made it to the front of the church, and the ceremony began.

~

"I've been waiting for this part all night."

Dante's lips sat next to Chloe's ear; his breath was a soothing caress on her skin.

Except that every person they knew, and every family member they had, were within a stone's throw of them.

Luca and Brooke had their first dance and then the wedding party was asked to join them.

Hence the lips-to-ear moment where everyone watched.

Where a photographer was busy snapping pictures, and Chloe smiled as if Dante was talking about his mother's dress . . . which was, quite honestly, the most daring thing Chloe had ever seen Rosa wear in her life. Maroon, a bit low cut . . . had Rosa lost weight?

"What are you doing?" Dante asked.

"Thinking about anything but what you're saying."

"Why?"

"Because people are staring."

Dante tossed his head, pulled her a little closer, his lips nearly touching her ear. "I'm dancing with my wife."

His words were meant to get a reaction, so she gave it to him.

In pain.

She dug her newly manicured nails into the hand that held hers.

"Zio."

They turned on the dance floor, and the photographer stopped them to snap a picture.

Alone again, they painted on smiles and talked under their breath.

"Don't tell me you haven't thought about Vegas this whole time," Dante said.

Chloe closed her eyes for a moment, felt the man in her arms as he moved her on the dance floor, and imagined in a brief fantasy if things were different.

Her forever crush finally returning the feelings she'd had her entire life, resulting in flowers and rings, churches and cake . . .

She leaned back enough to look into Dante's eyes.

The playful smile on his face fell and his steps slowed as the music started to fade.

"It's time to get this party started!" The DJ bumped the music, the beat changed, and the dance floor flooded with guests ready to let loose.

Salena grabbed Dante's arm and pulled him into a dance, and Chloe reached for the first glass of wine she could find.

CHAPTER TEN

Cotton in the mouth.

Burning light of the sun through the blinds . . .

Chloe was way too young to make a habit of this morning ritual.

She pulled her pillow under her head, realized it was in fact *her* pillow, and closed her eyes against the day.

Her brother was married . . . to the right woman this time.

The vows had been said, the cake had been cut . . . the bouquet tossed, which Salena had caught, and the rest of the night was a blur.

There was wine, dancing, and plenty of laughs.

And blur.

Chloe opened and closed her mouth a few times, the offensive pasty taste on the roof of her mouth suggesting she had in fact remembered to brush her teeth before climbing into bed.

"Auntie Chloe," Franny called from outside her closed bedroom door. "Are you still in bed?"

Chloe didn't have an opportunity to answer before Franny bounced in, bright and smiling. "What are you doing? It's late."

"Last night was late."

Franny climbed onto the bed with her, a habit she'd had since she could walk, and Chloe scooted over.

"Nonna said you should probably get moving since Papa and Mama will be here soon to open presents."

The newlyweds had spent the night in a hotel but were due home after noon. Because of Franny, they planned on spending Christmas in San Diego and leaving right after for their honeymoon. All of which meant that Chloe wasn't off the hook and able to break free quite yet. She'd signed up to take turns watching her niece and working extra shifts at the restaurant.

Chloe felt a finger tapping her shoulder.

She fluttered her eyes open to stare at Franny.

"You're not falling back to sleep, are you?"

"That's not possible with a human alarm clock." She pushed herself up on her elbows and looked at the time. Nine thirty.

She moaned.

Franny bounced off the bed and moved to the window, opened the curtains wide. "C'mon."

Her phone, which was set on silent, buzzed on her nightstand. "I'm moving."

"I'll tell Nonna you're up." Satisfied, Franny left the room.

Chloe sat up with a stretch, moved her head from one side to the other.

No headache. Which was a good sign.

Her phone buzzed again.

Looking over, she saw Salena's name pop on her screen with a text message.

Chloe opened her messages, only to find Salena telling her to call her. Three messages back to back, all saying the same thing.

Call me.

The minute you wake up. Call me.

Are you still asleep, you lazy . . . call me!

Chloe rolled her eyes, got to her feet, and dialed her friend as she padded to the bathroom.

Salena picked up immediately. "About time."

"Where is the fire?"

"Are you ready to give me all the details about Vegas?"

Chloe stopped short of the bathroom door, turned, and went back to her room. "Excuse me?"

"Vegas. Last week. You and Dante?"

Chloe lowered her voice. "What are you talking about?"

"Oh, don't even start that. You, my friend, were drinking last night, and somewhere between the Macarena and the Cupid Shuffle, you told me what happened."

No. No, she didn't.

That can't happen. Didn't happen.

"Wh-what did I tell you?"

"That Dante made more than a pass at you. You don't remember?"

Okay, yes, now that Salena mentioned it, she vaguely remembered talking about Dante kissing her. "Oh, that."

"Oh, that! You said there was a whole lot more to the story but you couldn't tell me last night. So here we are, the next day, so spill!"

Chloe shook her head. "Wait, what?"

"Spill. I've been up for hours and need *all* the details."

"All I told you was that he kissed me?"

"I know there's more, Chloe. Did you sleep with him?" Salena sighed. "Please tell me he is everything we ever imagined."

Chloe stood again. "We have to have this conversation later. Franny is right outside the door," she lied. "And I have to get ready for lunch and presents."

"You can't leave me hanging like this."

"You suck at keeping secrets."

"I do not."

"You do. And this can't get out. Please, Salena. You have to promise me."

"I promise."

Right. All good intentions, but Salena couldn't help herself. Much like Chloe when the party was right.

"We'll talk later," Chloe said.

"I'm holding you to that."

~

Two hours later Chloe stood to the side of the rooftop patio where her family gathered with just a few friends, mainly the wedding party, and ate lunch and watched Brooke and Luca open the hoard of gifts from the day before.

Franny fell to the side, playing babysitter to Carmen's son, which she ate up.

Dante and Gio hoofed gifts from the lower apartments to the roof while Brooke did most of the unwrapping.

Carmen sat to the side and wrote down the names and gifts for the required thank-you cards later.

Chloe made sure there was enough food, more wine, and other beverages available for everyone in attendance.

The outside heat lamps kept the roof warm, and the barriers they'd constructed for the outside dining area for the restaurant had been mimicked for their own personal use on the patio so the space could be used year-round.

"I thought we told everyone that we didn't need anything," Brooke said to Luca loud enough for everyone to hear.

"We didn't listen," Rosa said from her perch beside Mari.

Chloe looked over to find Gio and Dante both struggling to carry a massive box, which was obviously heavy, through the back door.

She moved to push a chair out of their way.

Dante smiled and winked. His motion wasn't new but twisted her gut all the same.

Chloe chided herself on her reaction to him.

Seriously, it had to stop. Look where all her fantasies had landed her.

"This is the last of 'em," Gio announced.

"Oh, good. There isn't enough room in the apartment," Brooke exclaimed.

Everyone laughed.

"It's time to do some redecorating anyway," Luca suggested.

Chloe agreed. Some of the things in the space had been there since his first wife. Probably out of sheer laziness. And it was time for a change.

"Where is your papa?" Rosa asked Brooke.

"Oh, he was wiped out after yesterday. He will probably sleep for a week."

"He looked like he held up pretty well, considering," Mari said.

The man had suffered a stroke, and he'd had trouble walking when they'd all first met him. The fact that he was able to walk Brooke down the aisle unassisted was a huge relief.

"He did." Brooke looked up at Chloe.

Without any words exchanged, Chloe assured her friend what she knew she needed to hear. "And don't worry. Franny and I will go by and visit him twice when you guys are gone and be on call if he needs us."

"Thank you."

Gio nudged by her, grabbed a plate, and started to pile on some food.

Carmen's husband lifted the portable coffee carafe. "Is there any more?" he asked.

Chloe reached for it. "I'll get some."

"I'll help," Dante said as he followed her away from the guests and off the patio.

"It's a one-person job," she said as they reached the stairwell.

He waited until they were down a whole level and stopped her.

"You hardly talked to me yesterday."

"That's not true."

His normal playful smile was gone, and what replaced it was something that looked a lot more like concern.

"Chloe, I—"

Noise from the top of the stairs stopped him.

She continued the descent to the bottom floor and whispered under her breath, "We need to talk." If for no other reason than for her to inform him that Salena knew about the kiss and would likely make more of it. And that would be enough to get the gossip going. They needed a game plan.

"Tonight," he said at the mouth of the kitchen.

"Fine. But far away from here."

He removed the carafe from her hands and smiled.

She paused and then looked away before allowing the flutter in her belly to show on her face.

Chloe turned on her heel to find Gio staring at the two of them from across the room, his brow furrowed. "Mama wanted two cappuccinos, one for her and one for Rosa."

"Okay," she said. Her smile came easy this time.

Gio shrugged and walked away.

Chloe and Dante exchanged glances and moved in opposite directions.

~

Dante couldn't remember the last time a woman picked him up.

Chloe pulled up to the curb like an Uber driver in the Gaslamp District, and he jumped into her car.

Saying nothing, she used the green light to make it through the intersection and through the holiday traffic.

"Hi," he said.

"Hey."

Her hair was slicked back in a simple ponytail. She wore a slim black turtleneck sweater that hugged her body and blue jeans. And she darted around traffic as if someone was on her tail.

"Is someone following us?"

"I wouldn't have picked you up if that was the case."

He laughed. "I was joking."

Chloe looked at him, then back at the road.

"Hoookay . . ." He turned to look out the passenger window.

"Is that what this is? A joke to you?"

He knew how he sounded, how the last few days looked.

"No. I just want to see you smile again. At me. Listen—"

She lifted a hand. "Not while I'm driving, okay. Let me just . . . Let's talk about something else until we get where we're going."

He watched as her hands gripped the steering wheel and her eyes stuck to the road.

"You know, I don't think I've ever driven in a car with you before. Not where you were driving."

That brought a slight smile to her lips. "A skill I learned a long time ago."

He looked around the space. "Is this the same car you've had since high school?"

She shrugged. "I don't use it much."

"I'm not judging."

Chloe glanced his way. "What do you drive . . . in Italy?"

"I call them coffin cars. In Naples I drove a car so small my knees touched the wheel."

That had a smile on her lips.

"And in Positano a scooter is practical, narrow streets, winding hills."

Chloe jumped onto the freeway and headed north. He didn't question where they were going.

"Do you like it there?"

"Positano?"

"Yes?"

He nodded. "I do. But there are other places, smaller islands and places along the coast, I like more."

She glanced at him briefly. "Oh?"

"Marco and I, we have three boats now. I know it's not a lot, but—"

"Three boats are three more than I have."

There was pride in her voice, and it made Dante sit a little taller. "Well, we'd likely have more, but things were hard for a while."

"It's been hard for everybody." The world hadn't seen the virus coming, and no one could predict how long it would hold on. There wasn't a person on the planet unaffected.

"We charter our boats for private tours and often shuttle them between Capri and Positano. Along the way there are smaller villages where we stop and help the locals. Sleepy coastal towns. The way San Diego once was, I suspect."

"It sounds lovely."

"It is. You'd love Marco and his granddaughter. She's all of six. Spitfire. Blonde."

"Really?"

"Yes. I have no idea where the blonde hair came from. Cute little thing."

Chloe switched freeways and cut over toward Ocean Beach.

Dante smiled, remembering some of the good times he'd had there.

She kept driving along Sunset Cliffs until she'd reached as far as the road would go.

The park at the end was closed off since it was after dark, but there were plenty of places to park along the road.

"Can you still walk down there?" Dante pointed toward the steps that led down to a long expanse of beach that only locals and surfers knew about.

"Yeah. But the tide is high right now."

Dante glanced over, caught her eyes.

"I checked," she clarified.

"Very thorough."

Chloe turned off the engine and the inside of the car quieted instantly. "I figured we'd notice anyone driving by or looking in at us out here."

With houses on one side of the street, and a cliff with the ocean crashing against it on the other, she wasn't wrong.

Chloe unhooked her seat belt and shifted in her seat to face him. "Giovanni suspects something."

Dante released his seat belt and leaned back. "I sensed that, too."

"And I, ah . . . might have said something to Salena."

Dante's head twisted so fast his neck spasmed, and he reached a hand to soothe the pain. "Said what?"

Chloe closed her eyes. "Yesterday . . . at the wedding. Your crack on the dance floor about dancing with your wife set me off. What were you thinking?"

"Wait? What?"

"I've been good. Great, even. I mean, it's Christmas and my brother's wedding. Everyone is celebrating and I'm practically Mother Teresa sipping tea. I know my limits." Chloe looked directly at him. "You know my limits."

"I'm . . . what?"

Chloe squeezed her eyes shut, then opened them. "Apparently I told Salena that you kissed me in Vegas."

Dante held his breath and waited for the punch line.

Silence filled the car.

"And?"

Chloe looked out the dark windshield. "I may have told her there was more to tell but didn't tell her the *more*."

He released a tiny breath. "So . . . we kissed."

"She thinks we slept together."

"You told her that?"

"No!"

"I'm confused."

Chloe rolled her eyes. "Salena *thinks* we slept together. Because apparently, when I was pissed at you for bringing up to me that we were married and dancing for the first time, I decided it was a good time to start drinking. I told Salena that you kissed me in Vegas. And . . . that there was more to the story. Which she called me first thing this morning to hear."

The pieces started to fall into place.

"Let me get this straight. You're blaming me for you getting drunk last night and spilling our little secret?"

Chloe narrowed her brows at him. "It's your fault. I was doing fine before the wife comment."

"So, you told her we slept with each other."

"No! Damn it. You're not listening. She *thinks* we did. Last night I told her there was more to the story, and she *assumed* we got naked."

And just like that, Dante imagined Chloe naked, and so did his body, and fucking hell . . . he was a shitty man.

Even sitting in a car all folded up in the seat, practically yelling at him, blaming him for her loose lips, he wanted nothing more than to see her skin, taste her lips . . . touch her . . .

". . . are you even listening to me?"

"Sorry."

"What the hell was I supposed to say to her? 'No, Salena, we didn't do the nasty, we got married'? Yeah, that sounds like a natural flow of casual conversation."

Dante blew out a breath. "You let her assume."

"I told her we kissed and said I'd talk to her later."

Dante buried his face in his hands. "If your brothers think—"

"I know . . ."

Chloe shifted around in her seat again, staring out the window. "I've thought about this all day. I think we keep it simple. I tell Salena that we were both drunk in Vegas, which isn't a lie . . . and that a pass was made. And if she says something, and it gets to my brothers, you can say that I made a pass at you and you didn't want to say anything to embarrass me. I'll . . . I'll back that story."

"They won't believe it."

Chloe started to laugh. Slowly at first, then with enough force to shake the car. "Trust me, they will."

"Chloe—"

"And the looks that Gio is giving me . . . us, can be explained."

Gio would gut him if he thought he slept with his sister.

Rightfully so.

Except.

"We only have to do this for a couple of weeks. Less actually," she said.

"What do you mean?"

Drops of rain started hitting the windscreen of the car as she spoke. "As soon as Luca returns from his honeymoon, I'm leaving for Bali. You'll be back in Italy . . . so . . . We'll fix this marriage thing. Nobody will be the wiser."

It was Dante's turn to narrow his eyes. "I'm not going back to Italy right away."

She turned to look at him. "You're not?"

"No. I thought I'd . . . How long are you going to be in Bali?"

Her jaw dropped.

The muscles in her throat contracted. "I canceled my return ticket."

"You what?"

She looked him dead in the eye. "I don't know if I belong in San Diego. You of all people know that. I don't think my family will understand, and in light of everything, I hope I can count on you to keep this to yourself."

"Chloe—" He reached for her hand.

She pulled away.

"Lying is not something that comes easy. If I do come home, this marriage will be behind us, and like you said in Vegas . . . we can laugh about it." Her attempt at a smile made his heart want to cry. "If I stay here, it's going to come out. And that isn't fair to you. This is a mistake we both made."

Dante's chin lifted and his shoulders pushed back. "I'll keep your secret."

"Thank you."

CHAPTER ELEVEN

Christmas came and went. The happy newlyweds, the ones everyone knew about, were off to the Bahamas to soak up white sand and sunshine, and Dante literally felt the walls of his childhood home closing in.

He'd come back for the wedding, a visit . . . and a heart-to-heart with his mother. A conversation he'd put off until after the celebrations.

The time had come, and what he really wanted to do now was bounce. Get away for a while, regroup.

Only he couldn't.

Once Nevada processed his marriage license, they'd send a copy in the mail. The last thing Dante needed was his mother intercepting it.

Dante's phone rang and Gio's face lit his screen.

"Hey," he answered quickly.

"What are you doing?"

"I'm wondering what I'm still doing here."

Gio laughed. "Been wondering that myself. I have the day off. Tacos and beer in PB?"

"Sounds perfect."

Ten minutes later, Gio pulled up and they were headed to Pacific Beach.

"You don't look good," Giovanni said as he merged into traffic.

"Long couple weeks."

"The hard part is over. You should be sleeping in and calling it a vacation now."

Dante ran a hand over his chin and turned to look out the window. "Except I have some shit I have to sort out."

"Oh?"

"About my father."

"Let's get that beer going and you can tell me all about it."

Twenty minutes later they were on an outside patio, heat lamps on high, music pumping, with craft beers in front of them, waiting on tacos.

"What's going on?"

Dante tipped back his beer, set it down. "I want my mother to file for a divorce."

Gio didn't look surprised. "I'm listening."

"My father's never coming back. I'm not even sure he can."

"Why not?"

"My *zio* Raul, the one I visited in New York before I met you in Vegas, he said my father made his bed and was living in it."

"What the hell does that mean?"

"I don't know," Dante said. "I asked him to explain. Raul stopped talking. I kept the conversation going . . . one-sided, and every once in a while he'd shake his head or squirm in his chair."

"Like you were close to the truth."

"Yeah."

"What did you say to him?"

"I told him the things I've told you over the years. That my father moves around a lot in Italy. Almost like he is running from me. He's not alone. There are women." Dante took a drink from his beer. "Bastard."

"That wasn't surprising the first time you told me. There's no way your mother doesn't know."

"Why stay married?"

Gio shrugged. "Cultural sting?"

"That can't be worse than being the woman whose husband lives in a different country that she never visits, and he never comes home."

"Maybe she's waiting for him to file."

"He doesn't live here. She's the one that would have to do it."

Gio narrowed his eyes. "Really? How do you know that?"

Dante let out a short laugh. "I took a crash course on divorce this week." The words were out of his mouth before he realized what he was saying. Thankfully Gio didn't think they applied to anyone but Rosa.

"If she files, he still has to sign. Can it all be done online? From afar?"

"Yeah. I think so."

Gio drank from his glass. "Your mother's young enough to find a man who will be there for her."

"If she did that, I wouldn't feel so damn guilty about not living here."

"You could move home, and the guilt would fade," Gio said.

"Believe me, I've thought about it."

Giovanni looked at him from across the table, surprise in his eyes. "Really?"

He shrugged. "I say that and yet I'm anxious to move."

"That's because there isn't anything you're doing here to occupy your time. I mean, yes, the wedding and all the parties, but that, while fun, gets old. Working, setting goals, reaching toward something . . . you're not doing that here. You do that in Italy."

"True. Staying with my mother isn't ideal."

"I know that. The upstairs apartment was a great step for me. Too bad your mother doesn't own a four-story building."

The waiter showed up with their food. "I noticed a block away from our place, two of the residential houses are gone and a new restaurant opened up."

Gio talked around his food. "Real estate has skyrocketed. Some people are cashing in and moving out of state."

"I wonder if anyone has approached my mother," Dante mused aloud.

"There isn't a month that passes that someone doesn't contact us, trying to get us to sell. And honestly, if it wasn't for Luca's passion for the place, I wouldn't put it past my mother. But since at least one of us wants to keep it going, D'Angelo's will stay in the family for another generation."

"You never consider taking over?"

Gio looked at him like he was crazy. "Please. I want a D'Angelo label on a wine bottle. And next spring I'm joining you in Italy, so don't move home quite yet."

Dante took in half the taco in one bite, chased it with his beer. "You're too involved with your family to stay in Italy."

"I said nothing about staying. I have things to learn, and perhaps investments to consider."

"Vineyards?"

"I'll start with one. Maybe a partnership. I need to start somewhere."

"That's how I felt with the boat tours. Now I want more. Want to start something here. Have my feet in both places."

Gio picked up his drink, waved it in Dante's direction. "Do you have the capital for that?"

"Marco and I are ready to buy a fourth boat. I suggested we consider diversifying or spreading out." Marco, his partner and the grandfather of the cutest girl on the planet, had jumped at the opportunity to go into business with Dante when he'd presented it to him nearly four years before.

"Spreading to the US is a stretch."

"Not really. And he wants his granddaughter to have a reason to come to America, have a financial stake here."

"Interesting perspective."

Dante finished the last of his tacos, signaled the waiter for another round of beer. "I wasn't planning on returning to Italy until I've determined if it makes sense to open shop here."

"You're just telling me this now?"

"You didn't ask."

Gio laughed.

"Except . . ."

"I knew there had to be a but."

Dante sighed. "But . . . I haven't lived with my mother for five years."

Gio's smile grew. "Now we're getting somewhere. She's putting a cramp in your sex life."

Normally, Dante would agree. But the thought of a random hookup hadn't occurred to him. And the reason for that was Chloe.

Giovanni leaned forward, and his smile fell. "Don't tell me that hasn't crossed your mind."

"People change, my friend."

"Not you."

That actually hurt to hear. "Right."

"Really, Dante. Two girls on prom night. C'mon. Not so many years ago."

A second beer was put in front of him. "I grew up."

The look on Gio's face said he didn't believe him. "Let's get through New Year's Eve, and if there isn't a girl on your arm, I might believe you."

"That won't be a problem." The only woman he wanted was out of his reach.

Gio rolled his eyes. "Sure. Whatever. As for Rosa's house? Rent an Airbnb. They're furnished, temporary. You can borrow my bike while you're here."

Dante hadn't thought of that. "Good idea."

"You know," Gio said as he folded his arms across his chest, "if your mama has you around, she might be more inclined to kick your dad to the curb."

"Maybe."

"I sure would like to know what went down with your parents."

"I don't think anything went down. Anna was born six and a half months after they were married. I showed up a couple years later. He played until he couldn't anymore. Then my father took off as soon as he could. Hell, he was only half-there when he was home." There was a day he felt sorry for himself over the facts.

Now Dante was simply pissed.

For his mother.

"What an asshole."

"If there was anything more to the story, your mother and mine would have talked about it."

Gio shook his head. "If Mama knows anything, she doesn't say."

Dante thought of Chloe and Salena and how family secrets eventually unravel. "If anything major went down, it will come out eventually."

"Skeletons never stay in closets," Gio said, laughing.

Dante chuckled with him and, at the same time, hoped his would.

~

"It wasn't a big deal. It just made everything since super awkward." Chloe sat at the park with Salena talking while they watched Franny and one of her little friends play.

"You didn't sleep with him."

"How many times do I have to deny that?"

Salena shook her head. "You're ruining all my fantasies for you."

"Sorry."

"I don't think you'd tell me if you did."

"But I didn't. So let it go."

Salena shook her finger in Chloe's face. "See there. Puts a question mark on the whole conversation."

This wasn't going anywhere. Salena was like a dog with a bone, unwilling to give it up. "I made the pass at him, okay?"

Salena's eyes widened. "What?"

Chloe kept her lie going. "At first, I thought he was into it, but then he pushed me away. It's embarrassing."

"I don't know, Chloe. The way Dante looks at you."

She huddled into her jacket even though the temperature was in the high fifties. "I know. It's strange now. It's like he feels sorry for me."

"That's crap and you know it."

Complete crap, but Chloe was sticking with her story.

Lucky for her, her cell phone rang, giving the necessary distraction to shift the conversation.

Eric's name popped up on her screen.

She wanted to ignore it, but Salena was staring at her.

Smiling, Chloe answered the call. "Hi."

"Hey. How are you? How was your Christmas?"

"It was good. Yours?"

"Crazy, as always."

"It's a busy time of year," Chloe said, keeping the small talk going.

Salena looked at Chloe, rolled her eyes. Obviously, she could hear what he was saying even with the phone pressed to Chloe's ear.

"Now that life is settled, are you up for that second date?" he asked.

Salena nudged her and nodded.

"I-I'd, ah, like that. I'm still kinda busy."

"Oh?"

"Yeah, my brother and new sister-in-law are on their honeymoon, and I'm on auntie duty with my niece. I'm working at night."

"Oh . . . what about New Year's Eve?"

"Tell him to come," Salena said in a hushed whisper.

The thought of Eric and Dante in the same room made her nauseous. Then again, it would stop any whispers of her and Dante.

Maybe she'd stay home.

Salena poked her shoulder.

"Uhm. I have plans, but—"

"If you already have a date—"

"No," Chloe interrupted. "You can't count my annoying best friend as my date."

Salena made a face at her comment.

"Do you want to join us?" Chloe wanted to revoke the invitation as soon as it left her lips, but with her bestie staring her down, she didn't dare.

"You sure?" Eric asked. "Is there room?"

"Yeah, absolutely."

"Okay, then. I'd like that."

Salena was smiling.

"I'll call you later with the details."

"I look forward to it."

She disconnected the call and dropped the phone in her lap.

"The best way to get Dante out of your head is to get another guy in it."

"Unless Dante shows up."

"I don't doubt he will. Which is even better. Let him watch another man with his hands on you, and then we'll see if he really meant to push you away." Salena sat back, arms crossed over her chest.

Chloe knew, deep down, she was playing with fire, and the one that was going to burn in the end was her.

CHAPTER TWELVE

Dante found his mother in their small backyard, trimming the dead out of the winter flowers. The sun peeked through the gray clouds and threatened rain by the end of the day. His mother looked younger, outside in nature, than she did standing in the kitchen. It helped that she was listening to music that even he was familiar with.

She caught him out of the corner of her eye and hesitated in her task. "Are you going to stand there staring all day or give your mama a hand?"

He stepped forward and looked around. "What exactly do you need me to do?"

"You can empty that bucket and bring it back," she said, pointing to the waste can at her side.

Moving quickly to do as she asked, he took the bucket around to the side yard and emptied it in the green waste. As he walked back, he stared again. This time looking at his mother with a different eye.

Could he actually see her with another man?

The image wiggled in his head like a worm and made him feel a little ill.

The thought of her living alone the rest of her life, however, made him downright sick.

"You're staring again."

Dante placed the empty bucket down and rocked back on his heels. "Papa's never coming home," he said without preamble.

To his mother's credit, she didn't stop cutting away at the rosebush.

When she didn't say anything, Dante started to repeat himself. "Did you hear me . . . Papa—"

"I know."

"Do you know why?"

She kept pruning. "We've had this conversation before, Dante."

"And you never answered."

"What he told me and what is the truth are different things."

"Which are?"

She turned to him now, gave him the eye. The one that said, *Don't pry.*

"When a husband and wife argue, they don't share with their children."

"This isn't an argument, Mama. He is living an entirely different life in Italy. If you were divorced, then fine! Who cares? But you're not and it isn't fair to you."

Turning back to the roses, she started chopping again. "He has never asked for that."

"He can't. Not really. Not without returning, and we both know he can't do that."

Rosa's head turned, and her eyes met Dante's. "What do you know?"

"Uncle Raul told me a few things."

She narrowed her eyes. "What things?"

Obviously, she knew something, and maybe if he pretended like he knew it, too, she would let something important slip. Or maybe he needed to pour a bottle of wine and she would channel Chloe and start singing the whole song.

"You know. Things. It doesn't matter. You live here, and you'd need to file for the divorce."

"Since when does a son encourage a mother to leave his father?"

Dante raised his hands in the air. "He's the one who left."

He could see energy gather in her jaw as she moved to the next bush. "He still sends a check. Quarterly now, but it covers everything. And more."

"So that's what stops you? It's called alimony. He provided for you in your marriage, he will be obligated to do so in a divorce."

His mother started to laugh and finally dropped her hands to her side. "Do you know how many women I've met who have a court mandate and no money?"

Dante narrowed his eyes. "No, actually, I don't."

"A lot. And how would I force your father if he stopped sending the checks? Run after him? Where is he this week? Rome? Naples?"

There was worry on her face.

"Mama, I—"

She put a finger in the air. "No. I don't ask much of you. Please drop this."

"I hate seeing you alone."

"I'm not alone," she argued. "I have my friends. My community."

"What about a man?"

She shook her head, looked at the earth and then the sky. "I had one of those. Have two beautiful children for the effort. Now I wait by the mailbox, wondering if this will be the month my *man* forgets me altogether. Trust me, I'm better off on my own."

That put an ache in his chest. "You're still young."

She laughed, stepped forward, and placed a hand on his cheek. "And too old to start over."

"That's not true."

"Oh, Dante. I know all of this comes from the heart."

"I worry about you."

"Well, stop. I'm healthy. My home is paid for, and the money your father has sent me is put away for the day it stops coming. I'll be fine.

You concentrate on you." She poked a finger in his chest. "Find a wife and make me grandbabies."

"Anna's the oldest," he said, deflecting that responsibility onto his sister.

Rosa rolled her eyes. "She can't make anything the way she goes about it."

That had them both laughing.

"They could adopt," Dante said.

"Too busy building careers. No, you are the one." She turned back to her roses.

And for a few minutes he thought about her position. "How much does Father send you?"

"That's none of your concern."

"It is if I'm going to take over for him."

Her lips fell in a thin line. "Do you have your own home?"

"I rent in—"

"Yes. I know. And do you have a windfall of money you haven't told me about?"

"No, but I—"

"Enough, then. I'm not hungry. The power is still on. Build your empire but do it for you and your future wife and children. If I'm in trouble, I won't be too proud to ask for your help, as I hope you would do the same to me. But stop running and trying to fix everything."

"What are you talking about?"

She shook her head. "You ran after your father to fix this. And you keep doing it. Stop. You know he isn't coming back, so leave it. You can't force him to provide if he chooses not to."

The thought brought his hands into fists. "He better hide deep if he decides to do that."

The lines on her face softened. "I love that you care so much."

And he hated that she was still alone. "I do."

"Now why are you bringing all this up now?"

He sighed. “I’m, ah . . . I’m leaving.”

She closed her eyes, and the muscles in her throat contracted. “I thought as much.”

“I’m moving across town. By the marina, actually.”

His mother found her smile. “What?”

“I’m sticking around for a while. I want to explore business options here in San Diego.”

Rosa’s mouth opened, and her eyes filled with tears.

“Don’t get overexcited. I haven’t decided anything yet. And I am most definitely returning to Italy and will even if we expand our business here.”

His mother stopped listening and threw her arms around him.

“This is how you make your mother happy.”

“Mama—”

“But you don’t have to spend money on a rental. Stay here.” She pulled out of the hug to look at him.

“I’m a grown man, Mama. I need my own space.”

“Oh. Yes, of course.” Her devious smile replaced all the sorrow and concern from earlier in the conversation. “Maybe you’ll find that wife.”

Chloe.

“You never know.”

She looked at her watch and clapped her hands together. “Let’s celebrate. I made some *limoncello*, add a little sparkling wine.”

Dante turned to follow her into the house. “You made your own *limoncello*?”

“Of course. A single woman such as myself needs to be frugal.”

“Mama!”

“I’m kidding.” She looked over her shoulder and shrugged.

Ten minutes later he accepted her homemade liquor and enjoyed every drop. “This is good.”

“I know.”

“No, I mean, you could bottle it up and sell it.”

"Who says I don't?" She sipped from the spritz she'd created.

"I think that's illegal." The ATF would have fun with that.

"If you're caught."

"Mama!"

She looked over the brim of her glass. "My son is coming home."

Dante shook his head and leaned back in his chair.

~

How was it that the coldest night of the year required women to wear the smallest amount of material?

The party was on the rooftop deck of a popular building in Little Italy. Heat lamps were everywhere, but the chill still managed to cut through.

Chloe had left Eric's name with the bouncer on the ground floor and had expected him to show up at nine. He said he was running a little late, but by nine thirty she was wondering if he was coming at all.

The party was wall to wall, with the DJ making enough noise to keep everyone on the block awake past the midnight hour.

Salena danced with just about everyone, single or not, attracting all kinds of attention.

And Chloe watched the entry to the venue.

She'd yet to see Eric, or Dante.

"What is this?" Giovanni walked up to her and motioned to the glass in her hand.

"Club soda."

"What is up with you lately?"

"I'm pacing myself."

Gio laughed, looked around. "Where is this date of yours?"

She glanced at her phone for the zillionth time. "No idea."

Her brother laughed. "My entire gender sucks." It was obvious he wasn't drinking carbonated water.

"Don't I know it."

He draped an arm over her shoulders. "Don't worry. I'll dance with you if no one else will."

She pushed him away. "Get out of here."

He stumbled a bit right about the time someone called his name, and he walked away. "*Bella*," he called out.

Chloe was about to give up on sobriety when she saw Eric walk through the entrance. *Nine thirty-five.*

He looked over the tops of heads and settled on her.

Smiling, she waved him over.

"I'm sorry I'm late. Everything was against me getting here on time. Parking is impossible out there."

"I imagine it is."

Eric opened his arms, and she had no real choice but to accept his hug.

When he pulled back, he kept a hand on her shoulder and looked her up and down. "You look fabulous. Aren't you cold?"

"It's not bad. Thanks."

"When you said outside, I thought sweater."

"You look good." Though the black sweater did seem to have a small something on the left shoulder. She nearly reached up to see if it was the light or lint or . . .

"What are you drinking?"

"Club soda, actually. I've been overindulging all month," she explained.

He nodded toward the bar. "You don't mind if I do? I don't get out that much."

"Of course not."

They turned, and his hand that he'd left on her shoulder moved to her back.

As they headed toward the bar, she felt, more than saw, another set of eyes.

Over her left shoulder, Dante stared.

But not at her.

At Eric.

Chloe redirected her eyes toward the line at the bar and ignored the heat on her back.

This was nothing new. She was at a party, with a date.

My husband is staring daggers into my back.

Who was she kidding? There was nothing normal about this.

"I don't remember the last time I stayed out on New Year's Eve," Eric started.

"Really, why?"

"Different priorities."

His answer felt strange to her ears. "To be honest, I probably would have stayed home if you weren't going to come. I feel like all I've done is party all month."

Eric moved to her other side, and when he did, Chloe pivoted so it wouldn't be as easy for him to touch her, as he'd been doing.

He let his hand drop to his side. "I was going to ask if this was your normal routine."

They moved forward in line. "No. But it's not every year my brother gets married."

"That would be a problem if he did."

They both laughed at the thought.

Eric's phone buzzed and he instantly reached for it. "Sorry, I . . ." He started typing and then put the phone back in his pocket. "How often do you normally get out like this?" he asked, looking around the open patio.

"Like this? Not much. You?"

"Couple times a year, maybe."

"I have to cough up more than that."

"I have early mornings," he said as they inched forward in line.

"Mine are more flexible."

"Right. Your family restaurant is close by."

"D'Angelo's. It's a couple blocks away."

It was their turn at the bar. "Are you sure you don't want anything?" he asked.

She shook her head. Not a chance.

Eric ordered an old-fashioned and leaned against the counter.

"Do you like to dance?" she asked. And as the question came up, she glanced at those moving to the music.

She saw Dante beside a busty blonde.

Figures.

Chloe looked down at her chest.

Busty . . . not even in her dreams.

"Not my thing. I, ah, will, if you want to. But—"

"It's okay." Not really, but whatever.

Eric paid for his drink and they set off to the opposite side of the roof, where they could hear each other over the music.

They nudged into a long counter where people could place their drinks as they talked.

"Hey, Chloe." She turned to find an old friend at her side.

"Hi, Pat. How are you?" They hugged.

"I'm good. I heard your brother just got married."

"He did. They're on their honeymoon." Chloe looked at Eric to see that he'd picked up his phone, so she didn't bother introducing him.

"Tell him I said congratulations."

"I will, thank you."

Pat walked away.

When Chloe turned around, she immediately explained who Pat was. "We went to high school together."

Eric looked up, smiled, finished his text, and set his phone down. "I bet you know most of the people here."

"Not really."

One of the waiters from the restaurant walked by, said hi. "A lot, I guess. I'm sure you have places you hang out where people know you."

He laughed. "At work."

"Oh, come on. What are your friends doing tonight?"

"Most are at home, watching the ball drop."

Chloe played with the straw in her club soda and tapped her foot to the music. "You need to get some new friends."

He smiled. "Isn't that what I'm doing?"

"I guess so."

Eric reached for his phone again.

She hadn't noticed that it was buzzing until he did.

Was that the third or fourth time he'd looked at his phone since he showed up . . . late?

He typed feverishly into the phone before putting it down. "I'm sorry. What were we talking about?"

Chloe glanced at the phone. "Is everything okay?"

"Yeah. Just a little thing going on at home."

She narrowed her eyes. "With your roommates?"

He nodded.

"What's the matter? It's already all over in New York."

Eric looked at her as if confused, then remembered what they'd talked about and laughed. "No, it's not that." He waved a hand in the air. "Never mind." He took a big drink from his glass and tried to smile.

It looked forced.

Chloe heard Salena before she saw her. "Oh my God, is this Eric?"

"Oh my God, are you drunk already?"

Salena pointed at her as she walked over. "Guilty."

"Eric, my best friend Salena. Salena, Eric."

Salena looked him up and down as a bestie should, without apology and with complete assessment. "You will do."

"Stop it," Chloe chided.

Eric was laughing. "I'll take it."

"I bet you will."

Chloe nudged her friend.

Eric's phone rang and he cussed under his breath. "I'm sorry. I need to take this."

What was she going to say, no? "Okay."

He turned away from them and lifted the phone to his ear.

"Wow, he's cute," Salena said when his back was turned and his attention was focused elsewhere.

"And he's been on his phone ever since he got here."

"Really?"

Chloe looked at the countdown clock on the wall, realized he'd only been there twenty minutes. "Constant texting and now a call. He got here at like nine forty."

Salena looked like she was going to say something to him and Chloe stopped her. "Don't. I got it."

"You know who's been watching you?"

Salena's question had Chloe searching the rooftop for Dante.

Sure enough, his eyes were zeroed in on them, even though he was dancing with a brunette now. "He looks busy to me."

Someone called Salena's name.

"You go."

"If you need me, just wave."

Chloe all but pushed her away.

After a full minute of looking at Eric's back, she approached him from behind to ask if they needed to try this another night. Or maybe not at all. Then she heard his half of the conversation.

"Christian, I told you I'd be home late. Go to bed like the babysitter told you. No. Just because you're older doesn't mean you get to stay up late."

Chloe let his words sink in.

Babysitter?

Eric's roommates were his kids.

What?

He looked over his shoulder and realized she was right there, listening.

His smile fell. "Because I said so, now go to bed."

I should have stayed home.

Eric hung up. "That was my—"

"Son?"

He nodded slowly.

"Your roommates are your kids?"

"Yeah."

"You were late because . . . ?"

"The babysitter was late."

"Great."

"Women don't like to date men with kids."

"And if it worked out you were going to . . . what? Keep them from me forever?"

"No."

"Ridiculous." Chloe put her glass down and turned to walk away.

"See, this is why I didn't tell you."

She stopped, looked him dead in the eye. "If you told me you had kids, I would have still gone out with you. But if you start out lying, there is no place to go but downhill. Happy New Year, Eric."

"What? Women don't lie?"

She pointed to her chest. "I don't have kids."

She scurried out of Eric's orbit to find Salena, tell her she was going home.

Eric walked by, shook his head, and headed toward the door.

"Hey, Chloe . . . wanna dance?"

"No." She didn't even bother to see who asked, her eyes searching the crowd for Salena.

Giving up, Chloe reached in her purse to text her friend instead.

She felt a hand on her elbow.

Dante was there, his beautiful golden eyes looking at her, filled with concern. "Are you okay?"

She shook her head. "I'm going home."

"I saw your friend leave."

"His two roommates are his kids! Kids he failed to mention. In fact, his profile said no wife, no kids." She stopped short. "God, what if he's married?"

One look at Dante and she started to laugh.

"What am I saying? I'm such a hypocrite."

"All right." He started pulling her away. "C'mon, let's go."

Irony kept her laughing. A little manic-like, but laughing nonetheless.

"Do you have a coat?"

She shook her head, and he pulled his jacket off his shoulders and placed it over hers before walking her out of the party.

CHAPTER THIRTEEN

Dante was ordering an Uber before they reached the ground floor.

With as many people showing up for the party using the same mode of transportation, they didn't have to wait long for a ride.

They walked across the street and hopped into a car.

"I should have stayed home. Warm pajamas, popcorn. I could have had a glass of wine at home. No one to ask me questions there."

Dante looked in the mirror at the driver and smiled. "Except your mother."

"Mama doesn't ask questions. She tells me I need to be out looking for a husband." One look at him and she started laughing again. "Rich, isn't it?"

It appeared to Dante that Chloe might actually be losing it. Clearly the secret inside her was too much to keep and she'd reached the boiling point.

"It's going to be okay."

"Right. Sure. There is no way people aren't going to find out. It's been what, three weeks?"

"Twenty-two days."

She nodded like a bobblehead doll sitting on top of a semi going over a bed of boulders. "Twenty-two days. We've been married for twenty-two days."

"Chloe." Dante looked at the driver.

"She doesn't know us." Chloe leaned forward. "We got married twenty-two days ago in Vegas and didn't tell anyone."

The driver glanced over her shoulder. "Congratulations?" It was a question.

Chloe started laughing again and flopped back in her seat.

"I can't do this. I'm not cut out for deceit. A little white lie here and there, fine. Sure, that color looks good on you when it looks like dirt, but not this, Dante. This is too big."

Dante switched to Italian. "We'll get through this. Together."

"Together? How do we do that when we're getting a divorce? And you live in another country."

The driver pulled onto the street where he was renting the Airbnb. "I told you, I'm not leaving right away."

The car moved to the curb.

"Where are we?" Chloe kept speaking in Italian.

Dante jumped out, ran around to her side of the car, and caught the door as it opened. "Thank you," he said to the driver.

"Congratulations."

Chloe started laughing all over again.

Dante placed his arm around her shoulders and walked her to the stairs leading to the condo.

"What is this?" she asked, this time in English.

"I rented a place." He fished in his pocket for the key, unlocked the door. Inside, he clicked on the lights.

"You did?"

"I love my mother. I can't live with her after living alone for five years."

Chloe moved through the open space, touching the white furnishings and stopping to look out the sliding glass doors. "You have a view."

"I like boats, what can I say?" The marina condo was a deal for this time of year and ideal for him.

"It's nice."

"Glad you like it."

She shrugged out of his jacket, and he swallowed hard.

The gray-sequined dress hung off the shoulder and stopped midthigh. The nude high heels she wore made her calves ripple with every step and made it hard for him not to stare or travel up her backside and over the curve of her ass.

"Have you been here long enough to stock it with liquor?" Chloe asked.

"First thing I did."

"Thank God."

He laughed. "What were you drinking at the club?"

"Water."

"Really?" He was sure she was half-lit.

"In case you haven't figured it out, alcohol is my truth serum." She turned, smiled. "You already know my secrets."

Dante set his keys on the counter, pulled his wallet and phone out of his pockets, too. "What do you want?"

"It's New Year's Eve."

"Champagne?"

She crossed to the small kitchen. "You have some?"

"I do."

He opened his fridge, pulled out one of two bottles he had inside. "I wasn't sure I'd make it long at the party and thought I might be toasting the New Year by myself."

"I saw you dancing. You wouldn't have been alone."

"Why does everyone think so little of me?" he asked as he twisted off the metal wire around the cork.

Chloe moved away from where he stood and started searching through the cupboards. "It's your reputation."

"I don't chase women as much as you give me credit for."

She moved to another cupboard, found two wineglasses. "Are you suggesting you're celibate?"

"No. But I'm not a man-whore." The cork popped free, and Chloe leaned a hip against the counter.

"I'm glad my *husband* has some self-control."

He took a glass from her, poured a generous portion for her, and handed it back before pouring one for himself. "That's really strange to hear."

"It's really strange to say."

"Well, *wife*. To the reluctant bride and groom."

Man, did he love to see her smile.

"*Salute*."

She pressed the glass to her lips and he watched her swallow.

Even that was breathtaking.

Dante joined her in the drink and pulled his gaze away. "Do they still let off fireworks over the bay at midnight?"

"Yes."

He crossed to the sliding door, opened it. "We should be able to see something, then." The crisp outside air helped slap his overexcited libido into control.

Chloe followed him.

A few of the boats in the marina had groups gathering on them. Music from at least one of the condos in the complex drifted their way.

"It's peaceful out here," Chloe said at his side.

"You mean aside from all the parties going on?" he teased.

"It's not bad," she said. "Quieter than Little Italy."

"That wouldn't take much."

"True."

"Last night was my first night here. Not a peep at all. It was nice waking to the sound of the water lapping against the boats."

She leaned against the balcony railing. "Was Rosa upset that you left?"

"She's happy it's down the street and not Positano."

Chloe shivered.

"We should go inside."

"I like the fresh air," she said and sipped more wine.

Dante set his glass down. "I'll get you something."

Back inside, he found a blanket on the back of the sofa and brought it outside.

He covered her shoulders and let his hands linger on her arms, moving them up and down to warm her.

He closed his eyes for a brief moment and willed himself to let go.

When he opened them, Chloe had twisted enough to catch his expression.

His breath caught hard when Chloe's eyes lingered on his and then moved to his lips. They parted just a small amount, and the tip of her tongue licked her bottom lip.

Awww, fuck. "Chloe."

"Don't talk." She was breathless. Her eyes caught his again.

Her chest rose and fell.

His kept pace with hers.

Neither of them said a word.

She was right. They didn't need to talk.

Dante reached for her. Their lips met with a spark so strong it hurt.

Her frame melted against his, from knee to lips, he felt her.

Fingertips grasped at his waist and circled his back, and the blanket he'd just wrapped around her fell to the ground.

If she was cold, he couldn't tell. Her tongue joined his in a dance older than time. His erection kicked into overdrive.

She tasted like salt air and champagne; the mix intoxicated every sense in his body.

Dante let his hands travel over her chilled skin and down her back. He dared to touch her hip and round the curve of her ass.

Her lips stilled, with a gasp. "Yes."

He squeezed and renewed their kiss with more fire, biting her lower lip and then kissing it gently.

Chloe placed both arms around his neck, and Dante lifted her from her bottom, her legs wrapped around his waist, and walked them into the house.

She shifted her lips, kissed him from another angle as he struggled to hold on to her as he slid the door closed behind them.

He heard one of her shoes hit the floor, then the other.

Her hands were in his hair, her hips pushed against his.

Dante finally got the damn door closed and nearly tripped over her shoe as he walked them into the bedroom.

His knees hit the bed, and they all but fell onto it together.

Maybe it was the jolt or the fact that their lips parted, but he drew away enough to look at her.

This was not the Chloe D'Angelo he'd known all his life. This was an entirely different woman. *Chloe Mancuso.*

Her hooded gaze kept his, her breath pushed her breasts against her dress in short gasps.

Dante wanted her so completely he could cry for the need of it.

Yet he had to ask.

"Are you sure?"

Her answer was one soft hand reaching for his cheek and the other tugging his shirt to pull him down on top of her body.

With her permission slip signed, he took what she offered.

His lips landed on hers, briefly, and danced over her chin and down her neck. "So soft," he whispered.

Chloe's hands reached inside his shirt. "So hard," she said back to him.

His erection pushed into her thigh and she let out a tiny laugh. "That, too."

He kissed the tops of her breasts that her dress didn't cover and let his hand roam down her waist to the edges of her dress. He'd never wanted a woman more. Part of him wanted to take all the time in the world, and the other part wanted to sample all of her right away and lay claim.

What would she taste like? How would she feel wrapped around him? All his questions would have answers by the end of the night. Caution tried knocking in the back of his brain, but he kicked that door closed and enjoyed the warmth of the woman in his arms.

And not just any woman.

Chloe Mancuso.

His wife.

He found the zipper on her dress and tugged. "I want to taste all of you."

She jolted against him. "I'm up for that."

Dante pulled at her dress.

She tugged at his shirt.

Tiny rosebud nipples, already hard and eager, popped away from her dress. Just enough, he thought as he filled his mouth and teased her with his teeth.

Chloe squirmed under him, fiddling with her dress, eager to get it off.

He stopped touching her long enough to help her shed the dress.

Once he dropped the material to the floor, he looked down. All she wore now was a tiny pair of panties and a smile.

"Oh, *bella.* How did we get here?"

Chloe leaned up on her elbows. "We opened the door."

"You're absolutely sure?"

Her smile grew and she leaned forward, placing both hands directly on his cock through his pants.

Dante's head fell back and his eyes closed.

She squeezed just a little and ran a hand down him, then worked the zipper of his pants.

Cool air touched his bare skin as she pulled him from his clothing. Fingers grazed and stroked. Dante was afraid to look. Fear of feeling too much in this moment. One where Chloe was seeing him like this for the first time.

Please don't let it be the last.

Then he opened his eyes and saw the moment her lips wrapped around him and took him in.

He cussed, first in English, then Italian, and did everything he could to hold back the tidal wave that surged forward in a rush of heat and desire.

He wanted to watch but felt himself losing it and closed his eyes.

This was good. She was . . . *Awh, fuck that.*

It was her moan that made him pull away. The vibration tore into him and tightened his whole body. "No more."

"Too much?" she asked, teasing.

He stepped back long enough to kick his clothing from his body and pushed Chloe farther up on the bed. While he wasn't rough, he was less than gentle.

She wiggled her eyebrows and bent one knee to the side. The movement displaced her panties enough to display the folds of her skin.

"My turn."

Both hands on her thighs, he pushed her legs up even more, opening her to his gaze.

Her hips shifted. Invitation? Anticipation?

Didn't matter.

Dante lowered his mouth to the top of her panties and kissed the delicate skin there. He traced the edges of the material, felt the heat coming off her center.

He used his breath, his fingers . . . touched everywhere but where she wanted.

Words fell off her lips. A mixture of languages, all giving him permission and begging.

The first touch and she gasped. But when he moved her panties aside and took hold with his lips, she all but levitated off the bed.

He pulled her bud into his mouth and moved it until it started to unfold under his tongue.

Chloe went back and forth between saying yes and no . . . and praising their maker and the whole time held the back of his head, pressing her to him like a life raft from the *Titanic*.

When the moment came where her body clenched and Dante heard his name ripped from her lips, only then did he ease his pace and let her breathe.

While she was lax, his body screamed.

But damn, she was beautiful. Her face flushed with pleasure, her hair splayed on his bed. Her legs open.

Dante pulled her panties all the way off and reached for his pants on the floor.

"I'm on birth control," she told him.

"Two is better than one," he told her and pulled a condom from his wallet.

Chloe plucked it from his fingers. "Then let me."

He let go and leaned back on the bed. Taking her time, she rolled it over the length of him with teasing fingers.

When she shimmied up his body and straddled his hips, he couldn't help but think that no matter what the morning brought, this moment, with this woman, was worth it.

Chloe lowered her body onto his, and he buried himself so completely he never wanted to come out again.

He grasped her hand, intertwined their fingers, rolled her onto her back, and latched his lips to hers.

CHAPTER FOURTEEN

Chloe couldn't remember waking up this deliciously sore, fulfilled, and lax in her entire adult life.

The sun was barely starting to rise, and Dante was still fast asleep beside her.

They'd made love twice. In the middle, they drank the champagne they'd opened and welcomed the New Year.

Chloe had left a message for her mother, telling her not to worry, that she was staying with a friend.

Her mother never asked, and Chloe never offered more than that in the past. Her mother knew she wasn't a saint, and since Chloe wasn't out all the time, the arrangement worked.

Making as little movement on the bed as possible, Chloe slid from the covers and pulled Dante's shirt from the floor before slipping into it.

She closed the bedroom door and tiptoed into the kitchen in search of coffee.

After finding what she needed, she started a pot and found her purse.

Sometime in the night, a message came in from Eric with an apology. Another from Salena, asking where she went.

Chloe ignored both. It was too early to be texting anyone on New Year's Day. Instead, she saw a charger on the kitchen counter and plugged her phone in.

Then she saw what looked like a rental agreement.

She picked it up and started reading.

Six weeks.

The condo Dante was renting was only his for six weeks.

And then what?

Chloe closed her eyes.

She knew what happened next.

Dante would leave. Return to Italy, where he lived.

Her heart kicked in her chest, and a tickle in the back of her throat made her swallow. Last night meant nothing. Perhaps not nothing . . . but . . .

Yes, it was a lifelong fantasy made a reality, but it changed nothing. Even as it was happening, she knew Dante was not hers to keep. And as she moved to return the rental agreement to where she'd found it, she saw another stack of papers. These ones were printouts about California divorce. In it and highlighted was a statement about one or both people having to be a resident of California in order to petition for said separation. In another stack of papers was information about annulments.

Dante had the bases covered.

She neatly stacked the papers together and ignored the moisture that threatened in her eyes.

In six weeks, if she hadn't gone to the court for the divorce, annulment, or whatever and applied, he could . . . so long as he was here. And then he'd be gone.

Grow up, Chloe!

She'd made a big-girl decision to sleep with the man the night before, so regretting it the next morning was childish. Pressuring him to be someone he wasn't or do something he didn't want to do because of it was infantile as well.

Lifting her chin, Chloe moved about the kitchen and poured a cup of coffee.

She took her time drinking it and even made noise, thinking Dante would wake up and join her.

As the hour moved on, she thought of that walk from the Uber to the back door of her home. She wanted to avoid seeing anyone in her dress from the night before. And she sure as hell wasn't going to try and wear anything of Dante's.

Chloe went back into the bedroom and retrieved her clothes and put them on. She was zipping up the back of the dress when she heard Dante stirring in bed.

"Hey."

Painting on a smile, she turned to face him.

"Good morning," she said.

"What are you doing?"

She walked over, sat on the side of the bed. "You slept in."

He looked at the clock. "It's still early."

"True, but, ah . . . I have the walk of shame to endure. I'd like to avoid an audience."

He placed a hand on her thigh and squeezed. "I should have taken you home last night."

"Too late now."

He ran a hand over his face, blinked his eyes open. "I'll call a ride."

"I got it. No worries. You get some sleep."

His sleepy smile was something she'd remember forever. "I'll call you later."

"It's okay. You don't have to."

He opened his half-closed eyes. "What?"

"Dante, if you start calling, people will ask questions. We can't have that. It's okay." She glanced at the bed, back at him. "This was fabulous—"

He shook his head. "Wait, what? You're . . . what are you doing?"

She tilted her head, smiled. "In six weeks, you'll be back in Italy and I'll still be here. If our families find out about us, they'll turn this into something dirty when we both know it wasn't." And just talking about it was making her want to cry, so she needed to wrap this up before the tears started.

"You're serious."

Chloe put on her brightest fake smile, lifted his hand to her lips, and kissed the back of it.

Without anything else, she walked out of the room, then rushed to find her shoes, purse, and phone and hurried out the door.

~

Franny ran past, nearly colliding, and had Chloe doing a double step to keep from dropping the plates in her hands. "Francesca!"

"Papa! Mama!"

Much as Chloe wanted to continue to scold the girl for running in the restaurant, she understood her excitement.

Luca and Brooke were walking through the back door, arms open wide to accept Franny's hug. The words *I missed you* and *what did you bring me* were out almost at the same time.

Chloe quickly took the food to the table and returned to greet her brother and Brooke.

Kisses, hugs, and compliments on their sun-kissed skin brought Mari out from the office.

Chloe peeled away and went back to work.

The presence of her brother and sister-in-law was exactly what she needed.

"Your brother looks happy," Julianne, one of the waitresses, said, watching the reunion from the workstation next to the kitchen.

"He does, doesn't he?"

"We could all be so lucky."

Chloe shook her head, pulling it out of the Dante cloud it had been in since she'd left his place New Year's Day. "Do you want to pick up a couple extra shifts next week?"

Julianne looked hopeful. "You giving yours away?"

"I am."

"Absolutely. Christmas about killed my savings account."

The buzzer on Chloe's hip let her know an order was ready. "Let's compare before you leave today."

Julianne offered a thumbs-up and walked away.

It was January third, and even though her original plan wasn't to leave for Bali for another week, she was changing her plans.

She'd switched her flight the night before and had yet to tell anyone.

And wouldn't, until the last minute.

Once her shift was over, she worked her way to the bank, withdrew a hearty amount of cash, and cleared her credit card for travel.

The yoga studio she taught at twice a week was a little trickier. The woman who ran the place wasn't happy about the late notice, and even more disappointed when Chloe expressed her extended plans.

In the end, either she took her off the schedule or Chloe would be forced to resign her position.

That night, she silently packed and tucked her suitcase into her closet. Later, she joined her family for dinner and to hear about Luca and Brooke's honeymoon. It took every effort for Chloe to keep from spitting envy at the marital bliss the couple was surrounded in. She pasted on a smile and acted as if nothing was wrong.

But it was all wrong.

She'd told Dante not to call, and he hadn't.

It was stupid of her to want him to defy her.

Asinine to think she would be different for him.

Yet she hadn't seen Dante at all.

He'd been around. Gio said as much about the two of them looking at boats and discussing business opportunities in San Diego.

Did Dante step one foot in front of her?

No.

It gutted her.

Chloe went to bed that night feeling just as deceitful about her plans for the next day as she did about her marriage.

Her phone buzzed.

The airline reminding her to check in for her flight.

As she did, she realized there was no turning back.

~

"I don't know what to do, and you're the only person I can talk to."

"Is my little brother in trouble?" Anna asked, laughing.

"I'm serious."

Anna sobered in a moment. "Are you okay?"

Dante ran a hand through his hair. He hadn't slept and had barely moved since she'd walked out.

He couldn't breathe and only had one person he could turn to.

"No."

"What's going on?"

Dante sucked in a breath, let it out. "Remember when I told you that you liked girls before you told me you liked girls?"

Anna sighed.

"Yeah."

"Remember how I kept it all to myself until you were ready to tell the world?"

There was silence on the line. "You're not gay, Dante."

He rolled his eyes as his head fell forward. "I married Chloe D'Angelo."

Anna started coughing as if she were drinking something and it went down the wrong pipe. "You"—cough, cough—"what?"

"Las Vegas. At the bachelor party. No one but us knows, Anna."

"Chloe D'Angelo?"

"Yes."

"Giovanni's sister?"

"Yes."

"Are you crazy?"

"Yes."

"He's going to kill you."

"I don't care about that right now. It's Chloe I'm worried about."

Anna stopped talking long enough that Dante thought maybe the connection had gone bad. "Interesting."

"Interesting? What is interesting?"

Instead of answering, Anna asked another question. "Why doesn't anyone know about this marriage?"

"That isn't important right now. What's impo—"

"Hold up. How is keeping your marriage a secret not important?"

Dante sat looking over the boats in the harbor, trying his best to tell his sister what she needed to know to offer advice without giving away every emotion burning through him.

"We decided that together. In case it doesn't work. It was Vegas."

"You were drunk," Anna said without censure.

He didn't admit or deny. "It was Vegas."

"Do you regret it?" she asked immediately.

"No." Dante paused. "Yes."

"Which is it?"

He squeezed his eyes shut. "Because I married Chloe, I might have lost my chances with her."

Anna's voice rose an octave. "Interesting."

"Why do you keep saying that?"

"I've never heard you like this."

"Like what?"

"Frazzled," she said. "Over a woman."

"I don't want to lose her, Anna. I need a woman's perspective here."

"Okay, then. What are you doing?"

He turned from the balcony and walked back into the condo. "Nothing. And it's making me crazy."

"Why?"

"Because it's what she wants."

Anna laughed. "When did that ever stop you?"

"It hasn't before. But it's different this time."

Anna sighed. "Because it's Chloe. I know, I understand. But if there is a superpower you have, little brother, it's getting women to fall at your feet. That isn't going to happen if you fade into the background. There is a fine line between giving a person space to figure out what they want and space that makes them think you don't care. It's obvious you care, so you better get to narrowing that space or your *wife* is going to think the two of you were nothing but a mistake."

Dante rubbed the back of his neck with his free hand. Nothing his sister said was new information, but he needed to hear it from someone else's lips. "If that backfires?"

"Can you live with it if you don't try?"

Dante shook his head. "No."

"Get to it, then."

Yeah . . .

It was time to get off his ass.

~

"What is this?"

Chloe rolled her suitcase into the living room at nine in the morning.

Her mother stood, jaw slacked, staring as if she was looking at a spaceship and not a rolling bag that carried clothing.

Chloe pulled enthusiasm from the air and sprinkled that shit everywhere. "You won't believe what a wonderful opportunity I've been given."

"Where are you going?"

"Mama, don't look so surprised. Bali."

"That isn't for a week."

"I know. But the airline was offering business class for an extra hundred dollars, and how could I pass that up?"

Her mother looked at her like she was crazy. "It still costs money to stay there."

"Pennies compared to here. I already found a co-op."

"A what?"

Chloe walked over to her mother, kissed her cheek, and then checked her phone. Her Uber was five minutes away.

"It's a guest housing thing. Then the yoga retreat and the training I've been putting off. Don't worry. I've covered my schedule."

Mari stood there, completely dumbstruck. "You're leaving now?"

Chloe took a deep breath, blew it out. "I need this, Mama."

"But—"

"Haven't you ever needed to just get away? Burst out of the box the world has put you in for a while and just be you?"

Her mother's face softened. "Chloe."

"I'll be back. I need a little zen time."

Mari looked around. "I'll take you to the airport."

"No. My ride is almost here. Tell everyone I said goodbye, okay?"

"This isn't like you," her mother said.

"I know. Exciting, right?"

Chloe kissed her mother's cheek and pushed into her jacket. She swung her backpack over her shoulders and rolled her suitcase to the door. "I love you," she said.

"Love you, too, *tesoro*."

Chloe made it down the flight of stairs without encountering anyone.

On the ground floor, she wasn't as lucky.

Luca had the door leading to the back of the restaurant open, and he caught her trying to escape.

"What in the world?"

Her phone buzzed. One look told her the Uber was at the back door.

"No time to explain. Mama has the details. Ciao."

She rolled the bag to the car.

The driver jumped out to help her.

"Where are you going?" Luca asked from the door.

"Bali."

"But—"

She waved off his questions. "It's time for *my* vacation," she said with a laugh.

As the driver pulled away, Chloe settled into her seat and let her smile fall.

"Bali? Wow, that sounds exotic," the driver said.

"Yeah. It should be."

Little Italy disappeared behind her, and within ten minutes she was at the airport, checking her bag in for her flight.

She placed her coach ticket into her passport and thought of the little lie she'd given her mother. Better that lie than all the ones that would pile up over the next six weeks with Dante in town.

For the second time in less than a month, she passed through TSA security and into the main terminal. Because the airport was small, there wasn't a reason to check in three hours early for an international flight. Not that there was anything direct about getting to Bali. Her first leg was to San Francisco, then Hong Kong, then Bali. She was in for over twenty-five hours of flying and layovers.

In coach.

She walked into an airport bookstore, bought a large bottle of water and a neck pillow, and then called Salena. Now that there was no risk of someone stopping her, she was free to tell someone she was leaving.

"Hey, girl. You've been quiet lately. What's up?"

Chloe hoisted her backpack higher on her shoulder and walked to her departing gate. "You'll never guess where I'm at."

"I won't even try."

"The airport. I'm going to Bali early."

"What?"

"I know. Crazy."

"What?" Salena repeated the question.

"I'm leaving early and staying late."

"What the—"

"I needed to do something for me. I put this trip off forever. Now that Luca is married and the restaurant is covered . . ." Chloe found her gate and sat.

"How long are you going to be gone?"

Chloe thought about lying. "I don't really know."

"Jesus, Chloe. This isn't like you."

"Second time today I heard that."

"Well, it isn't," Salena said. "Does this have anything to do with Dante?"

"Oh, please."

"It does, doesn't it?"

Chloe closed her eyes, saw him smiling at her over a glass of champagne. "Dante and I are just fine, okay. This has nothing to do with him."

"Is it Eric?"

"Please, Eric has two kids he didn't bother telling me about. I nixed that before midnight on New Year's Eve."

"Oh, snap. I thought for sure when you disappeared you were with him."

"No."

Salena let out a long sigh. "Aren't you a little scared, traveling all that way alone?"

"More excited than scared. But smart enough to want someone to know where I'm at. Which is why I'm calling you."

"Oh?"

"I'm sending you a Friend Finder request. So someone knows where I am."

"What about your family?"

"No way. I don't need them trying to drag me home if I don't want to come right away." Chloe watched the other passengers pile into the chairs, most of them grabbing their phones to avoid talking to anyone.

"I guess that means you don't want me to tell anyone where you are," Salena confirmed.

"Of course not. Just like you're not going to say a thing about Vegas and you know what."

"I haven't said a word."

"Good. Now, I have a nine-hour layover in Hong Kong. I'm going to try and get out of the airport for a few hours and see the city, don't freak out."

"That's nuts."

"I know. I'll send pictures."

"Be safe, okay?"

Chloe shrugged. "I'll think about it."

Salena laughed and Chloe hung up.

As soon as she did, she went onto Friend Finder, then added Salena and silenced Gio, Luca, and her mother.

Dante was still there . . . flashing like a red light at an intersection.

She deleted his name and took a deep breath.

She turned to look out the window and at the airplane that would start her journey. One away from the crazy mess she'd made of her life.

CHAPTER FIFTEEN

Dante pulled the motorcycle into the back lot of D'Angelo's and parked it behind Chloe's car.

He'd put off coming by the restaurant as long as he could, but if he didn't lay eyes on her soon, he was going to go out of his ever-loving mind. Besides, Anna was right, it was time to win Chloe over.

It had been four days and three nights since he'd had the single best experience of his life. One he wanted to repeat over and over until he died.

And she'd walked out.

How fucking poetic was that?

"This was great, don't call." And left.

How many times had he said that in his life?

How many women?

Fucking karma was kicking his ass every hour, every minute, since Chloe walked out of his door.

Dante used the excuse that Luca was back in town and he wanted a dish of his famous lobster ravioli to show up for dinner.

He planned on sticking around until Chloe made an appearance. However long that was.

Since her car was in the lot, it appeared he wouldn't have to wait.

Using the back entrance, he greeted the staff he knew and walked on through.

He found Giovanni and Brooke standing by the bar, glasses of wine in their hands. "Look who's back," he said, kissing Brooke's cheek.

"We had such a fabulous time."

"The weather cooperated?"

"It only rained briefly a couple of days."

Dante turned to Gio, shook his hand. "What are you drinking?"

"Whatever that is will be fine."

Gio walked behind the bar and poured it himself.

"I'm surprised you're still here," Brooke started. "We were excited to hear it when Gio said you had rented a condo."

Dante found himself looking around the restaurant for the familiar frame of a tall, dark-haired woman with full lips and eyes that peered into his soul. "There's no reason I can't have a home in Italy and here."

"That makes everyone very happy."

Gio handed him the wine.

"Did you tell him?" Gio asked Brooke.

"About Chloe?"

The mention of her name had Dante's head darting Brooke's way. "What's up?"

"She left for Bali this morning," Gio told him.

The information went in but didn't really connect with Dante's brain. "What?"

"Bali!" Giovanni repeated.

"I thought that wasn't for another week."

"According to Mama, she got some deal on a business-class ticket and jumped at it."

"It's a long flight. I'd jump, too," Brooke said.

Dante tried to hide his surprise behind the glass of wine in his hand. All the while his heart thumped in his chest so loud he thought everyone within five feet could hear it. "She's never traveled alone, right?" he asked.

Gio shook his head. "I know. Luca and I have talked about that. We have her on Friend Finder, but it hasn't updated since she was at the airport."

"Do you know what flight she was on?"

Gio shook his head.

Fuck.

Brooke laughed. "Look at you two. Chloe's a big girl, she is capable of taking care of herself."

"She's the baby in the family," Gio said.

"Not a baby anymore," Dante pointed out.

Gio lifted a finger at him as if in warning.

"Listen, I've flown to Bali, it's eighteen hours from the West Coast to Hong Kong or Singapore and then another six or so to Bali. That's if she went that way. She might have gone the other way around, through Europe or the Middle East."

Dante damn near dropped his glass. "What the fuck? The Middle East?"

Brooke rolled her eyes. "Doha in Qatar is a perfectly safe airport."

Dante stared at Gio.

Gio grabbed his phone.

Dante scrambled to his side and looked over his shoulder, saw he'd pulled up Friend Finder.

Chloe was there with *location unavailable* in big, bold letters under her name.

"When did her flight leave?" Dante asked.

"She left here before ten this morning. I'm not sure when her flight took off."

"My guess is she had to catch the long flight from LAX or maybe San Francisco. Maybe even Seattle. That's if she went the short way," Brooke told them.

Dante narrowed his eyes. "How do you know so much about this?"

"I traveled a lot with my . . . in my life before Luca," she said.

Gio leaned in. "Brooke's ex was a travel blogger."

"Oh. When do you think Chloe will land in Bali?"

Brooke sipped her wine, set her glass down. "If she went through Asia or even Australia, twenty-five hours, give or take. If she went through Europe or the Middle East, it could be as much as forty."

"Damn."

"Makes that business-class ticket look mighty good."

Gio shook his head. "Yeah, but usually you get that information about your flight the day of the flight, or even right before you board . . . not a week before. This feels all wrong coming from Chloe."

Dante nodded but kept silent.

"Ever since I met your sister she's talked about this trip." Brooke looked Dante in the eye and smiled. "I'm sure Chloe had her reasons for extending it."

Oh, shit.

Gio put his phone away. "It's going to be a long night."

Brooke laughed.

Dante wanted to throw up.

~

Chloe could not remember a time in her life when she felt as exhausted as she had walking into her room after twenty-eight solid hours of travel. Three more hours than expected, due to delays. Once she landed in Bali, went through customs, and found a ride to her hotel, all she wanted to do was shower and fall into bed.

She'd read that the first couple of days would kick her ass, so she booked low-key accommodations with minimal amenities.

Translation . . .

Cheap.

And then, because it was midmorning once she was settled, Chloe forced herself to stay awake for as long as she could stand it.

When she couldn't keep her eyes open any longer, she pulled the blinds and slept.

She woke to the sound of rain beating down on the windowsill.

Still dark, she looked at her phone to check the time, certain she'd woken up in the middle of the night.

No, it was nearly five in the morning. She'd slept for thirteen hours straight.

Even though it was raining, an air conditioner ran in the room.

Chloe padded barefoot to the sliding doors and looked through the glass. Even her cheap accommodations afforded her a small terrace.

She took care of her needs in the bathroom before searching for some type of hot morning caffeine. Finding a kettle and a tea bag, she made do before settling into a chair to watch the sunrise.

"I'm in Bali."

Just saying it brought a smile to her face.

She'd done it.

Jumped the gun by a week, likely shocked the hell out of her family . . . but she'd done it.

Her phone tugged at her to pick up.

But no.

She'd texted Salena when she'd arrived at the airport and told her to relay to her family that she was unplugging until jetlag had passed.

After all, that's why she was in Indonesia to begin with.

To unplug.

Slowly the tea helped open her eyes as the sun pierced the gray clouds in the sky. The rain let up to a drizzle, but from the looks of it, there wouldn't be a lot of dry spells to catch.

She didn't expect many.

It was the rainy season, after all.

Besides, the rain would hide the tears. The ones she hadn't planned on having on this trip but knew she'd shed once given the chance.

Six weeks.

She had six weeks to mend her heart and prepare herself to return home. By then Dante would be gone, and by the time he returned, she'd have moved on. One way or the other.

Chloe pushed out of her chair to get into the shower and start the first day of restoring balance in her life.

As cliché as it was to do it in Bali, it's what she was doing.

~

There's a scene in every movie where if the guy likes the girl, he plays it cool in front of his friends and then runs around the back of the building to read the text or make the call or some such gesture that screams to those watching that the guy is in over his head.

That was how Dante felt walking into the restaurant Salena worked at to try and squeeze information out of her.

He saw her almost immediately, smiled, and sauntered toward the bar. Right away he saw another familiar face . . . The name of the woman he didn't remember, but something told him he probably should. *Brenda? Linda?*

It was early and a weeknight. The bartender smiled. "Dante, right?"

He reached out a hand. "Sorry, I forgot your name."

"Chad."

"Hi. IPA?"

"Coming right up."

Brenda . . . or Linda . . . kept looking over.

Dante turned away, hoping she'd get the hint. Two years ago. Yeah, that's when he'd met her.

Salena acknowledged him with a nod as she walked by several feet away but didn't stop what she was doing to say hi.

His beer came and Brenda/Linda stared so hard the skin on his neck crawled.

Thirty minutes passed and his beer was nearly gone before Salena graced him with her presence.

"Hi."

He smiled.

Her lips sat in a flat line. "What did you do?"

"Excuse me?"

"You know what I'm talking about."

The hair on his arms stood up.

But if there was one thing Dante was good at, it was keeping his mouth shut.

If there was one thing Salena wasn't good at, it was keeping her mouth shut.

So, he waited her out.

Salena shifted her weight to her other leg, placed a hand on her hip. "There are three kinds of breakups for women." She lifted her hand, extended one finger. "The ice cream breakup, a pint of ice cream and you're over it. The tequila breakup, a good night out with your girls and a decent hangover and it's all 'fuck that guy.' And then there's the Vegas breakup. The one where it takes a weekend and maybe a random hookup to get him out of your system. Chloe left the fucking country!" Salena tossed her words at him like an accusation. "So let me ask you again. What. Did. You. Do?" With each word she poked her finger in his chest.

"Chloe and I aren't—"

Salena stopped him from continuing by getting right in his face.

"I know about Vegas," she said in a whisper. "I also know that Chloe's been crazy for you since her ovaries started popping eggs. She didn't run away to Indonesia because you pushed her away from a kiss." Salena shook her head. "No, no. That would have been a tequila night. Chloe's been off her normal axis for weeks, and now she's gone, so there is more to the story and you know what it is."

Dante leaned back enough to breathe. “There is, but I promised her I’d keep it between us.”

Salena stepped back. “It had to be something huge for her to take off for so long.”

He shook his head. “What do you mean? She’ll be back in a couple of weeks.”

“Yeah. That’s what she told everyone else.” Salena leaned forward again, lowered her voice. “But since you’re so good at keeping secrets, know this. Chloe isn’t coming back. Not until you leave. Wanna convince me that you’re not the reason she left?”

Dante’s heart sank. “What?”

“Six weeks.” Salena pulled her cell phone from her back pocket and showed Dante a text message from Chloe. After next week’s retreat, I’m renting a small place in Ubud for a month. Longer if I have to. The place is stunning.

Dante tried to scan the rest of her messages but Salena snatched her phone away.

“She can’t just leave,” Dante said.

“Why? You do.”

It was different now.

“Salena!” Someone from the restaurant staff called her name and waved her over.

Dante grabbed her arm as she started to walk away. “Where is she?”

“Bali.”

“Where in Bali?”

She pulled away. “No. I’m not that easy.”

Fuck!

CHAPTER SIXTEEN

"It's beautiful, isn't it?"

Chloe made a necessary phone call home, but dialed Brooke's number since she was the one most likely not to give her a hard time about leaving the way she did.

The text messages that her brothers had sent her were pissing on her choices but laced with concern for her well-being. No one knew she was extending her stay, and they wouldn't until after the retreat.

"It's indescribable," Chloe told Brooke. Truth was, it had rained most of the time she'd been there, and she hadn't ventured very far. "Very lush."

"What part are you in?" Brooke asked.

"I've been in Kuta, but I leave this morning for the retreat, which is north of here." Kuta was busy, and inexpensive. Then again, she'd discovered that everything in Bali was dirt cheap. Yeah, you could spend a lot if you wanted to, but for the budget traveler, you could find a bed for twenty bucks a night. Not just a bed, but one with a pool and views of the rice fields. Although those were everywhere.

"I can't wait to hear all about it when you're back."

"We'll have plenty to talk about. Listen, I called because one of the goals of this retreat is to unplug. It's the reason I took everyone off my location. Salena knows where I'm at, and if there's an emergency, she will get ahold of me. Can you make sure everyone knows that?"

"Absolutely. We all need to do that once in a while."

"Thank you. And tell Luca to keep me off the schedule. Coming here has opened my eyes to a few things."

"Are you having a Julia Roberts moment?" Brooke teased.

Chloe watched the falling rain. "Not yet. But I'm looking for it."

Brooke paused. "Are you okay?"

"I'm fine. Send my love to everyone. I'll call next week."

"Enjoy."

"Ciao."

Chloe ended the call and looked at her phone.

Several messages from Dante had come through right after she left.

Where are you?

Are you okay?

We need to talk.

Call me.

She ignored them all.

Her family knew she was okay, Salena knew exactly where she was. In turn, Dante knew she was safe, and as a lifelong friend, that's all she owed him.

Chloe had one more call to make before she truly turned off her phone for the week.

Salena's phone went to voice mail.

"Hey, baby!" Chloe put cheer in her voice that she had to fake. "As promised, I'm unplugging for seven whole days. I have never done this. My location tracker will be on, but unless I leave the retreat, my phone will be off and in my room. I only plan on leaving the retreat twice with the group. Thanks for being the buffer for my family. I owe you. I know you're dying for details, and I'm sure I'll spill them all, but right now I need to do this. Anyway . . . I'm rambling. Love you."

Chloe hung up and tossed her phone on her bag.

She'd spent a week in Bali feeling sorry for herself.

That needed to change.

Gathering her belongings, and double-checking every drawer and closet, she worked her way out of the room.

Less than thirty minutes later Chloe walked into gardens of the women's yoga retreat and the training that she'd been planning for years.

The two women that greeted her were all toothy smiles and hellos.

"Miss Chloe. Finally, you are here."

One of them took her bag and started walking.

She was encouraged to follow. "I'm excited."

"There are two of you who have arrived for the week so far. The others will come later. My name is Eka. One of the hostesses."

They walked past an open-air dining area that hosted a long table in the center and several smaller tables around it.

"All of your meals are here. Breakfast is anytime before class begins. We break for lunch. And gather again for afternoon healing, meditation, and of course, yoga, then dinner. But I'm sure you read the itinerary."

"Dozens of times."

"Everyone this week is already certified and expanding their training, like you. I believe you'll leave here much fuller than you are today," Eka said.

"I can hardly wait to begin."

The other woman with her bag disappeared and Eka continued to show Chloe around the retreat. There was a covered outdoor yoga *shala* and an indoor space to practice as well. Water features and reflecting ponds with Buddha statues and various imagery of chakras and people meditating were tucked in corners or peppered along the pathways.

There were three huts where massage tables were set up. Part of the wellness package included an unlimited amount of massage and skin treatments. All of which she planned on taking full advantage of.

"The swimming pool for your afternoon and evenings if you like."

"When it's not raining," Chloe pointed out.

Eka nodded and smiled. "We will have several dry days this week."

They rounded a corner to a path that led to the rooms. Eka opened the door to hers, where her bag was waiting. High ceilings, bright colors. Air-conditioning with netting around the bed to help keep the nighttime biting bugs away. Through the room was an outside shower surrounded by walls and plants. "It's better than I imagined," Chloe told her.

Eka placed her hands in front of her. "The kitchen is open anytime today until our welcome ceremony at two. You can enjoy a massage, go for a swim, meditate in the gardens . . . whatever you'd like."

"Thank you, Eka."

Once Eka left, Chloe fell onto the bed, arms stretched wide.

This was truly a yogi's paradise.

~

How does someone actually unplug?

Seriously, who does that?

There was nothing worse than the silent treatment, especially growing up in an Italian family, where expressing one's emotions, loudly, was a way of life. This quiet shit was for the birds.

And that was the crux of the problem. Dante had not had an opportunity to say what he needed to say to Chloe, and it was eating him up inside.

He and Gio had checked out several boats that would be acceptable to start a San Diego charter business, but Dante couldn't pull the trigger.

How could he, not knowing if he could show his face in San Diego once Chloe returned?

So many times he'd been tempted to blurt out what he and Chloe had done, and each time he held back. It wasn't just his life he was messing up. It was hers, too.

Twice Gio had called him out on not acting like himself.

Three times he'd been looked at funny for asking if anyone heard anything from Chloe.

Brooke knew something was fishy, he could sense that a mile away.

Luca seemed pleasantly clueless.

All of them would hate him soon.

He'd really fucked things up.

In all of this, there was one person he couldn't stand to have hate him. And she was 8,700 miles away.

He knew what he needed to do, but he had to have a little help in doing it.

Dante waited by the door of the restaurant that Salena worked at and rubbed his hands together to ward off the cold night air.

One by one the employees exited the building until finally he saw her walk out the door.

He pushed away from where he was perched and jogged to her side, calling her name.

She hesitated at first, surprised, noticed who it was, then kept on walking. "I haven't heard from her and the answer is no."

"Hear me out."

Salena walked fast, and he doubled his step to get in front of her.

She jogged around him as if he was no more than a pile of crap in the street. "Go away."

Sadly, the metaphor was an accurate description of his self-loathing feelings.

Dante stopped walking. "I'm booked on a flight to Bali in the morning."

That halted Salena's forward momentum.

She turned, stared him down. "I'm listening."

He pointed to his chest. "I need to fix this. I can't do that if she won't talk to me. So you can either tell me where she is so I have a fighting chance of finding her, or I get there and put an ad in the local paper for a missing person."

The frown on Salena's face that seemed to be permanently etched there when she looked at him lifted ever so slightly.

"An ad in the paper?"

"Or the police, or something." He ran a hand through his hair. "I need to see her."

"If you're lying to me, I'll cut off your balls myself."

Said balls recoiled in his pants.

But hope flared in his chest. "I'm not."

Salena removed her phone from her back pocket, and within a couple of clicks, his phone buzzed. He opened his messages, and Chloe's location came up on his screen.

A tidal wave of relief washed over him.

A second image followed the first.

"That's where she is staying after the retreat. In case you miss her at the first place."

Dante rushed forward, kissed Salena hard on the cheek, and backed off. "Thank you. I owe you."

"Don't fuck this up."

He tilted his head. "I already did that. Don't tell her I'm coming. She'll bolt."

"Then you might want to get to her before she turns her phone back on. I'm loyal to her before you."

That was fair. "And don't tell anyone else where I went."

Salena actually laughed. "No worries. Watching everyone spin in circles trying to figure out what the hell is going on is half the fun."

"I owe you," he said again.

"You do. Don't think I won't collect."

Dante looked up the dark street and moved to her side. "I can at least walk you home."

She rolled her eyes and muttered, "Must have been one hell of a kiss."

He looped his arm through hers and almost danced her to her front door.

~

Giovanni woke to a message on his voice mail from Dante. It was as cryptic as it was brief.

"Hey, bud. I have an emergency I need to deal with. I'll be back as soon as I get everything fixed. I left a key under the planter by my door. Your motorcycle key is on my kitchen counter. You know my mom, she'll worry. Stop by and see that she's okay, will ya? Shit, that's my flight. I gotta go. Ciao."

Gio pulled his phone away from his ear and stared at it as if it were a foreign object.

What the hell was up with the people in his life?

He heard footsteps in the central staircase, followed by the door opening to the outside rooftop deck. The only person who came up there that early in the morning was Chloe. To do yoga.

He quickly opened his door, hoping it was her.

Brooke was rolling out a mat.

"Oh, hi."

"Don't sound so disappointed."

He laughed, stepped farther onto the deck. "I thought maybe Chloe came home."

"Not yet. Does anyone know her flight information?" Brooke asked.

Gio shook his head. "The only one that knows anything is Salena."

Brooke lifted her arms over her head. "I'm sure Chloe has her reasons. And judging from how often Luca has asked about her since she left, I'm starting to understand them."

"What? We're used to watching out for her."

Brooke rolled her eyes. "Don't look at me, I know nothing."

"Yeah, yeah." Gio walked back into his apartment, poured another cup of coffee, and texted Salena.

Where is my sister?

A few seconds later she replied. Do you know what time it is?

It was early. The day is half over.

Seven thirty. I worked late last night.

He wanted to feel bad. He didn't.

What day is she coming home? She didn't tell any of us.

The dots on the screen lasted entirely too long before Salena's message finally came through.

Ask me in two days.

Enough of this. Gio dialed Salena's number. When she didn't immediately pick up, he thought she was going to ignore the call.

Thankfully, she didn't. "You're a pain in the ass, Gio."

"What happens in two days?"

"Nothing. She'll tell me in two days."

Gio counted the days she'd been gone on his fingers. "I thought she was on lockdown or unplugged or whatever for the next five."

Salena was quiet for a moment. "Right. Uhm, okay. I can tell you more in two days."

"You know when she's coming home but you're not telling me."

"No. I absolutely do not know exactly when she's coming home."

Now he was even more confused. "Then what are you going to tell me in two days?"

"Whatever my best friend wants me to tell you. Now, if you don't mind, I need at least two more hours of sleep."

And just like that, Salena hung up.

"What the actual fuck?"

CHAPTER SEVENTEEN

Chloe partnered up with two women a few years older than her, Fiona, from Sydney, and Tina, an ex-pat who lived in Spain. Both women were full-time instructors in studios and both of them wanted to open their own places. The three of them shared that vision of finding a future in doing what they loved to do for a living.

During the busy times of the day, Chloe didn't have time to think about the problems at home. In the quiet, however . . . which happened every morning during group meditation, and again at night when she closed her eyes, her mind drifted to Dante. Had their wedding certificate arrived in the mail yet? She'd have to call him sooner or later to discuss signing the divorce papers.

Not today.

Today the sun was out, and she, Fiona, and Tina were taking their afternoon by the pool.

"How many times have you been here?" Tina asked Fiona.

"Bali, several times. It's so close for us. This is the second time for this retreat. My original certification was done here."

"You'll have to give me a list of things to do," Chloe suggested.

"You're really staying for another month?" Tina asked.

"That's the plan."

"You're smart. Travel before you get married or have kids. It's much more complicated after that," Fiona said.

"You're managing."

"True. But my mum is with the kids during the day and switches with my sister when my husband works late. It's a bit of a shuffle when I'm not there."

Tina laughed. "I just leave my son with my mother-in-law and have my husband visit her."

They chuckled with that arrangement.

"What about you, Chloe? Are you seeing anyone?" Fiona asked.

Chloe instantly thought of Dante. "It's complicated."

Fiona lowered her sunglasses, looked over the brim. "When a woman replies like that it means he's married or otherwise committed to someone else."

"Oh, God no!" Chloe spit out. "I once unknowingly dated a man who was married. Figured it out on the first date. Then a recent guy had 'two roommates,'" she said, air quoting the roommate part. "Who he failed to mention were his children. But no. I don't date married men."

Tina, who was sitting on the steps of the pool, her body submerged, with a hat covering her face, swam closer. "Then what's complicated?"

Chloe looked between the two of them and realized she'd likely never see these women again in her life, so what would it hurt to open up?

"I-ah . . ." She took a deep, cleansing breath, blew it out slowly, and closed her eyes. "I accidentally got married last month to my brother's best friend while we were in Vegas celebrating my other brother's bachelor and bachelorette party. And no one knows about it." Once the words were out, the weight of them lifted from her shoulders.

Chloe opened her eyes to find the other women staring.

"How do you *accidentally* get married?" Fiona asked.

"We were drinking. There was a chapel. Dante bribed the minister, or whatever he was, to call his buddy who worked with the courts . . . We managed a license and, yeah. I didn't remember much until the next morning, to tell the truth. Woke up with this fake ring and a green finger and a killer headache."

"Beside Dante?" Tina asked.

"No. He got me back to my room. We didn't . . ." Chloe sat up, folded her legs under her. "Dante is the guy you look at and dream about but know he can't be *the* guy. Besides, my brothers would kill him if he ever tried with me. If you looked up *player* in the dictionary, you'd see his picture. I've never dated him. We're not like that."

Fiona swung her legs off the side of her chaise lounge and focused her attention. "I'm starting to see the problem."

"We immediately saw the error in our ways and scrambled to stop what we started, but it was too late." Chloe looked out over the water, saw a gecko on the other side of the pool. "I'm close with my family and have recently learned that after a couple of drinks, my ability to keep a secret is shitty."

"You let the cat out of the bag," Fiona said as if she knew.

"No. Not completely. That's why I hopped on the quickest flight I could and why I'm staying here until Dante leaves."

"Wait, he doesn't live in San Diego?"

Chloe shook her head. "Italy."

"Oh."

"He can go home, and then I can go home. We get the annulment, and everything will be fine."

Fiona started to laugh. "Wait, wait . . . I think you skipped something here. You two got *married*."

"Yeah, so?"

"*Married.* Two people don't just do that even if they've been drinking. And if this was a deed done because you were both pissed out of your minds, you would have told everyone, laughed about it, and been on your merry way. Not be a million miles away on an island in Indonesia."

"Well . . . that's what I did."

Fiona narrowed her eyes. "What possessed you to say yes to his little game of *let's say I do*?"

Chloe felt the smile on her lips. “He kissed me,” she said with a sigh. “I knew he was a player, but that didn’t stop me from wanting that kiss ever since I stopped thinking boys were dumb.”

Tina lowered her chin on her folded hands and sighed. “Sounds romantic.”

The tight knot that had been sitting on her for weeks lifted. “It feels so good to tell someone about this.”

“We’re easy. You don’t know us.”

“The only person I could talk to was Dante and that was ruined, too.”

“Why? Did he turn into an ass?” Fiona asked.

Chloe shook her head. “No. We just . . .” The memory of him touching her, his lips, his body. The way he lifted her as if she weighed nothing and took her to heights she didn’t know existed.

Tina lifted a hand in the air with a laugh. “I can guess what he did.”

Fiona nudged Chloe’s knee. “You did consummate your marriage.”

Chloe shook the image from her head. “I think it was inevitable under the circumstances. It changes nothing. He will be back in Italy in four and a half weeks, and by the time he comes back to San Diego, who knows where I’ll be. Or who will be in my life.”

“You really think you’ll be able to laugh this off?” Fiona asked.

Chloe lifted the fruity iced tea to her lips. “I’m staying in Bali until I can.”

Tina pushed away from the side of the pool to float on her back. “At least you picked a beautiful place to pout.”

“I’m not pouting.”

Fiona put her legs back on her chair. “At least now we know why. Getting that out was important. Now you might want to work on being truthful with yourself.”

Chloe sipped her tea. “I’m working on that.”

Fiona leaned back. “I know.”

~

Giovanni waited until eight in the morning, because he was a nice guy.

But the second his phone turned over, he dialed Salena's number and counted the rings.

"You suck" was how Salena answered the phone.

"Two days. It's been two days."

"This is exactly why Chloe ran off. You and Luca micromanage her way too much," Salena yelled.

"We do not."

"You drilled her prom date like he was an ex-con with a weekend pass."

Gio shook his head. "Fake news."

"You had him open his wallet to see if there was a condom in it."

True.

"Our father told us to protect our sister before he died. It's our job."

"Then why isn't Luca calling me asking when Chloe is coming home?"

"Because he's distracted with his bride. And lucky for my sister, she has two brothers."

"Fine. Listen, Chloe is staying in Bali for a while."

The news rolled around in Giovanni's head like a pinball game, only it kept hitting the bumper that lit up the word *what.* "Excuse me?"

"A couple weeks, a month . . . longer. I really don't know. When I talked to her, she didn't have a return ticket."

Ding, ding, ding. "What?"

"The only reason I'm telling you and she isn't is because she doesn't want the argument and she didn't want to leave the restaurant without staff if someone put her on the schedule. So don't let anyone do that."

"What?"

"Do you want me to say that all again in Italian?"

"A month?"

"Yeah. I don't know. Maybe longer. Depends."

"Depends on what?" Something didn't feel right about any of this, and the hair on his neck was itching.

"I don't know. Enlightenment. It is Bali. Don't they do that there?"

"God, you're a smart-ass."

"And you're blind. Your sister needs a break. Let her have it."

"A break from what?"

"Goodbye, Gio. Have a nice day." Salena hung up.

"A break from what?" he asked the empty room.

~

Dante stood outside the yoga retreat, rain beating down on him.

He'd found a hotel a half a mile down the road the night before and slept like the dead. He didn't think his body would ever recover from the flight, but here he was.

He'd looked up the information about where Chloe was staying, hoped that he was arriving at a time where she'd be in one of the activities scheduled for those attending the retreat and not possibly walking by.

One of the many scooters drove by behind him, splashing water on his ankles, as if telling him to move. Instead, he stood there with his phone pressed to his ear, talking to his sister.

"I found Chloe." He'd called Anna the day Chloe had run off and promised to call when he had an update. "I'm in Bali."

"What?"

He looked up at the pouring rain. "I'm crazy."

"You are. But I love you more for it."

"Tell me I'm doing the right thing."

"You are."

Another scooter drove by and threatened to drown him in road water.

"I'll call later."

Dante hung up before walking through the doors and into an open lobby.

A Balinese woman sat behind a desk and smiled when she saw him. "Good morning."

He removed the hood of the raincoat he wore and shook some of the rain from his hair. "Good morning." He stepped farther in. There didn't seem to be anyone walking around. "I'm here to see my . . . I need to see one of your guests." Dante looked at the woman's name tag. "Eka."

"This is a retreat. Our guests come here to get away. If there is an emergency—"

Dante shook his head. "No. You don't understand." He smiled, which normally charmed any female within twenty feet, and tried another approach.

"This is a women's retreat, right?"

"Yes. Women only."

Dante placed a hand on his chest. "My woman." He stopped, shook his head. "Chloe Mancuso . . . D'Angelo." He purposely stopped smiling, looked Eka in the eye. "We had a fight. I flew all the way here, Eka. I need your help."

Eka's smile turned into this puppy look of mush and love, and Dante knew he had an ally.

~

"Miss Chloe?" Mawar, the director of the retreat, stood beside Eka outside the dining room as Chloe, Fiona, and Tina were walking out.

"Yes?"

"There has been a special request made for you tonight."

Eka and Mawar exchanged glances before Eka stared at her feet.

Chloe looked between Fiona and Tina. "What request?"

"An unusual one. Perhaps you can come and see. If you choose not to, of course we will respect that. The plea was made with so much heart, we had to listen."

Chloe nudged Fiona. "Do you know what this is about?"

"Don't look at me."

Mawar and Eka started walking and she followed.

When Tina and Fiona didn't, Chloe waved them toward her.

They scrambled to catch up.

"What's going on?" Chloe asked.

The ladies smiled but didn't answer.

They led her through the grounds to one of the huts that offered massages. The tables had been removed from what she could tell, and someone stood there with their back turned. The torches outside were lit, the scent of bug repellant thick in the air.

Balinese meditation music mixed with the night sounds that were coming to life as dusk started to rise and the sun moved toward the horizon.

A chill moved up Chloe's spine and the hair on her arms stood on end as she neared the hut.

A man . . . tall, olive skin.

Broad shoulders.

Slowly, he turned.

She stopped dead in her tracks. Air caught in her lungs in a sharp inhale.

"Holy shit," Tina whispered.

"Is that Tall, Dark, and Italian?" Fiona asked.

"The husband, nonhusband?" Tina added.

Chloe slowly nodded, lost for words.

"I'm three months pregnant just looking at him," Fiona teased.

"A man who flies here and does this doesn't want you out of his life," Tina said as she nudged Chloe forward.

Mawar and Eka parted.

Dante's eyes collided with Chloe's. Her feet started to move. "What are you doing here?"

"You disappeared," he muttered. "I couldn't leave it like that." Dante looked over at the small crowd watching them.

Mawar questioned Chloe with a tilt of her head and a lift of an eyebrow.

Chloe nodded and the four of them walked away.

Dante waved a hand at the floor. "They offered cushions to sit on."

"We do a lot of meditating here." Dante was standing in front of her, in Bali. How the hell was that possible?

He wore a long-sleeved white cotton shirt, something that looked like it came from a local vendor. His pants were equally casual and loose-fitting. Chloe moved to sit on the floor first and watched in amusement as Dante made his way down. The last time he sat on the floor must have been a long time from the looks of how he was sitting there.

In addition to the mosquito repellant, she noticed the scent of incense burning close by.

She closed her eyes and took a deep breath, instantly calming her nerves that threatened to ping on high.

Silence had her opening her eyes to find Dante staring. *"Sei bellissima."*

Chloe shook her head.

"No. You are. I haven't said it enough, not out loud to you. I've always feared you'd think it was a line, or more . . . I've feared you'd believe it wasn't and see the truth."

"And what *truth* is that?"

"That you're the most beautiful woman I've ever met and that ever since we were teenagers, I've cursed the fact that you were Giovanni and Luca's sister."

She found that hard to believe. "You haven't looked at me twice."

"Because I've grown accustomed to my balls being attached to my body."

Okay, that was funny.

She grinned and studied her hands that rested in her lap. "I'm still their sister."

He hummed. "True. But you're something else."

She looked up.

"You're also my wife."

"Dante—"

He raised his hands. "We didn't go about it the way most peop—"

"*Any* people."

"Most. There are arranged marriages in the world. Close families make matches for their children. Our mothers are practically sisters. You have always been welcomed in my home, and me yours."

"Dante—"

"We didn't go about it the way maybe we should have, but we *did* go about it. For a couple of weeks there, you convinced me that it was a colossal mistake. And then . . ." His words drifted off, his shoulders softening.

"New Year's Eve."

"New Year's Eve," he repeated. Dante reached for her hands, pulled them out of her lap, and squeezed them between their crossed legs. "And you left. Good God, you left."

"I had to. I can't fall any deeper for a man who is going to leave. Sex wasn't going to change that."

Dante lifted her hands to his lips, kissed her fingertips. "Sex? No. You're right. Sex changes nothing. Making love to the right woman? That's an entirely different thing."

It wasn't cold, yet her body shivered.

"What we shared didn't feel like sex. And I've never chased a woman halfway around the world to beg her to give me a chance."

"A chance for what?"

"To know you. To date you. Not my best friend's sister, not the girl next door . . . not the girl I can't . . ." He squeezed his eyes shut, opened them again. "I think we might be perfect for each other."

So much of her wanted to jump and say "Yes, let's try," and an equal part knew the man she held hands with would leave her empty when it was over.

"What if it doesn't work?"

"What if it does?" he asked.

"My family is not goin—"

"They're not here, Chloe. They don't know where I am. I said I had an emergency and had to leave, and I'd be back. Now we can come clean with everyone. Put all the facts on the table. And maybe that's what we end up doing. But right now, they're not here and can't reach us . . . and can't say yes or no to us being together." He squeezed her hands. "And I want to try. I want to date Chloe D'Angelo and see if she likes me as much as I like her. And not worry that her brothers are going to beat the shit out of me when I kiss her at the back door."

Both the image of him kissing her at the back door and a fistfight between her brothers and Dante made her chuckle. "You could probably take Gio. Not Luca."

Dante shrugged. "I wouldn't hit back. The things I've imagined doing to you . . . I deserve to get the living shit kicked out of me."

Her jaw opened with a tiny gasp. "Dante."

"You added fuel to that fire on New Year's."

Chloe couldn't help but ask herself if this could work. "And if the flame burns out? If we try and it doesn't work? The fallout isn't just you and me. I would hate if you and my brothers were at odds."

"This is going to be hard for them to choke down anyway." He paused. "I truly believe they'll get over it. And for one very good reason."

She looked deep in his eyes. "Why is that?"

"This isn't casual. Never was."

He was taking down her fences faster than she could build them. "I have so many questions about how this looks when we get home."

"Can I take you on a first date before we think about that?" he asked.

She choked out a laugh and smiled with a nod. "Yes."

Dante squeezed her hands tight. "Can I kiss you?"

Another nod.

He drew her in so fast, her head spun. With a tilt of her head, his lips pressed more, tongue asked for acceptance, which she granted until they were both breathless.

Dante eased his hold, lingered with a few peppering kisses before she opened her eyes. "You flew all the way here," she whispered.

"You're worth it." He stood, helped her to her feet.

"How did you find me?"

"Salena."

Chloe shook her head. "I knew she couldn't keep a secret."

Dante rubbed his hands along her arms. "If you don't want your family to learn of our marriage, you better hope she can."

"You told her?"

He stopped rubbing. "You did."

"I did not."

"She said she knew about Vegas."

Chloe rolled her eyes. "She knows we kissed. That's it. I told you that."

His shoulders relaxed. "She made it sound like she knew more."

"She doesn't. Well, the first kiss, but no more."

Dante placed his arm over her shoulders as they walked from the hut. "You're here for a few more days?"

"I am."

"Okay. I'm going to leave you alone. Do your yoga, zen thing. I'll pick you up when you're done and start our date."

"One date?"

Chloe thought she saw Fiona and Tina watching from the other side of the gardens but kept the observation to herself.

"It's going to be a long one. A few days, maybe a week or two. You rented a place in Ubud, right?"

"Did Salena tell you everything?"

"Is there more?"

"Not really."

"Good. I'll see you in a few days." They reached the front door. He turned and kissed her briefly and placed his lips to her ear. "I'm right down the street if you need me . . . Mrs. Mancuso."

CHAPTER EIGHTEEN

Gio was officially stalking Salena.

He walked into the club he knew she spent time in on Friday nights and found her with one of her friends, drinking at the bar.

The Gaslamp District was alive with activity and faces he didn't recognize. Which he was pretty sure was why Salena hung out there.

The second she saw him, she rolled her eyes and turned away.

"You wouldn't be ignoring me, would you?" Gio asked as he approached her from behind.

"I swear, if you ask me one more thing about Chloe—"

"No. I came to buy you a few drinks and apologize for being a pain."

Salena closed her mouth and looked him dead in the eye. "Excuse me?"

"Early-morning phone calls and drilling you for information. You were just being a good friend. We could all be so lucky."

She twisted on the barstool, tilted her head. "What's your angle?"

Her healthy distrust was one hundred percent warranted. But instead of saying so, he gave her the wounded-male act with a pout followed by a smile. "What are you drinking?"

"It's margarita night."

Gio clapped his hands together. "Tequila it is." This was going to be easy. He lifted a hand to the bartender and ordered her another, and him the same, with a couple of sidecars.

Salena indicated her friend. "You remember Lisa."

He smiled, looked at what she was drinking. "Want another?"

"I'm pacing myself. Maybe later."

"You got it." Gio reached over, into Salena's space, and grabbed a handful of bar nuts. "You guys work together, right?"

"We do."

"Do you guys come here a lot?" The dance floor was filled with plenty of twentysomethings, many who were probably there with their big brother or sister's ID.

"You already know the answer to that," Salena said. "You did find me here."

"Guilty." He winked.

"I'm waiting . . . by the way."

"For what?" he asked.

"For that apology."

Gio had to smile. Salena was a ballbuster.

He took both her hands in his, kissed the back of them, and made the grandest gesture he could summon. "Salena, my lifelong friend and bestie to my loving sister, can you ever forgive me for being such an ass?"

"Huh."

Their drinks came at that moment and she pulled her hands away. "I'll think about it."

Lisa busted into laughter, and the bartender asked for Gio's credit card to open a tab.

He handed it over and picked up the shot. "Maybe a few of these will put me in your good graces."

"Bring it."

Gio brought it with a smile, a couple of whirls on the dance floor, several shots . . . He almost felt bad when Salena was holding on to his arm as they walked back to their perch at the table they'd found between songs.

"Why don't I hang out here more often?" Gio asked her.

"Because you don't like playing in the same place your sister and I do."

Lisa bounced in, took a sip of her drink, and grabbed her jacket. "I think I'm going to take off with . . ." She looked over her shoulder to the guy she'd been dancing with.

Salena looked the man up and down. "You sure?"

Lisa lifted an eyebrow.

"Okay. Let him know I have you on Friend Finder and I have links to the Italian mafia."

Lisa, who wasn't Italian, laughed. "Will do."

"Wow."

"Wow, what?" Salena asked.

They watched Lisa and her new friend walk out of the club. "I forget how different it is for women."

"The dating scene?" Salena asked.

"Dating . . . hooking up. I leave a bar with a woman, I don't ask Luca or Dante to follow me on an app or make up lies about my family."

She started laughing. "Who said I made up any lies?"

Gio had known Salena since puberty. Her family had zero ties to the mafia.

She had a damn good poker face, though.

It made him look at her twice. "Very funny."

With a smile and a laugh, she broke character and reached for her drink.

He joined her. "You can understand why I worry so much about Chloe being in a foreign country."

Salena sucked her drink down until the ice rattled at the bottom of her straw. "Chloe's going to be fine."

"Going to be?" Gio stopped the waitress, ordered more drinks.

"Men make you do crazy things, but we always pull it together . . . eventually. Remember when I put in blonde highlights?" Salena had coal-black hair. The highlights were her first year out of high school, and they came out looking muddy and gray. They looked ridiculous.

"Yeah?"

"A guy." Salena pointed her straw at him as if accusing him for her hair mistake. "Chloe was the one who talked me out of going completely blonde. Thank God."

"A guy drove Chloe to Bali? I should have guessed." Gio sat back in his chair as if he was uninterested in what Salena could possibly say next, when in reality, he'd been waiting all night for her to be tipsy enough to rattle on and on . . . and hopefully on.

She rolled her eyes. "You always seemed so smart. How can you be so stupid?"

"Hey now." He was about to ask if the guy in question was Eric when the waitress returned with their refills.

Salena latched on, took a big drink. "Chloe has been crushing on Dante forever. You might be blind to your hot sister, but no one else is."

With slow and even movements, Gio sat forward and pulled his drink to his lips. "Dante knows better."

Salena laughed and spit part of her drink from her mouth before grabbing a napkin.

Her reaction brought heat to Gio's face and tension to his neck.

"Are you saying Dante did something to Chloe?"

"No, sir. I did not say that. I may be drunk, but you did not hear that from me. Chloe may have made a pass at Dante, and she says he turned her down, but between you and me I don't buy it. Nope. Not buying that at all. I see how he looks at her." Salena tried again with her drink. "Are these getting stronger?"

"When did this happen?"

"Vegas. Don't you remember how they got all weird after we all went clubbing? Chloe wouldn't drink. You know she can't keep a secret when she's drinking."

Gio lifted his glass in the air. "Not like you."

Salena's smile was so big he questioned everything he thought he knew about the woman. "I know all kinds of things I'm not telling you."

"Like what?"

She opened her mouth, closed it. "Nice try. I'm not that drunk."

He pushed his margarita to her side of the table and folded his hands under his chin.

~

Ubud was slightly cooler, steeper, and felt a lot less like California than the beachside area where Dante had been staying. The rental that Chloe had booked was vacant leading up to her stay, and he was taking advantage of that by arranging a welcome for her she wasn't expecting.

What surprised him was that the terrain was flat and full of rice fields on one side of the road, and up a little way and around a corner, you were in a tropical jungle with steep cliffs and monkeys peeking through the lush landscape unaffected by the urban sprawl that invaded their space. It was utterly fascinating driving around on a scooter where nearly everyone else was doing the same, even with the threat of rain.

The host of the Airbnb accommodated Dante's request with a huge smile and plenty of assurance that everything would be taken care of. Dante was pretty sure the amount of money he was giving the man to do so was overboard, but with the exchange rate of the rupiah to the dollar being so far apart, it made it impossible to figure out what things cost. It also meant that Dante had a wad of cash on him that made him feel like he'd just robbed a bank.

Dante did what he could to scope out local places and those off the tourist traps to keep Chloe entertained for as long as she wanted to stay on the island.

Dante sat outside his room with a map of Bali spread out on a table in front of him and a beer at his side when his phone rang. He saw Marco's number light up and he answered right away.

"*Pronto*," Dante answered with a smile.

They both spoke in Italian, an easier language for Marco since his English wasn't second nature.

"I haven't heard from you all week."

"I know, I'm sorry. I had a change of plans."

"What? You didn't find anything worth our while?"

Dante looked up and saw the ocean and boats, just not the boats Marco was talking about. "I found something worthwhile, but she can't be purchased."

"What? Everything has a price."

Dante sat back, switched the phone to his other ear. "Remember when I told you about my best friend's sister?"

"Ohhh, we're talking about a woman." Marco's voice came down an octave, his words slowed down.

"Not a woman . . . *the* woman."

"If it's the best friend's family, she better be *the* woman or you lose them all."

Dante grabbed his beer. "I know."

"A woman is more important than a boat, so take your time . . . but not too much time."

Dante laughed. "I won't. How is everything there?"

Marco clicked his tongue. "The weather this time of year." His statement was a complaint with only his tone. "A few charters, but you know how it is. Our dance card is filling up for spring. How is tourism in San Diego?"

"It buzzes all year round. Plenty of people on the water, even in winter."

"Good, good."

"I'll call you in a couple of weeks," Dante said.

He had no sooner disconnected the call and set the phone down than it rang again.

Dante picked it up, still speaking in Italian. "Did you forget something, Marco?"

"Do you want to tell me what the hell is going on?"

Not Marco.

"Giovanni?"

"What happened between you and my sister?"

Oh, shit.

Dante pushed his beer aside, sat up. "Who have you been talking to?" Not that he had to ask. There was only one person in San Diego that knew anything.

"You're not going to deny it?"

Dante could hear the heat in Gio's voice.

"It's not what you think."

"It damn well better *not* be what I think. It damn well better be what I'm being told."

"What's that?"

"Damn it, Dante."

"What rumor are you pissing about?"

"That Chloe made a run at you and you pushed her away. And that's why she's sulking in Bali."

"And that's what you *want* to believe."

Gio was silent.

Dante took a breath.

"What happened between Chloe and me—"

Gio hit his edge, and his voice went over. "Awh, fuck, man, no. No. There is one goddamn rule, Dante. Don't fuck with my sister. One fucking rule."

"Gio . . ."

"The next time I see you I'm kicking your ass."

Dante lifted his chin. "Fine, take the first swing, the second. Eventually you'll have to stop and listen."

"Fuck you. I know you. I know how you use women and throw them away."

That hurt. Especially coming from Gio. "It's not what you think," Dante repeated.

"Do us all a favor, stay in Italy." And Gio hung up.

Dante threw the phone on the table with a curse.

CHAPTER NINETEEN

"Promise to keep in touch," Chloe said to both Fiona and Tina. They stood in the foyer of the retreat, their bags at their sides. Their bodies relaxed, their smiles huge, with a bit of moisture in their eyes with their goodbyes.

"Are you kidding? I need to know how this story ends!" Fiona opened her arms for a hug.

"I'll let you both know."

Tina moved in next. "I already know. I just want the details."

When the hugs were done, Chloe stepped back. "If you're ever in San Diego."

Tina pointed her way. "Or Barcelona."

"Or Sydney," Fiona ended.

"Looks like we have some traveling to do."

Chloe felt the weight of someone's stare and turned to find Dante watching her.

"Details," Tina whispered as she walked by.

"All of them," Fiona added.

Dante smiled at the ladies as they passed and moved forward to take Chloe's bag from her. "You ready?"

"I am."

Then, with a strange hesitant move, Dante placed a kiss on her cheek and waved at the women behind the desk.

"We hope you come back soon," Eka said.

"Thank you for everything."

Dante opened the door and led her outside. "I hired a car to get us to Ubud."

"It would have made for a long walk," she teased.

He laughed. "I rented a scooter but didn't see holding a suitcase on one."

Even though the locals seemed to manage, Chloe didn't see trying. "Good call."

The driver retrieved her bag and put it in the front seat while Dante held the door open for her.

Chloe pulled out the paper with the Airbnb location and went to hand it to the driver.

"I got it," Dante told her.

"Oh?"

"Salena."

"That's right, my best friend who gave away all my secrets." She settled into her seat as the driver pulled onto the road. "I haven't turned on my phone. I'm almost afraid to."

Dante moved his legs to one side, then the other. The back seat had little room for his frame. "It's probably a good idea if you hold off on that."

"Oh no."

He gave up trying to get comfortable and reached out his hand. As strange as it was to see it there, it was even more awkward to place her palm in his.

But once they touched, his fingers curled around hers like a sea urchin capturing its prey.

"Giovanni called me."

The stoic delivery of his words told Chloe it wasn't a social call. "And?"

"He knows there's something going on between us."

"Does he know you're here?"

Dante shook his head. "He thinks I'm in Italy and believes you're staying here to get over me."

"Well . . ."

"I know. Not far from the truth. I hope that when you turn your phone back on and listen to whatever people are saying, you still give us a chance." He squeezed her hand.

Chloe looked out the window. "Last night, when I was packing, I considered turning on my notifications. Looking at my messages, emails. The crap on social media. For the last week I've only used my phone to take pictures on occasion, but for the most part it's been shoved in my suitcase, completely forgotten. And you know something?" She glanced at him.

"You didn't miss it."

"I didn't. I know that was the purpose of this retreat. Get away from technology and noise to breathe and focus on what's important. But I didn't expect that I'd go a whole week and not miss the leash of it all." Chloe twisted in her seat to give her full attention to Dante. "My family is important, they are." She pointed to her chest. "But so am I. And I have lived most of my life doing for them. I don't regret it. I really don't. Taking this time for myself. For us, to figure us out. We get to do that. And if it's a mistake—"

"It's not," he interrupted.

"If it is, it's mine to make. Mawar, back at the retreat, said to me, 'Regrets are made in the things in life you don't do, not in the things you do. Everything leads you to who you are meant to be. Doing nothing is not a life lived.'" Chloe paused. "She's not wrong. I want to live my life. I'm going to make mistakes and I'm going to make great decisions that bring me joy as well. What I'm not going to do is sit around and let others tell me what I can and can't do."

Dante stroked her palm with his thumb, his shoulders relaxed against the seat. "All this from a yoga retreat?"

She shrugged. "There's also this guy who is breaking the bro code to be with me."

He grinned. "That's big."

"Huge." Chloe smiled. "When we get settled in Ubud I'll text Salena, tell her to call Mama, tell her I'm good, not to worry, that I'm having the time of my life. Then I'm putting my phone away. You are the official photographer," she told him.

"I can do that."

She looked out the window, pointed to a monkey sitting on the seat of someone's scooter. "Did you see that?"

"No."

Their eyes met and Dante smiled.

~

He encouraged her to wear a dress.

Even though they were sharing the small one-bedroom home with a private pool and equally private outdoor shower and lanai, there were four other mini-homes on the property and a host that greeted them when they arrived.

Dante had already been there and arranged a special welcome.

Chloe was met with flower petals on the bed and in the tub. The refrigerator was stocked with local fruits and vegetables, bottled water, and juices. A small bar had a host of alcohol to mix drinks, but as she had already learned after being on the island for two weeks, good wine was hard to come by. Dante procured a couple of bottles of champagne, to which he said after pointing them out . . . "How bad can it be?"

Guess they would find out.

Chloe stood in front of the mirror, playing with her hair. She hadn't brought makeup to Bali. All she had with her was one tube of lipstick that had been buried in her purse and lotions.

Preparing for a date without the war paint was an entirely new experience. "You know," she called out to Dante, who was on the other side of the wall getting ready himself, "men have it easy."

"Far be it for me to argue with you on our first date, but what are you referring to?"

"I left all my makeup, hair spray . . . everything back home." She applied the lipstick. "Almost all of it," she corrected herself.

"Yes!" Dante said under his breath.

Chloe looked at the rose shade of lip coloring with a smile. "What does that mean?"

"You don't need it."

"All men say that."

"I've known you since before you wore a bra. I remember the pimple stage."

Her jaw dropped, but she found herself smiling in the mirror. "I remember yours, too."

"I couldn't hide it with makeup."

Chloe plucked a small white flower off the arrangement on the counter in the bathroom and placed it in the clip in her hair, turned to look at the back of the sundress . . . and walked behind the partition that separated the two of them.

"I never thought of that. I guess it sucked a little to be a boy during puberty."

Dante turned to stare.

She wore a white spaghetti-string summer dress that gathered at her waist and fell to her feet. Sandals and simple jewelry finished out the look. Nothing fancy, and perfect for a night out in Bali.

"Wow."

Chloe looked down at herself. "What?"

"You're wearing white."

"It's Bali."

He shook his head.

"On our wedding day you wore red. When I danced with you for the first time you wore silver. When I made love to you the first time you wore gray sequins, and now . . . on our first real date, you're wearing white."

A knot formed in the back of her throat and chills ran up her spine. "How do you remember all of that?"

"I remember a lot of things." He bumped his arm out for her to grab hold of. "Shall we?"

"Do I need a coat?"

"We're not going far."

Chloe accepted his arm and fell in line beside him.

The moment they stepped out the door she noticed things had changed. There were lanterns lit, even though the sun had yet to set, and flower petals, similar to those left in the room when they had arrived, trailed the path that he led her on.

"You've put in some effort."

"I flew all the way to Bali."

"You did."

The gravel path led them past the other "homes" that mimicked theirs until they spilled out on a veranda that looked down on a cliff surrounded by a lush tropical jungle. A covered lanai sat at the end of the path, and in it, a single table set for two welcomed them.

"Wow."

Dante pulled out her chair before taking his own.

"This is beautiful."

Dante shook his head. "*You're* beautiful."

She looked away. "It's strange hearing you say that to me."

"Why?"

"I didn't think you looked twice."

Dante pushed in closer to the table. "I wasn't allowed to. I'm okay with that. I was an asshole in high school."

"I don't know about that . . ."

"I couldn't commit. My longest relationship was what, two months?"

"It was high school."

"I deserved the reputation I earned." Dante reached across the table, took one of her hands in his. "The rules about you were set then, and understandably so."

"Well, Dante Mancuso . . . I'm interested in hearing what's changed."

He leaned back, pulled his hand from hers, and waved it in the air. "We might need alcohol for that."

Their host approached the table and brought two drinks in pretty glasses with flowers and fruit garnishing the brims.

His toothless smile reached his eyes. "My name is Ketut."

Chloe had to stop herself from rolling her eyes.

"Your husband take care of everything. If there is something you don't like. No problem. I bring something else," he told her in his slightly broken English.

Chloe smiled at their host and then Dante. "I'm sure whatever is on the menu is perfect."

The man nodded and walked away.

She started the chuckle once he was out of hearing range.

"What?"

"He's the second man who has told me his name is Ketut."

"Isn't it a common name here?"

Chloe laughed. "You never watched *Eat, Pray, Love*?"

"That's a chick flick."

"I take that as a no."

Dante shook his head.

Chloe leaned forward. "There was a Balinese healer in the book and the movie . . . his name was Ketut. I think the locals use the name to . . . I don't know, give the feeling of trust, of familiarity. Probably to gain more tips."

Dante grinned, looked over his shoulder. "Well, *Ketut* hasn't stopped smiling since I arrived. I also have no idea how much I've been tipping him."

Chloe picked up her drink. "Wait, what?"

Dante shrugged. "I get the general idea—"

"You didn't look up the average salary or customs for tipping?"

He placed an elbow on the table, stared into her eyes. "I chased you to Bali. I have no idea what I'm doing."

Chloe shook her head. "You need me."

He picked up his glass. "To needing you."

"I can drink to that."

The flowery fruit drink wasn't too sweet or too strong. Ketut, or whatever his real name was, did a great job.

Chloe put the glass down and leaned forward.

"Okay, Dante Mancuso. I want to know about the women in your life."

Dante coughed on his drink.

She laughed.

Once he managed a deep breath, he cleared his throat, moved his head from side to side.

"I've made you uncomfortable."

"Yes."

"Good."

He laughed.

Chloe took another sip and waited him out.

"You're serious."

"I want to know about the hearts you've broken."

Ketut stepped forward, this time with an appetizer.

Dante looked relieved and dug in once their host walked away.

"Tastes like chicken."

Chloe took a bite. "Pretty sure it's soybean."

"Really?"

She laughed. "So . . . the women?"

Dante wiped his lips with his napkin, took a swig from his drink. "You want the truth."

It wasn't a question.

She looked him in the eye, her smile fell. "Do you want to start this relationship on lies?"

Another swig of his drink. A big sip of air.

"My first year in Positano was as you'd imagine. I was young . . . single." He smiled. "That got old," he said.

"What changed?"

"I don't know. Marco maybe. We became partners and my life filled with schedules and boats and insurance and employees. Marco became the barometer for who I dated. I couldn't date anyone who worked for us."

"I would hope not."

"No." Dante shook his head. "Eventually I started to date with purpose."

"For a relationship?"

He nodded. "My first attempt was my second year in Positano. I thought she was a visitor from another part of Italy, she assured me she was moving to Positano." He lifted a forkful of food to his mouth.

"That wasn't the case."

"Mmm . . . no," he said around his food. "I tried again a year later . . ."

A whole lot could have happened in that year, but Chloe didn't pry. "And?"

Dante shook his head. "We dated. Nothing bad happened. It just didn't work."

Ketut arrived with the second course, removed the first, and quickly disappeared.

The soup was spicy and full of flavor.

Two sips in, Dante asked, "What about you?"

"I'm sure you've heard it all."

"Are you kidding? Luca and Gio never talked about you when I called. I'd ask, but they'd only say you were fine, or bitchy . . . late for a shift. I had to come home to see you to gather any information. I couldn't do that by asking your brothers."

"I suppose that would blow your cover."

"Asking your friends felt like adolescence."

It was Chloe's turn to set her spoon down. "My high school boyfriend taught me that boys lie."

Dante narrowed his eyes. "Ty . . . Tyler?"

"You remember his name?"

"I hated that guy."

Chloe chuckled. She placed a hand to her chest, looked up at the sky. "I thought I was in love . . . I wasn't."

That had Dante's frown growing to a smile.

"Then there was a guy my first year in college. That's when I learned to keep as much information from my brothers as possible."

"Why? What did they do?"

"There was a frat party, I was only nineteen . . . Gio showed up." Chloe shook her head and continued. "Half of the man pool disappeared when the world went virtual. I found myself online with everyone else. The clubs are full of tourists and one-night stands."

Dante lifted his brows.

"Don't look shocked." Chloe sipped her drink. "Not that many of those. Truthfully, if I was going out with someone for a while and things evolved and we'd . . . ya know . . ."

"Sleep with him . . ."

"Yeah . . . and then poof, gone. Most of the guys I met online were already in a relationship and cheating or they just got out of something and only wanted sex. Womanizing, patronizing, look nothing like their profile, lie about their age, unemployed . . . the list goes on and on."

"It couldn't be that bad."

"You're right. I was worse. If I found someone that didn't fall into that category, Giovanni or Luca would find something wrong, point it out, and then that's all I would see and eventually it would end. Then there's Mama . . . 'You need a family man, Catholic, Italian.'"

"Our mothers drink the same Kool-Aid."

"Mama stopped preaching that when Brooke came around. She's not Italian or Catholic and look how well she fits."

"But you're the daughter."

Chloe pointed at him. "That's sexist."

Dante laid a hand on his chest. "I'm also Italian and Catholic, and fit half the requirements."

"Dating sucked."

"Cheers to that." Dante lifted his drink.

Chloe sipped, looked him in the eye. "You never seemed to be without a woman on your arm when you came home for a visit."

"I had to find someone to hang off of or someone would see me drooling over you."

"C'mon." That sounded like a line.

Dante reached out and captured her hand. "I'm serious. I can't tell you exactly when it happened, I just know that you'd walk into the room and my brain and body would short-circuit. I'd go back to Italy and couldn't stop thinking about you."

"You have a damn good poker face." Although right now he wasn't trying to hide how he was feeling. The soft look in his eyes, the tilt of his jaw . . .

"When I came home, I kept up the facade of *Dante the guy who hooks up with whoever*. Until last year."

"What?"

He shook his head. "I haven't slept with anyone in the States, other than you, in two years."

"You're kidding?" Dante visited every year.

"I know how it looked, but I didn't. I wasn't a saint in Italy, but I couldn't in San Diego. Not with you down the street."

Ketut arrived with their main course, another semi-spicy dish, this one with chicken and rice and plenty of local vegetables and fruits.

Chloe picked up her fork as she spoke. "I've dated enough to know what I don't want."

"I'm listening."

"I don't want someone who is so absorbed in his work that he forgets where he is laying his head at night, or who is important in his life. I want someone I can build a life with, not be a placeholder in theirs . . . ya know, like a piece of their puzzle that they need to move on to the next accomplishment." She took a bite of her dinner.

Dante nodded. "I know people like that."

"I don't want someone who is insecure or jealous. That's impossible to deal with."

"You have experience."

Chloe nodded, swallowed. "Yeah, that guy sneaks in and then third date, or after you get naked, boom, 'Where you going? Who are you going with? Did you look at him? Was he looking at you?' Screw that. No, no, and no!"

Dante sat forward, looked over his shoulder. "I don't know . . . I saw how you were looking at Ketut."

Chloe stopped smiling, acted like she was standing up. "Okay, I'm outta here."

He grasped her hand with a laugh.

It was hard to believe they were sitting there, together, talking so openly. For a few moments they simply ate. "It's about trust," he concluded.

"A hundred percent. And that is earned over time, not given with the third-date pass. Like us. I've known you long enough to know you're not here doing all of this to play me. You have too much to lose."

"We're starting out ahead of the game."

That made her laugh. "We got married before we unwrapped the cellophane from the box holding the game."

Dante cracked a smile. "We're crazy."

"Certifiably."

"We've been doing a whole lot of crazy ever since," he pointed out.

Chloe looked around with a nod. "No kidding."

"I think it's good. If this was too easy, it wouldn't be right." Dante reached across the table and placed a hand on her chin.

The butterflies that she'd felt only when looking at him now flourished with his touch.

"Are you ready for dessert?"

"Is that metaphorical, or is there something with sugar on the menu?"

His gaze flared with excitement. "We can skip the next course."

Forging innocence, Chloe leaned back, out of his reach. "No, no. I don't want to be too easy. I hear when you work for it, it makes it better."

Dante shifted in his seat with a growl.

Ketut removed their dinner plates and brought a light sponge-type cake with fruit and cream.

"Isn't this lovely." She pulled off a tiny portion of the cake and placed the tip of her tongue on the cream but waited until Dante looked up to wrap her lips around the food.

He lifted an eyebrow.

"Thicker than it appears," she said, stabbing a berry as she chewed.

He finally took a bite as he watched her.

The berry became a vessel for the cream that she spooned onto her tongue slowly.

Dante moved to the left.

The right.

The tart berry exploded in her mouth and she went for another. She loaded it with cream and Dante captured her hand.

She set the fork down.

"Ketut," Dante called out. "Thank you for everything."

He pulled her to her feet and walked them toward their rooms.

As soon as they were alone Chloe found herself up against the door, Dante's body on hers, his lips locked on, with no oxygen to be found.

It was glorious.

Her body was lax from the week of yoga and Balinese massage, not to mention the cocktails they'd had with dinner. Her heart was filling with every gesture Dante was putting in to give the two of them a shot. And her soul was screaming *Finally.*

"I want to touch you," he whispered.

"Yes."

"All the time. Tell me I can." His hand slid down her hip, cupped her sex.

"Yes." Her chin fell back.

"And kiss you when I see you." Dante placed his lips on her neck, nibbled.

"I'd like that."

"Hold you."

Chloe stroked the length of his erection through his clothing. "Yes, to all of it. And I get to do the same."

Dante smiled, dragged her to the bedroom, and tossed her on the bed.

CHAPTER TWENTY

Dante woke with his chest pounding.

He shot straight up in bed; his hand flew out to the side.

Chloe wasn't there.

He looked left, right. "Chloe?"

When she didn't immediately respond his heart skipped a beat. His feet hit the floor and he half ran out of the room. She wasn't in the living space that opened to the kitchen.

"No . . . C'mon."

The bathroom was empty, the outside shower . . . empty.

He ran a hand through his hair as his thoughts started to spiral.

That's when he saw movement out of the corner of his eye in the outside lanai.

Chloe.

She was on her yoga mat, contorted in a way he didn't think the human body could actually achieve.

Dante covered his face with both hands. "Get a grip."

He gave himself a moment to get his shit together before opening the door and walking outside.

She didn't notice him at first, so he soaked in the image of her.

There was grace and beauty in how she moved. And strength. No wonder she was able to bend the way she did when they made love.

"You can grab a mat and join me."

He smiled. "I like this view."

"Scared?"

"That sounds like a challenge."

"It was." She folded in two, lifted her arms above her head, and brought them back down to her chest as if she were praying.

"If the guys back home found out about it, I'd never live it down."

She turned to him, smiled. "I won't tell."

He looked her up and down, swallowed hard. "I woke up and you weren't there. It scared the hell out of me."

Chloe lost the amusement on her face and walked over to him. "I wouldn't do that to you. Ever."

He buried his head in her neck and she wrapped her arms around his waist.

"How about some coffee?" Chloe suggested.

~

"I want to know everything!" Salena squealed into the phone.

"I'm only giving you the highlights. The rest has to wait until I'm home." Chloe sat with her feet dangling in the pool.

Dante was inside making them breakfast, so Chloe took the opportunity to call Salena and get that chore out of the way.

"When are you coming home?"

"We have no idea."

"'We'?" Salena squealed again.

"Yeah. We."

"I knew it was more than a kiss."

Chloe smiled so hard. "It's been murder not being able to tell you. I couldn't risk my brothers finding out."

"Yeah, about that . . ."

"I know about Gio. It's okay. But if he asks, you don't know where Dante is, okay? He thinks he is in Italy and we want it to stay that way.

We want to find out if we can work without my family trying to dictate if we should or shouldn't."

Salena scoffed. "A good friend would remind you that Dante is a playboy."

"I'm not exactly Mother Teresa."

"You are compared to him."

"People grow up and change." She saw him walk past the window, the muscles in his back slick with the moist Bali heat.

"You sound happy."

"I am."

"Is he everything we talked about?"

Chloe felt her skin warm. "Be jealous, my friend. Be very, very jealous."

"Bitch." But Salena laughed.

"I need you to keep running interference. If I call home, there will be questions I don't want to answer."

"I'm sure. What do you want me to do?"

"Just tell my mother I'm having the time of my life, meeting new friends, and staying off the phone. Which I am going to do. Emergency calls only, okay? And call Dante's phone. I'm leaving mine behind."

"I'm your girl."

"Thank you, Salena."

They said their goodbyes and Chloe disconnected the call. She glanced at the number of text messages but didn't open the app. Same thing for her emails. They were piling up, but she ignored them.

Dante walked through the back door with a tray of food and set it on the outside table.

"How is Salena?"

"Great." Chloe stood, moved around the pool to join him.

"And everything at home?"

"I assume fine, she didn't let on that it wasn't."

"Then we won't worry." He pulled out her chair.

"I could get used to this."

He leaned over, kissed her. "Me too."

"What do you want to do today?" she asked.

He looked up at the clear sky. "Let's take advantage of the nice weather and go for a hike . . . find a waterfall."

"I'm sure we can find one."

Chloe picked up her fork and dug in.

~

"I need you to go over to Rosa's. She needs help with her sink."

Gio sat across from his mother in the office and was currently staring down at the schedule. Chloe's name was there with a line through it for the next two weeks.

It boiled his blood looking at it.

"What's wrong with it?"

"I don't know, she said it's loose."

"Is it the kitchen or bathroom?"

"Kitchen, I think. Does it matter? It's a sink. You and Luca fix sinks all the time. She needs help, I send one of my sons."

Right, because her son wasn't there. Before Dante went on his shit list, Gio would've considered any help for Rosa a gift to both her and Dante. Now, Gio was only doing it for Rosa and his mother.

"Go."

"Now?"

"Yes. I need you for the early-dinner rush."

Gio moved to his feet. "Fine."

He first went to the storage room, grabbing a toolbox and what he thought he'd need, before climbing into Chloe's car and driving down the street to Rosa's.

He knocked three times, heard her yell to come in, and did so.

So far, he'd told no one what Salena had revealed.

Luca would be just as furious, and to give him this stress while he was still basking in the glow of his wedding . . . no, Gio couldn't do that.

"Giovanni, thank you for coming." Rosa motioned him to the kitchen, where she'd removed everything that lived under her kitchen sink. Wet towels sat under a dripping pipe.

"Anytime."

"I don't know what happened. I noticed the water when I was doing my dishes this morning."

He dropped to his knees, climbed under the sink. It took him ten minutes to figure out what was wrong and another hour to fix it.

When he was done, his back hurt like hell, and Gio decided for the tenth time in his adult life that he never wanted to be a plumber. "If it leaks again, turn the water off under here." He pointed out the valve to shut it off. "We'll have to get a replacement for you if what I did doesn't hold."

Rosa offered him something to drink, food . . . Gio refused.

"Can you do me another small favor?"

He smiled, despite the worry of what that favor would be.

"Sure."

"Can you take Dante's mail to his place and make sure everything is good over there? I know he's only renting, but I'd hate if he came home to rotten food on the counter and bugs. He told me you had a key."

A key Gio wanted to toss in the ocean.

Rosa handed him a pile of mail as if he'd already agreed.

"Absolutely."

"Such a good boy."

Gio used the sink he'd just repaired to wash his hands before gathering his tools and walking out the door.

Outside, he looked at Dante's mail, slapped it against his thigh, and walked to the car.

Fifteen minutes later, Gio sat in the car, looking up at the condo complex that housed the place Dante had rented, with heat boiling under his skin.

"Get this over with," Gio said to himself.

Gio found the key where he'd left it after retrieving his bike . . . and unlocked the door.

The place looked the same.

Cold, since the heater had been turned off, and even though it was San Diego, it was still winter, and the nights were nippy.

Gio thought about what Rosa said in regard to food spoiling and looked in the fridge.

Milk.

He smiled and left it.

There was fruit rotting on the counter.

Yup, that ought to attract a few ants.

Gio thought about Chloe and wondered if Dante had rented the space for her . . . to be there with her.

He squeezed his eyes shut, slammed the mail on the kitchen counter, and cussed his friend. Former friend. Former *best* friend.

Gio would never have gone after Anna. Yeah, Anna was a lesbian, but that was beside the point.

Opening his eyes, Gio pushed the mail across the counter and stopped.

A pile of papers sat close to the mail. On top of them was a printout that said something about filing for a divorce in California.

Gio picked it up and started reading . . . confusion swept over his brain. What the hell did Dante need with information about divorce?

His mother . . . Rosa.

Only the next set of papers talked about annulment.

What the hell was that about?

Then, because why the hell not, Gio started snooping. He looked through the stack of papers, found the rental agreement for the condo.

He went into the bedroom, rifled through a few drawers, didn't find anything important, went back to the kitchen.

"What do you need to know about annulments, Dante?"

If he'd gotten married and was trying to hook up with Chloe and had a wife in Italy, he'd kill him. Is that why Dante was sticking around? What was the emergency in Italy that he had to go back for?

Gio's head spun.

As it did, he pushed through the papers, the mail . . . there had to be a clue . . .

State of Nevada, Clark County: Official Document.

The post from Nevada stood out, and the hair on Gio's arms stood on end.

"Vegas. Don't you remember how they got all weird after we went clubbing . . ." Salena's words echoed in Gio's ears.

He lifted the envelope, looked at the seal.

Gio was ninety-nine percent sure it was illegal for him to open someone else's mail without their permission.

Gio was also ninety-nine percent sure he didn't give a flying fuck.

He found a knife and made a neat slice across the top of the envelope and removed what was inside.

One look and his blood ran cold, and the knife fell to the floor.

~

Chloe regretted the bite the moment it passed her lips. "Oh my God, that's hot." She reached for the water and sucked it down. Her eyes teared up and Dante laughed at her.

"You should see your face."

She fanned her lips. "How do they eat this?"

They were at a local market brimming with street food. Small carts filled with all kinds of choices, local spicy varieties that she and Dante were determined to try.

"Okay, smarty-pants . . ." She pushed the plate his way. "Let's see you do better."

Dante filled a fork with shrimp and the chilies it was cooked in. The amount alone was impressive, and once it hit his mouth, Chloe started counting.

One . . .

Two . . .

His eyes started to water.

Three . . .

He swallowed, coughed.

Four . . .

Then reached for the water as fast as she did and downed what was left in the bottle. "Holy hell."

"Told ya."

"That's gonna hurt in the morning."

Chloe moved that paper plate to the side and scooted the next one between them. "You first."

"Which cart did we get this one from?" he asked.

She swiveled around and pointed. A child stood in line, giving her hope that this plate wouldn't be as bad.

"What is it?"

"Chicken, I think."

He opened another bottle of water, rubbed his hands together. The chicken was on a stick and smothered in sauce. Dante put it to his nose first.

Chloe leaned across the table to sniff, then looked at what they'd just tried. "I think that burned my smeller out."

"Mine, too."

She pushed his hand closer to his mouth. "It looks good."

He offered it to her. "You try it."

She nudged it back his way. "Age before beauty."

"Ladies first."

Chloe shook her head.

He took a bite and she counted. By six he took another bite. "Not bad."

She put out her hand and accepted the dry end of the stick. Unlike the last bite, she nibbled this one and waited for the heat.

"Not bad." She took off a bit more and Dante grabbed her hand.

He shook his head. "The heat comes later."

Without ceremony, she found a napkin, spit out the food, and reached for the water.

Dante started laughing, and before long she caught his joy as if it was an out-of-control virus and laughed right along with him.

"We're going to starve."

That made her laugh harder.

Up next, a bowl of rice with something shredded, red, and chunky piled on top. Just looking at it made her tongue curl.

Dante shook his head. "I can't."

She covered her mouth, unable to stop laughing. "We may need to find a McDonald's."

He looked at her as if she were crazy, reached for the bowl. "How bad can it be?" Dante brought the food to his nose and shook his head.

Chloe couldn't stop laughing.

Dante twisted out of his seat, piled the food into his hands, and took it to the closest trash can and dumped it. After dusting off his hands he reached out for hers. "We can say we tried."

Instead of eating, they walked through the market, dodging vendors. Chloe picked up a trinket or two for Franny, something for her mother and Brooke.

Chloe was looking at a shirt that screamed *Bali for men* when she asked, "Do you think Luca and Gio will feel left out if I don't get them anything?"

Dante's gaze lost focus before he looked away. "No."

Her hand dropped and she stepped away from the clothing. "What's wrong?"

He looked at the shop, then back to her. "I think when they realize we were here together, whatever you buy them they'll either burn or make a voodoo doll out of using my hair."

She looped her arm in his and walked away from the men's shirts. "It won't be that bad."

"Your brothers know me better than you."

Her hand slid over his hip, touched a part of him only a lover would. "I doubt that."

Dante swung his arm over her shoulder, kissed the side of her head, and pulled her close. "They're going to hate us."

"They'll get over it."

The weight of Dante losing his friendship with her brothers weighed on him. No matter how much she wanted to assure him that it would work out, she knew that the only way to prove it was with time.

Chloe swatted the side of her arm where a mosquito was having dinner. The sun was just starting to lower on the horizon, which meant it was time to reapply the bug repellant. "The thing I won't miss about Bali are these bugs," she said. Chloe reached into her purse and pulled out her spray.

"Have you thought about when you want to go home?" They'd had over a week together and several more days planned out.

She shivered. "No."

They kept walking.

"Maybe that's irresponsible of me." Chloe shook the bug spray as she spoke. "I haven't even asked you how this unexpected vacation is affecting your bottom line."

"I'm okay. I wasn't expected back in Positano for several weeks."

"There's the day-to-day work, but the flight . . . that wasn't cheap."

"I have miles saved."

She narrowed her eyes. The airlines that frequented Bali weren't the same as those that went back and forth to Italy from the States. At least not the ones that were most economical.

Dante pulled her close. "Don't worry about it."

"Fine. I won't worry, but I know you're not getting rich off your boat business."

"Not rich, but we do okay."

She swatted at another biting bug and pulled him away from the passing crowd. There, she sprayed her exposed skin and handed him the bottle. "At least you have a direction in your life. I'm floundering."

"You've been working at the restaurant."

"I know. But that's my mother's and, arguably, Luca's."

"He wouldn't agree to that." Dante sprayed his arms, gave her back the bottle.

"He's the main chef. Mama steps in when it's absolutely necessary. The two of them take care of the books. Gio and I have waited tables, hired and fired staff. Take care of some of the operations, but Mama and Luca, they take on the bulk of it. It runs without me. And it runs without Giovanni. You know that."

"It's a good thing Luca enjoys it."

"It is. Gio and I've talked about it a couple of times privately, how we are the lucky ones that don't feel tied down to the family business. We've always known it was an option for us to come or go."

"Luca assumed you'd get married and move out," Dante said.

They looked at each other, laughed.

"Gio won't stay forever either."

"No. He won't."

They started walking again. "I know business. I know restaurants. I know yoga."

Dante reached for her hand again, added to her list. "You speak two languages and are beautiful."

"Unless I'm applying for a stripper position, I'm not sure what beauty will get me."

"Much as the world wants to deny it, beauty opens many doors."

"I don't know if I like that."

"Those same doors close if you're not intelligent enough to keep them open. Confidence is attractive and you have that in spades. You can do anything you set your mind to, Chloe. I just don't think you've given yourself the space to try."

She gave him a sideways glance, a half smile. "You've never said anything like that to me before."

He shrugged. "I also have never walked a market in Bali with my wife before. I'm all full of firsts this month."

"No."

"What, no?"

"We're just dating this week."

"We're married."

"I'm aware. I was there. That doesn't feel real. *This* does." She squeezed his hand. "Talking about what we want to do with our lives, what's possible."

"Whatever makes you happy."

Chloe laughed. "You know what would make me happy?"

"What?"

She moved in front of him, stopped. "Food. I'm starving."

"Let's find McDonald's."

Her feet didn't budge.

"Joking."

Chloe smiled and let him pull her away from the market and toward the busy street where the restaurants lived.

CHAPTER TWENTY-ONE

"What now?"

Giovanni cornered Salena at work. Low move, he knew, but he'd kept the Dante and Chloe marriage certificate information to himself for two nights, and he was beating his head against the wall.

"I need you to call Chloe."

"She's not answering her phone." Salena stared at him, a tray of drinks in her hand, glaring.

"You told our mom that if there was an emergency you could get ahold of her."

Salena tilted her head to the side. "Who is dying?"

Dante, as soon as Gio wrapped his hands around the man's neck. "I have to talk to her."

Salena rolled her eyes, started to walk away.

He jumped in front of her.

"I'm working, Gio. And you're losing it."

"Please, Salena, it's important."

On an exacerbated sigh, she said, "Chloe is due to call in a couple of days, so I'll tell her what you said. But unless someone is sick or hurt, I'm not interrupting her zen."

"Fuck."

She walked around him and out of sight.

Gio stormed out of the restaurant and down the street to D'Angelo's.

It was the middle of the week, not terribly busy, and Gio walked through the back entrance and went straight to the storage room adjacent to the office, where they kept the liquor. He grabbed a bottle of his preferred whiskey, signed for it on the inventory list, and turned to see Luca at the door.

"Thirsty?" he asked.

Signing for alcohol wasn't new . . . the expression on his face was.

"Bad day."

"You've had a few of them. Wanna tell me what's going on?"

Gio looked left . . . right, then lifted the bottle in his hands. "Join me upstairs. You're going to need this."

Luca's eyes widened. "Give me thirty minutes."

With a nod, Gio took the back stairs and made his way to the top floor.

Outside, it started to drizzle, matching his mood.

He was on his second drink before he heard Luca's footsteps outside his door.

"Come in," Gio called out, not that he needed to.

Luca stepped in.

"Close the door behind you."

In the small kitchen in what used to be a guest suite of their home, Gio poured a generous portion of whiskey over a single cube of ice for his brother and handed it to him.

"Looks serious," Luca said, taking a seat in the living room.

Gio sat opposite him on the edge of an overstuffed chair, his drink dangling from his fingertips. The ice in his glass melted slowly, diluting the color of the liquor. He wasn't quite sure why that thought popped into his head.

"Gio?"

He looked up. Sighed. "I've been sitting on some information for a couple of days. It's in here spinning." Gio placed the cold glass to his forehead. "I can't fucking believe—"

"Spit it out."

He shook his head, took a drink. "Remember Vegas?"

Luca snorted. "Of course."

"Remember how Chloe and Dante were so hungover they ditched us the morning after we were all out doing the bachelor party thing?"

Luca's lips fell into a line. "Yeah."

"Remember how strange Chloe acted at the wedding? The rehearsal dinner?"

"No. Not really."

"I remember. In fact . . . Chloe hasn't been acting like herself *since* Vegas."

Luca pointed at him with his glass. "You wanna skip to the good part here?"

Gio stood, put his drink on the coffee table, and moved to the counter in his kitchen, where he'd placed the marriage certificate.

"I had reason to believe that Dante had made a run at Chloe."

From behind him, he heard Luca choke on his drink, sputtering and coughing. The sound put a smile on Gio's face. Nice to know his brother felt the same way about that. "What the f—"

"Yeah. And that she'd run off to Bali like she did to get over it. Get over him. Then Dante leaves. Back to Italy. Pretends he's coming back, but who the fuck knows?"

"Did you talk to him?"

"Yeah. He didn't deny it."

"Son of a bitch."

Gio waved the envelope in his hands. "Then Rosa asks me to drop off his mail at the condo. I find this." Instead of reading it, he handed it to Luca.

Luca set his drink down and read. Slowly, Luca went from anger to fury. Nose flared, face white. "Is this what I think it is?"

Gio flicked the paper in Luca's hand. "They got married. In Vegas at your bachelor party. And you know what's really fucked-up?"

"She's pregnant?"

Gio shook his head. "Don't fucking say that. No, not that I know of. The fucked-up part, Dante is already planning the divorce. I don't know what the hell this was. A damn permission slip to screw our sister or what? But the divorce papers were right next to this on the kitchen counter. While Chloe is off in Bali recovering from whatever it is he's done, he ran back to Italy before any of us could find out about it."

"I'm going to kill him."

"Get in line," Gio said.

"No wonder Chloe isn't talking to any of us."

"And no wonder she isn't coming home for a month. Dante's lease on the condo is six weeks. She's coming back right when he is supposed to leave. Tell me that's a coincidence."

"What the hell are we going to do?"

"I know what I'm going to do."

Luca looked up from the paper in his hand. "What?"

"I'm going to Italy. Dragging his ass back here. Going to make him face everyone. There is no way he is going to shame our sister and not stand up and take it like a goddamn man."

Luca kept shaking his head. "I can't believe this. Even for Dante."

"They got married before you did."

His brother looked at the paper again, put it on the coffee table, and finished the liquor in his glass.

"What do we tell Mama?"

"I don't know. You're the oldest. You decide."

Luca lifted his middle finger, stood, and walked to the kitchen for the bottle. He brought it back to the living room and poured more in each of their glasses. "Brooke will know what to do."

"What the hell was Chloe thinking?"

"Chloe always had a thing for Dante," Luca said as if that explained it all.

"And Dante has a thing for anything in a skirt."

Luca looked at the marriage certificate again. "Maybe there's an explanation."

"If there is, I'm going to get it. In person. No matter what, Mama knows nothing until I'm in Positano. I don't want him knowing I'm coming."

"You think he'll run off?"

Gio stopped his glass halfway to his lips. "Maybe he's more like his father than we've given him credit for."

Luca sighed. "I hope not, Gio. For Chloe's sake."

~

Tirta Empul was a sacred water temple not far from Ubud that had been on Chloe's must-do list from the moment she planned her trip to Bali.

Never in her wildest dreams did she imagine she'd be waiting in line beside Dante. Both of them wore sarongs that went past their knees, and she kept another over her shoulders as she had whenever she entered any of the other temples they'd visited on their tours.

As they moved closer to the pools of water, Chloe wrapped her hair on top of her head as the instructions told them.

"What exactly is this supposed to do again?" Dante asked.

"It's for prayer and purification. You stop at each spout, say your prayer, and duck under the holy water and let it wash over you."

The woman in front of them in line overheard their conversation and stood there nodding.

Dante held their offerings in his hand. "And these are for?"

Chloe shrugged. "Part of the ritual. A gift to the Hindu gods, I think."

They watched the other people entering the pool and slowly making their way through the many lines in front of each spout of water. Surrounding the stone pool were statues of all shapes and sizes, massive ones that looked like dragons and others that had faces of praying

Balinese people. The temple itself had been there since AD 926, which made Chloe walk softer somehow and lower her voice, almost as if she were inside a cathedral in Rome. "It's fascinating, isn't it?"

Dante nodded. "I never thought I'd be doing this."

The woman in front of them, midforties if Chloe had to guess, looked over her shoulder. "Women will have you doing all kinds of things you never expected."

That had them both laughing.

It was obvious the woman was American, so Chloe asked, "Where are you from?"

"Salt Lake. You?"

"San Diego," Chloe answered for the both of them.

The woman smiled. "Are you here on your honeymoon?"

Chloe tripped on her answer, looked at Dante as if he was the only one who knew it.

"Was that a difficult question?"

Dante used his free hand and placed his arm over Chloe's shoulder. "Technically, yes."

Ms. Salt Lake looked at Chloe's left hand, narrowed her eyes.

Chloe waved her hand. "My ring was loose, I didn't want to drop it in the pool."

"Oh."

Dante shook his head. "Truth is, we eloped. We haven't bought rings. Spent all the money on plane tickets and temple offerings."

Ms. Salt Lake looked like she was going to melt into a pile of adoring mud right there. "That's so romantic."

The word *eloped* did have a tender feel about it. Yet somehow that wasn't quite what they'd done.

"Congratulations."

"Thank you," Chloe and Dante both said together.

It was Ms. Salt Lake's turn to step into the water, and even though there was room, Chloe and Dante held back.

Dante read the sign, pointed to it. "The last two spouts are for the dead."

Chloe did a double take. "What?"

"Don't duck under the last two spouts. Bad mojo."

She looked down the long line of waterspouts, noticed no one at the last two. "Treat it like mass. Stand up, sit down, kneel . . . just follow the leader and we should be good."

They stepped into the fresh water and into the first line. Algae and small fish hovered at the side of the pool. While many of the people there were tourists like them, there were plenty of locals participating in this ritual as a part of their prayer . . . their church.

And as they moved closer to the first spout, Chloe let the calming noise of the water and quiet whispers of people drift around her. It dawned on her that for hundreds of years, people had come here in some way searching for answers. Maybe for absolution. No different than when she went to her church and, arguably, her god.

She stepped up to that first waterfall of holy water, put her offering on the ledge as everyone before her had done, and placed her palms together, bowing her head. That simple movement made her heart open, and her eyes teared a tiny bit.

Let me be okay with whatever is going to happen.

She repeated her prayer in her head, in English, in Italian . . . and ducked under the water.

It wasn't cold, it wasn't hot. But it did shock her body enough to feel as if someone had heard her.

Chloe smiled at Dante as she walked into the line at the next spout.

From there she watched him as he stood like she had.

She couldn't tell if he had a moment of divine anything, but after he ducked under the water and walked into the next line behind her, he kissed the side of her neck and left a possessive hand on her shoulder as they waited their turn for the next.

In silence they moved through several more spouts . . . At each one, Chloe repeated her same prayer, and by the end it felt less like a request and more like a given. As if the prayer had already been granted.

They stepped from the pool and away from the crowd.

Dante stopped without saying a thing and pulled her into his arms.

He was trembling, and she realized, in that moment, that she was, too.

They quietly held each other, water dripping from their clothing, their hair. Tears, which had no place but felt perfectly normal because of where they were, fell silently from Chloe's eyes.

When Dante did speak, he spoke in Italian. "That was unbelievable."

Chloe nodded against his shoulder.

"Thank you for bringing me here," he whispered.

She leaned back to look at him.

Dante placed a thumb under her eye to dry her tears. And then he kissed her. A soft kiss with promise.

~

"You're sure about this?" Luca asked Gio. They stood outside the airport.

"If you didn't have a new wife and a daughter . . . and a restaurant to run, you'd be on this plane."

Luca started to nod. "You're right."

"You take care of everything here. I'll take care of Chloe."

Luca spread his arms wide, pulled him in.

A kiss to the cheek. "Give him a chance to explain."

"I'm decking him first."

"It takes two," Luca said, his voice stoic.

"That sounds like Brooke."

He shrugged. "Without her I'd be looking for blood. But she's right. It takes two. Yes, Dante is older, yes, we all agreed Chloe was off the table for him to fuck with. But she did this, too. She said 'I do.'"

It was hard to see Chloe as anything but innocent in this.

"Still going. Still dragging him back."

"No argument here."

Traffic behind them started to pile up in the drop-off line.

"I'll call you when I land."

CHAPTER TWENTY-TWO

Three layovers, eighteen hours, and a hangover later, Gio was on the taxi ride from hell from Naples to Positano. The driver drove as fast as he talked. Between the sleep deprivation and cottonmouth, Gio wasn't sure if he should get a hotel and sleep for a day before confronting Dante or use the nasty feeling inside of him as fuel.

Nasty won, and he'd given the driver Dante's address and they were driving along the coastline at breakneck speed.

It had been a long time since he'd been to Italy, and although he'd planned on coming later that year to spend time with Dante at the coast and then go inland to the heart of Tuscany, he would have to alter all of that now.

With nothing to do but think and drink on the flight over, Gio vacillated between anger and hurt over what Dante had done.

The worst part was no one saw this coming. When had Chloe and Dante even had time to see each other, let alone get close enough to consider getting married?

The only time he'd ever seen them touching was dancing at the wedding, and even then, it was brief. In fact, they were barely in each other's orbit. And hadn't Chloe gone out on at least two dates with that Eric guy? Yeah, the whole thing baffled Giovanni's mind.

The road hugged the coastline and narrowed as they drew closer to Positano. Down below, the blue water of the Mediterranean Sea sparkled like diamonds as the sun bounced off the ripples fighting against the current.

As angry as he was about the reason for his visit, it was hard not to smile at the beauty of the Amalfi Coast.

Once they entered the actual city, the one-way traffic had them circling around, dodging pedestrians, scooters, and other cars, until they finally stopped at the building that housed Dante's rental.

Unfolding from the back seat of the small car never felt so good.

Handing over a crap ton of euros for the ride, on the other hand, sucked. Gio made a note to have Dante pay the bill.

Asshole.

The driver sped off and Gio stood looking up at the six-story building. Everything in Positano was vertical. The cliffside city only had room to grow up. And even that was limited due to restrictions. As it should be.

Gio sucked in a leveling breath and lifted his suitcase up the stairs. Inside the entry level of the building, he walked the short path to the elevator, pressed the button, and waited.

The memory of why he and Dante never used the thing returned. The rusty sound of it reaching the bottom level preceded the opening of the doors. It was dark, someone had obviously smoked inside of it recently, and if you suffered from claustrophobia, you wouldn't step into it for a thousand dollars.

Gio was tired, so he rolled his suitcase in, pressed the third floor, and suffered through the smell on the short ride up.

The elevator opened to a large hallway with tall ceilings that had been there for a couple hundred years.

Gio pushed the thoughts of architecture and elevator aside as he stopped in front of Dante's door.

His chest rose and fell rapidly at the thought of seeing him.

Gio left his suitcase at his side, clenched his fist, and knocked on the door. He held his breath, legs braced for the door to open, ready to knock Dante into next week without warning.

Seconds went by.

He knocked again.

Nothing.

He put his ear to the door, rattled the doorknob.

Shit. He wasn't home.

Of course not. It was the middle of the day.

Gio left his luggage in the hall and found the staircase leading to the rooftop patio for the residents. It was empty, probably because even though it was Italy, it was still winter and not exactly sit-in-the-sun warm outside.

He looked around for the statue of a famous naked woman and looked behind her. After tilting several pots of plants, he found the key . . . the one Dante had placed there for emergencies.

Gio tossed it in the air, caught it, and made his way back inside.

Much like helping himself to Dante's mail, he did the same with his apartment.

He unlocked the door and let himself in as if he were invited.

In truth, he would be, that was, until he put a fist through the man's jaw. "Hey, asshole, I'm home," he called out to the empty room.

He left his bag at the door and walked around the living room, ducked his head into the bedroom that appeared as if a housekeeper had just been there and left it spotless.

The apartment was cold, he realized, moving to one of the old radiators. It was turned all the way down. Jacking it on high, Gio used the bathroom before making his way into the kitchen. Much smaller than anything standard in the States, the kitchen held a refrigerator half the size than even Gio had in his small space. The only thing in Dante's was a few condiments and two beers.

Gio grabbed a beer, wondered why there wasn't a perishable in the thing. The counters were free of fruit, bread . . .

There was a rack with wine, but that said nothing. The pantry had some dried pasta, a few canned goods, a few jars . . . but again, nothing that would mold or go bad.

Gio slowly twisted off the cap of the beer and took a drink.

The curtains were half-closed.

He opened them and let in the light and took in the view of the ocean below.

Something felt off.

Gio set the beer down and moved back into Dante's room and opened the wardrobe. Rooms like his didn't have a closet like most places in the US, this was more of a freestanding piece of furniture that took up the side of the room.

Lots of hangers were free of clothes, the space where shoes sat was empty.

He rifled through drawers and found the same thing. And when he looked for a suitcase, he came up empty.

"What the hell?"

Grabbing the key, Gio left the apartment, locked the door behind him, and took the stairs as he walked out of the building.

He crossed the busy street and found the first of many staircases that would slowly bring him down to sea level.

He couldn't tell from his position if the vessels that belonged to Dante and his partner were bobbing in the water, anchored to one of the many buoys.

The tiny office space that housed their business was down an alley and sandwiched between a restaurant and a tourist-trap gift shop. The door was open, but no one was at the desk.

"Hello?" Gio called out in English.

"Be right there." It sounded like Marco and not Dante talking from the back.

As Gio waited, he looked around the space.

Pictures of Dante and Marco standing beside their first boat, and then the second. Each with champagne in their hands, smiles on their faces.

"Can I help you?"

Gio turned.

Marco's eyes narrowed. They'd met, of course, but it had been a while.

Gio switched to Italian. "I'm Dante's friend, Giovanni from San Diego."

Marco's jaw dropped, a smile lit his face, and his arms opened.

Leaving Gio little choice but to move in and accept the hug, which he did. He immediately apologized. "I just arrived, I'm sorry."

"No, no. Goodness. You look older." He tilted his head. "Or maybe that's tired."

"I'm sure that is it." He laughed.

"Did he know you were coming?"

He shook his head. "It's a surprise."

Marco patted Gio's arm and switched to English. "Then the surprise might be for you. Dante is not here."

Damn.

"Do you know where he is?"

Marco lifted his hands. "With you in San Diego. At the wedding."

"Which wedding?"

That left a furrowed brow. "Your brother's. Was there another?"

Gio ran both hands down his face. He needed a shave.

And ten hours of sleep.

"He didn't return to Italy?"

Marco shook his head. "He hasn't returned to Positano."

Gio let out a curse and a moan. All that money . . . all that way.

"Why not just call him?"

"I will have to do that now."

Marco smiled and walked to the front of the office. "I have a key to Dante's home. I'm sure he won't mind you staying there."

"I've already been. When he wasn't there, I came here."

"Good. You look like you need some sleep and food, eh?"

He nodded. "In that order."

"Go. Shower, sleep. We'll grab a late dinner and you can tell me what made you fly all the way here to surprise your friend with so much anger in your face."

Gio's jaw slacked open.

"You don't have to—"

"I insist."

Thirty minutes and what felt like a million flights of stairs later, Gio was back at Dante's under a hot stream of water.

Once he was out, and a little more pulled together than when he'd arrived, he picked up the phone.

~

Dante had never been an early riser, and yet he felt the bed shift when Chloe lifted her small frame from the mattress to start her day. He'd gotten into the routine of motivating his butt about thirty minutes after she did so he could catch her finishing her yoga routine.

He was utterly fascinated with how she moved and even more when she would sit in complete stillness, sometimes for half an hour, when she was done. The longer they were there, the more absorbed she became in her meditation.

Some days, like this one, it was raining, but that didn't prevent Chloe from picking a dry spot and rolling out her mat. The rain would blow in, but she didn't stop.

Dante sat with his cup of coffee, watching her from inside.

His phone, which he'd been checking his email on, rang at his side.

Giovanni's name came up on the screen along with his picture.

Dante's smile fell.

He slid the button over to answer and put the phone to his ear. "Hey."

"Where the hell are you?"

Dante looked out the window. Chloe was hands down, butt high on her mat. "I'm sorry?" he asked as if he didn't understand the question.

"I come all the way here to drag your sorry ass back to San Diego to face what you've done and you're not here. So let me ask you again . . . where the hell are you?"

Dante's morning brain hadn't had enough coffee to catch up. "Wait, what? Come all the way where? Where are *you*?"

"Positano, asshole. Running up your power bill. Where you robbed me of kicking your ass."

Dante stopped watching Chloe and turned away. His amusement started to fade. "You flew to Italy to fight me?"

"No. That would have been the bonus. I flew here to drag the coward who is trying to disgrace my sister and my family home to face what he's done."

Yeah, the amusement was gone, and Dante's breath started to come in short waves.

"I would never do that to Chloe or you and your family."

"Oh yeah?"

"Yeah. You know that."

"Then why did you marry my sister, not tell anyone, and leave town as fast as you could?"

Dante closed his eyes. "How did you find out?"

"Does it fucking matter? Now where are you?"

He looked up, saw that Chloe had moved into her meditative pose. "You're in the wrong country, Gio. You're going to have to fly a lot farther to kick my ass. Or you can wait until we come back to do it."

Then, because Dante had nothing more to say without talking to Chloe first, he hung up.

His phone immediately rang again.

He ignored it, put it on silent.

Leaving his coffee and phone on the table, Dante padded barefoot through the small house, out through the sliding doors, and into the misty rain.

When he was a few feet from Chloe, he saw her peek through the corner of one eye as the corners of her lips lifted. "Decided to join me after all?"

He pulled a cushion from a chair, set it on the floor in front of her, and moved down to her position. "I think a little peace and tranquility might be in order."

Chloe opened her smiling eyes and watched him as he crossed his legs. He pointed to hers. "I can't do that." Hers were doubled onto each other.

"Give me a year and I bet you can."

"Let's start with meditation."

She smiled and wiggled her hands. "Just relax. Place your hands in your lap, on your knees. Whatever is comfortable."

He followed her lead, put them on his knees.

Chloe lifted her shoulders up and let them drop. "Deep breath, lift your shoulders . . ."

He followed.

"Let them drop."

They did that a couple of times.

"Now close your eyes."

She was quiet for a few moments.

"Listen to the rain. Listen to your breath. Try and let all thoughts of everything else go."

Chloe was quiet again.

Listen to the rain . . . Yeah, it's raining. But my back hurts already. Shouldn't the cushion help? When was the last time I sat on the ground? Elementary school? Didn't we play games sitting on the ground all the time? When had sitting in chairs become a thing?

"When other thoughts come into your head, acknowledge them and try and push them away. Bring your attention back to the air going into your lungs and out of your lungs," Chloe instructed.

Shit. Okay . . .

He took a deep breath in, moved his head from side to side, let the air out.

Air in.

Air out.

Air in . . .

Air . . . He peeked at Chloe again. Her face was calm, her body completely relaxed, sitting there like a pretzel. What was she thinking about?

Bali had agreed with her. He liked her without makeup, he decided. Would she go back to wearing it every day when they returned home?

Shit.

Gio.

Dante closed his eyes and gathered his hands in his lap. No amount of meditation was going to keep the world from caving in. Gio calling him a coward was a sharp knife in his side. Him flying to Italy to drag him back to honor his family . . . damn if that didn't smack of exactly what Dante had tried to do with his own father.

His throat constricted as the anger over Gio's words puddled into his own emotions over what it was like to feel like someone who had abandoned their responsibilities.

I'm not my father!

Dante looked up to find Chloe staring.

Her smile slowly faded. "What's wrong?"

"Am I that transparent?"

She reached out, took one of his hands in hers. "You didn't used to be."

He squeezed, took that deep breath she'd talked about. "Gio just called."

"And?"

"Apparently he is in Positano."

Chloe's brows lifted.

Dante went on. "Said he flew there to first kick my ass and, second, to drag me home."

"He did not."

Dante placed both his hands on hers. "He knows about our marriage."

Chloe sucked in a long breath and then slowly deflated, almost like a massive balloon, spitting out every last drop. Her eyelids slowly fell, and an expression of peace washed over her face. "Do they all know?"

"I'm not sure. I didn't ask."

She nodded a few times.

"Are you upset?" Dante questioned.

"Resolved, I think. It was only a matter of time. Even if we don't work and we decide a divorce or annulment or whatever it is one does after this"—she looked around the backyard Bali haven they'd called home for the past couple of weeks before squaring her attention on him—"is what we want, we couldn't keep the truth to ourselves. Not forever."

"You're taking this better than I thought you would."

"We knew if the truth got out, my family would be pissed. We're Catholic and Italian, we don't elope. Hell, we weren't even dating. Catholics don't get divorced, so this whole scenario is going to crush our mothers, who might be the only ones okay with you and me being together, despite the lack of a big wedding. None of this is going to make anybody happy."

Dante moaned. "Gio flying to Italy shouldn't come as a surprise."

"No. It shouldn't."

"What do we tell everyone when we go home?" he asked.

"The truth. I'm done lying."

Dante smiled. "I'm glad you said that. It's time to go back and face reality."

Now she moaned. "A couple more days . . ."

He kissed her hands, nodded. "I'll figure out the flights, you plan our parting activities."

Chloe leaned in and kissed him.

CHAPTER TWENTY-THREE

"Dante talks of you and your family all the time. You're a brother to him."

Gio all but rolled his eyes at Marco's statement.

Marco had dragged him out to dinner. The little local restaurant was tucked away, outside of view of the main street, and didn't host a breathtaking view of the sea.

The bottle of house wine that cost all of ten euros, even Gio, with his educated palate, couldn't find fault with. What he wouldn't do to bring that to America. Effortless table wine that was affordable.

"My visit here wasn't social," Gio confessed.

Marco laughed. "Oh, I know. This is about your sister."

Gio stopped looking at his glass of wine. "You know about Chloe?"

"Hmm, while Dante speaks of you and your brother as brothers, he has never spoken of Chloe as a sister."

"How does he speak of her?"

"Fondly. With respect. But not as a sister."

Gio tilted his head. "Are you suggesting they had a relationship?"

"Not that I've been told."

The waiter came, set down the specials, and walked away.

"What are you trying to say, Marco?"

He shook his head, filled his mouth with a forkful of pasta.

Gio could either watch the man eat or join him.

He took a bite, nearly moaned. *So good.*

After a few moments, Marco started talking again. "My daughter is the love of my life."

That made Gio smile. "How does your wife feel about that?"

"She agrees. One day you will know the feeling." Marco lifted his wine, paused. "Or maybe you already have a taste of that . . . with Chloe."

"I love my sister."

"Of course you do. But you both lost your father. And you and your brother became that in a way for Chloe, did you not?"

Gio nodded.

Marco continued. "Fathers set rules and sometimes they make mistakes. That is hard to swallow. My wife, she reminds me all the time how imperfect I am. You and Luca made a rule about Dante never dating your sister, am I right?"

"I know where you're going with this. And with all respect, I know Dante. We've run together since childhood. He's broken many hearts. I can't stand by and do nothing as he does that to Chloe."

"I'd hope not."

Good. Marco understood.

Gio picked up his wine.

"How do you know he will break her heart?"

"It's what he does."

Marco leaned forward . . . looked left, then right.

Their eyes met. "It's what every man does . . . until he doesn't. Ask yourself this: Is Dante a cruel man? Does he hurt women on purpose?"

Some of the air went out of Gio's lungs.

Marco sat back in his chair.

"I didn't think so." He picked up a piece of bread, pushed it around his dish. "Maybe it works with your sister. Maybe it doesn't. But Dante wouldn't have risked your friendship for a fling." Marco pointed the bread in Gio's direction. "And you know that."

~

Chloe stood beside a massive airport window, her earpieces snug in her ear.

Dante was stretched out a few yards away on a phone call of his own.

She'd already texted Brooke and knew her sister-in-law was awaiting her call. It wasn't a surprise she answered on the first ring.

"You're coming out of hiding." Brooke's voice was full of bounce and happy. Not at all what Chloe would get from her brothers.

"We are."

"We? I take it Dante is with you."

"He is." For the first few minutes, Chloe explained how Dante had come to be in Bali before getting to the real reason she was calling.

"What am I walking into?"

"Luca and Giovanni are pretty upset."

"I knew they would be."

"They have a lot of questions."

Chloe turned to watch the tarmac. "Does Mama know?"

"No. The plan was to wait until Sunday to tell her. Gio came home late last night. No one told her where he was. Luca can't lie, and I've been hiding since we heard about Vegas."

"It would be better coming from me. But if she finds out, she finds out. I don't expect everyone to keep that secret. That's why I left. And why I didn't tell anyone."

"I know that. Luca does, too."

"We're in Hong Kong. Our flight leaves here in a few hours. A three-hour layover in San Francisco, then home. We plan on going to the condo, getting some sleep."

"You'll need it."

Chloe took a long breath, blew it out. "Can you ask Rosa over? We want to talk to everyone all at once."

"Not a problem. Text me the time."

"Thanks."

Brooke cleared her throat. "Now, are you going to tell me how you're doing?"

Chloe leaned against the glass, let a smile linger on her face. "I've just had the most amazing time of my life with the most incredible man."

"That's wonderful."

"It is."

"Then why do you sound sad?"

Chloe's eyes started to sting. *I don't know if it's going to last.* But Chloe couldn't say that out loud. Not to Brooke, or anyone . . . even herself. "I hate that I've upset my family," she said instead.

"Give it time."

"Thank you for your help."

"Anytime."

Chloe took a couple of minutes to clear the worry from her voice and face and walked back to Dante's side.

"How did it go?" Dante asked when she sat down. He reached for her hand, intertwined their fingers.

"It's good. Mama doesn't know yet. Safe to guess your mama doesn't either."

Dante nodded.

"Gio is home."

"I know."

Chloe questioned him with her eyes.

Dante waved his phone, which was in his other hand, in the air. "I was just talking to Marco. He says hi, by the way."

That made her grin. "I've never met Marco."

"You will."

She did a double take. Those two words hitting her hard.

Dante went on about how Marco tried talking sense into Giovanni, but Chloe didn't hear much of what Dante was saying.

She just kept hearing "you will" as if Dante knew something so completely that she didn't.

". . . hopefully he listened."

"Yeah." Chloe had no idea what Dante said.

"We'll find out soon enough."

"Um hmm."

Dante squeezed her hand. "Did you hear anything I just said?"

She shook her head and looked up. "Wh-what are we doing?"

"I don't understand the question."

"When we get home? I mean, other than telling our family that we got married before we even started dating . . . what are we doing? As soon as Mama knows I'm your wife, she's not going to understand if we're living in two different places."

Dante blinked a few times. "Is that what you want? To live at home?"

"No . . . I don't know. This is all backward." Chloe heard her own voice rising, looked around and noticed people watching them. Then, because English was more common than Italian, she switched languages. "I don't want to assume anything. We talked about going home and facing the music. That's it. Now what?"

"Are you asking if I want to stay married, *cara*?"

"God, that sounds pathetic. No."

"It's not pathetic, it's a legitimate question."

"Maybe later I'll ask that."

Dante was smiling now.

"What do we do? If I'm at home, Mama is going to be on me every day, asking me what is going on . . . and why are you smiling?"

There was laughter in his eyes. "You missed your yoga and meditation this morning."

"So?"

"It shows."

Chloe tried to pull her hand out of his.

He didn't let go.

She tugged harder.

Dante kissed the side of her cheek. "Chloe D'Angelo Mancuso, will you please move in with me? I know your family won't approve if we're not married, but under the circumstances, they can't argue."

She stopped tugging her hand. Took a sharp breath in . . . a sharp breath out. "I think, *under the circumstances*, that would make everyone's life easier."

Dante sat back and slowly started chuckling.

His laugh became contagious, and it wasn't long before she was laughing, too.

~

By the time they reached San Francisco, Dante swore he'd never get on an airplane again. Three hours later, they were on the final leg to San Diego.

They'd managed some sleep on the long haul, mainly because no one was in the seats beside them and they could stretch out. But it wasn't enough, and it wasn't sound.

They landed just after eight in the morning and were walking into the condo thirty minutes later.

Dante smelled the garbage the moment they opened the door. "You take the first shower." He kissed the side of her head, gave her a little shove.

Chloe left her bag by the door and walked, much like a zombie, to the bathroom.

He made quick work of removing the crap he'd left out to rot and nearly everything from the fridge. He tied off the bag and ran a washcloth through warm water to clean the counter and noticed his mail.

It was addressed to his mother's house.

It was scattered. On top of it was the information about divorce in California that he'd gathered for his mother. The annulment paperwork for him and Chloe.

Dante heard the shower turn off and picked up the papers.

The last thing he wanted was Chloe to see this and think he was planning their end.

He opened the garbage bag, shoved the printouts inside, and tied off the bag a second time. Next, he saw the rental agreement.

Dante entered the phone number into his cell and grabbed the garbage.

Outside, he called the rental company.

When he returned, he felt a little of life's weight lifted from his shoulders.

The next twenty-four hours were going to suck. But as he ducked his head into the silent bedroom and found Chloe headfirst in bed, one of his T-shirts tossed over her shoulders, sound asleep . . . he could only smile.

Maybe it wouldn't be that bad.

CHAPTER TWENTY-FOUR

An Uber driver dropped them off outside the restaurant.

For the first time in over a month, Chloe was home, and yet everything about it felt different.

No . . . the place wasn't different.

She was.

Dante stood beside her, his hand in hers. "You ready for this?"

"No."

His laugh was short. "Me either."

"Someone might throw a punch."

"I know it."

"I won't let them."

Dante turned her toward him. Both hands on her shoulders. "Let men be men, *bella.* Don't interfere."

"But—"

He placed a finger to her lips.

She nodded.

They turned, facing the building.

Hair on the back of her neck stood on end.

Chloe turned, looked behind them, half expecting to see someone looming over them.

"What is it?" Dante asked.

"Nerves."

She felt his hand reach for hers and instinctively pulled away.

Dante wanted nothing to do with that and took it anyway. "We have nothing to hide," he said in her ear.

Chloe lifted her chin, squared her shoulders. "You're right."

The family was on the roof, according to the last text from Brooke. Everyone but Rosa and her mother knew they were coming. Franny was spending the night at her friend's, in case things got out of hand.

Chloe thought things might have remained more "in hand" if Franny was around, but she certainly didn't want her niece to be scarred for life because of any drama created by her.

She and Dante walked through the front door of the restaurant and were immediately hit with pleasantries by the hostess.

"Oh my God, where have you been? How was Bali?"

Chloe kept it simple. "Family first, we'll talk later."

They passed the bar. Sergio did a double take. His eyes went to her, then Dante.

Dante moved his hand from hers to her waist.

Was that a smile on Sergio's lips?

Approval?

Concern?

Sergio's eyes drifted up. "They're upstairs."

"Grazie."

He winked.

They moved to the back, past the kitchen.

Staff watched them.

There were smiles, then hushed conversations.

"We have this," Dante said in her ear as they reached the staircase that led to their family home.

As they passed the first floor, the sounds of the restaurant below started to fade.

"Breathe in. Breathe out."

Chloe had to laugh. "Who is the teacher now?"

"I'm talking to myself."

That made her laugh even more. And in doing so, some of the tension in her body faded.

It was short-lived.

As soon as she heard her family outside the final door, her feet stopped moving.

Dante turned her toward him. "You're coming home with me, regardless of what happens. We started this together . . . we do this together."

Chloe painted on a smile and pushed through the final door.

The sound had everyone turning.

Her mother squealed first and stopped whatever she was doing to move to Chloe's side.

Even as Chloe was hugging her mother, Chole's eyes tracked Gio as he zeroed in on Dante.

Dante took a few steps away from Chloe, and all hell broke loose.

Gio pulled back, his fist flew.

Rosa screamed.

Mari twisted in Chloe's arms.

Before Gio could come back for more, Luca was there, holding Gio back.

"What on earth are you doing?" Mama screamed in Italian.

"You get one, Giovanni. Then I hit back."

Gio waved his fingers in a *c'mon* motion.

"Enough!" Luca yelled.

Chloe pushed past her mother.

Brooke stood close, a napkin in her hand. Chloe grabbed it as she passed and moved to Dante's side.

Rosa, who had surged closer, stopped.

Dante took the napkin, placed it on his bloody lip.

She wanted to hold him, show sympathy. She didn't. Chloe hoped the look in her eyes reflected her concern.

Instead, she turned to her brother. "You done?"

Mari stepped forward, yelled in Italian. "No violence in my home." She shoved Gio, both hands on his chest.

The contradiction would have been funny if Chloe's heart wasn't beating so fast.

"What is this about?"

Gio waved a hand toward Chloe and Dante. "Ask them."

Chloe felt Dante's hand take possession of her waist.

Brooke smiled.

Luca braced himself.

Gio shook his head.

Rosa hesitated, then grinned.

And Mama . . . her eyes moved between the two of them, confused . . . then her mouth opened with a full smile.

She turned to Rosa, reached for her hand. "Look at that!"

"Don't get too excited, Mama," Gio warned.

That had Mari's head snapping back . . . that same smile faded, and her eyes drifted to Chloe's abdomen.

"You made her think I'm pregnant." Chloe broke free of Dante's arms and slapped Gio full in the face. "No, Mama. I'm not pregnant."

"Then what's not to get excited about?" Rosa exclaimed.

While Rosa and Mari stood together in excitement . . . the rest of them held back.

Rosa spoke first. "What are we missing? Everyone clearly knows more than the old women in the room."

"And it's pissing me off!" Mari had both hands on her hips.

Chloe's eyes opened wide. Her mother never said things like that.

Chloe circled back to Dante's side, and his hand rested on her waist.

"Chloe and I eloped."

Rosa and Mari gasped.

Gio and Luca groaned.

Brooke kept her silence.

"Maybe *eloped* isn't exactly right," Chloe said, looking him in the eye.

His smile made the words easier. As did his nod.

"You're married?" her mother asked in a breathy voice.

"Yes," they both said at the same time.

Rosa slowly moved closer to Mari's side.

"But you didn't elope?"

"This ought to be good," Gio said.

Chloe glared at her brother.

"We were in Vegas," Dante started.

Mari groaned. "Oh, God no."

"There wasn't a priest?" Rosa's voice grew loud. "If there wasn't a priest, there wasn't a marriage."

"They're married," Gio insisted, his hands thrown in the air.

"And how do you know that, exactly?" Dante asked.

"I opened your mail, asshole. Sue me." Gio leaned forward.

Luca put a hand out to stop him.

Chloe felt Dante step forward, held her ground so he couldn't move without nudging her.

"I don't see a ring," Rosa yelled. "Who gets married without a ring?"

Two giant steps and Mari was in Chloe's face, her hand grasped Chloe's left hand. Looked at it, then her.

Gio said something to Luca.

Rosa was shaking her head.

"No ring, no priest . . . none of us were there? Vegas is garbage." Her mama all but tossed Chloe's hand out of hers and turned around.

"None of that matters. We did marry, Mama. It was Vegas and admittedly less than thought-out," Chloe said.

"What are you saying?" her mother turned and asked.

Gio laughed. "She's saying it was a mistake."

"No, I'm not," Chloe yelled.

Everyone paused . . . took a breath.

"Are you staying married?" Luca slowly asked. Only he wasn't looking at Chloe; he was staring at Dante.

"Of course they are," Rosa said for them.

Gio glared at Dante. "Tell them why we're really angry. Tell them how divorce is on the table."

"This isn't happening." Mari made the sign of the cross over her chest and rolled her eyes to the sky.

Dante moved away from Chloe and stood in front of Gio and Luca. "I knew if I told you I wanted to date Chloe you'd react like this. I saw that chapel, grabbed her hand, and thought there was no way you could ever doubt my sincerity if it started in marriage."

Chloe heard his confession for the first time. Somehow, she'd thought that the whole thing had been a complete joke to him, but the way he just described it, it almost sounded as if he'd thought it out.

"You instantly considered divorce. I saw the papers right next to the marriage certificate."

Dante stood back, looked between her brothers, and lifted his chin. "Because I woke up and realized it wasn't either of you that needed to approve my intentions." He turned then, looked at their mothers, offered a soft smile to Chloe. "Truth is, we haven't decided what we're going to do."

"When we do," Chloe added, "we'll let you know."

Mari lifted her hands in the air. "What kind of mess is this? What do we tell people? Rosa, where did we go wrong?"

"I'm sorry, Mama. Rosa. We didn't mean to hurt anyone."

Her mother shook her head and turned her back to her.

The movement put a knife in Chloe's chest.

Dante was by her side in an instant, arms around her, a kiss to her forehead. "We should go," he whispered in her ear.

His hands slid off her shoulders, captured hers, and they turned toward the door.

"That's it? Do your damage and then leave?" Gio yelled.

Brooke, who had stayed silent the entire time, spoke up. "Emotions are high right now. Let's give Mama and Rosa some time to digest what we've all known for a few days. We've heard what Dante and Chloe have to say. No amount of yelling, or hitting"—she stopped and stared at Gio—"is going to change anything." Brooke waved a hand toward Chloe and Dante. "It's obvious they care for each other. I can think of worse situations."

Luca blew out a breath. "Brooke is right. I'm not happy about any of this," he said, pointing at Dante. "But Gio and I wouldn't have approved if you'd asked permission. We need to own some fault."

"The hell I do."

"Gio!" It was Brooke who scolded him. "You flew off to Italy to drag him home, and you were wrong about that."

"Italy?" Mama asked. "When did you go to Italy?"

Chloe looked between her brothers and Brooke.

They looked everywhere but her mother's eyes.

"That's where I went last week."

"You went to Napa. A wine something or other . . ."

Gio studied his shoes, shook his head. "Positano. I thought Dante had left Chloe to deal with this on her own."

Rosa blurted out an obscenity. "My son may have made a mockery of this marriage, but he is not a coward. I'm disappointed in you, Giovanni. Thinking Dante would do such a thing." Rosa looked at her son. "He is not his father."

Dante's hand squeezed hers.

"I'm sorry, Rosa. I was angry and not thinking."

She clicked her tongue. "I should say so. But it isn't me you owe an apology to."

Gio looked at Dante. "Oh, hell no."

Brooke moved into the space between them. "Okay. That can wait for another day. Every family has their drama. This is ours today."

Luca moved to Brooke's side. "I think we should eat."

Mari shook her head. "You eat. Rosa . . . you and I deserve time alone to discuss this."

The two of them walked past them and off the terrace.

"We're going home," Dante told them.

"'We'?" Luca asked.

Chloe nodded. "Married women don't live at home with their parents."

Brooke stepped forward, opened her arms for a hug. "This will all get better. I promise."

She moved to Dante, hugged him, and whispered something in his ear that only he heard. He attempted a smile and looked at Gio and Luca.

Everyone was silent and no one moved.

Chloe tugged on Dante's hand. "C'mon."

CHAPTER TWENTY-FIVE

Forty-eight hours later, Luca reached out to Dante.

It came in a text message and felt more like a demand and less like a request. He sent an address and a time and said they needed to talk.

Dante looked up from his phone, saw Chloe folded up on the sofa, staring into her cell phone. The circles under her eyes hadn't been there in Bali, he wished he could erase them.

"Your brother is requesting an audience," he said with a laugh.

"Which one?"

"Luca."

She wiggled her phone. "Must be divide-and-conquer time. Brooke just sent a text and asked if I wanted to meet with her and Salena for lunch."

"I'll Uber. You take the car."

Chloe leaned her head to the side. "If the coast is clear, I'll drop in and pick up some of my things."

She was still wrapped up in spandex and Bali, not that Dante minded. They'd been home long enough to start a new routine.

But both of them were itching.

Chloe hadn't gone back to work . . . was waiting for the chaos to settle.

And now that Dante was more invested in starting a business in San Diego, he began looking at slightly different angles on how to go about it.

That left them both with energy to burn . . . which they did, with each other.

He smiled into that thought.

"What are you all happy about over there?" Chloe teased.

"I'm remembering this morning's shower."

Her cheeks started to turn red. "Probably best you don't bring that up at lunch," she said.

Dante rubbed the side of his face that Gio took a run at. "I'd like to keep all my teeth. Thank you."

Her phone buzzed.

"Ohhh."

"Oh no."

Chloe looked up, winced. "Mama is requesting an audience," she said, using his words. "Both of us on Sunday."

"Dinner?" he asked.

She shook her head. "Church."

Dante lost his smile. "Oh, boy."

"It's one thing to piss off Mama. It's another to piss off God." Chloe started to giggle.

"I'm not sure what's funny."

His phone buzzed.

A text from his mother.

I'll see you at church on Sunday. Both of you.

"Our mothers are talking." He moved to the sofa, showed her the text.

Chloe leaned over, kissed him briefly. "Don't look so worried. It's not like they can force us to get married."

He laughed. "Been there . . ."

"Done that," she finished.

"They can't stay mad at us forever," he told her.

She nudged her shoulder against his. "Gio will come around."

Dante nodded. "I miss him. I have this amazing girl in my life, and I want to tell him all about her, but I can't."

She placed a hand on his thigh. "That sucks."

"It does."

"You can tell me."

His shoulders folded in with a laugh. "And give away all my secret thoughts? I don't think so, *bella*. When a woman knows everything, a man has nothing left."

"You have that wrong. When a woman knows all, a man has everything."

He stared at her, those lovely dark eyes sucked him in. Maybe she had a point.

Her phone buzzed, and their moment dissipated.

It buzzed again.

"Who needs us now?" he asked.

Chloe slapped her hand on her phone, turned it up to read the text. "Oh my God."

"What?"

"Eric," she said with a laugh.

"Who?"

"You know. New Year's Eve guy. The one with two kids." She started typing, hit send, and dropped her phone to her side.

He felt his jaw tighten. "The guy you dated right after we got married."

"That's not fair."

He shook his head. "No. It wasn't. I'm sorry." But damn, the thought of her with that guy snapped his spine straight.

Her eyes narrowed. "You're still looking at me funny."

The phone buzzed.

Dante stared at it. What the hell was the guy saying?

"You're jealous."

He looked away from the phone. Leaned back on the sofa. "I'm fine."

The phone buzzed.

His jaw clenched.

Chloe laughed.

"It's not funny. That guy is tapping you."

"Tapping? What do you mean, tapping? He never touched me."

Okay, that he needed to hear. Thank God for that. Another man touching his wife would require a bit more than an understanding husband, even if they were pretending not to be married at the time.

"Tapping . . . he is . . ." Dante tapped his finger against Chloe's thigh a few times. "Texting, tapping . . . to see if there is any chance."

"I know what he's doing. I told him I'm with someone."

Dante shook his head. "That doesn't matter."

"Yes, it does."

"Not to a guy. When a guy wants you, another guy isn't even a roadblock. He may pretend it is, but he'll tap again in a week, a month. I know. I'm a guy."

Chloe looked him up and down. "Really? I had no idea."

He nudged her. "Tell him you're married."

Chloe shrugged, picked up her phone. She huffed out a laugh.

"What did he say?" Dante asked before she started typing.

"He told me to call him if it didn't work out."

"Told you."

Chloe typed, put her phone down. "Happy now?"

He crossed his arms over his chest. "Yes. I know guys like that. Hell, I was that guy."

She pulled at his arms and moved to straddle his thighs.

Some of the steam in his jealousy engine started to shift south. He placed both hands on her hips.

Spandex was his most favorite fabric in the entire world.

"Dante Mancuso is jealous."

He ran his thumbs up her hip bones and down. "I trust you, *cara.* I don't trust him."

"It takes two. And I'm taken." Her pelvis pushed against his.

That was all the invitation Dante needed.

He lifted her from him, flipped her onto her back, and covered her body with his. "Yes. You are."

~

Salena sat there with her jaw on the floor. "The secret to Vegas is that you got married? Holy hell. I just thought you got laid."

They were at an outside café in Liberty Station, surrounded by strangers.

"That didn't happen until New Year's Eve."

Brooke did a double take. "Seriously?"

"Hand to God."

"Whoa."

For ten minutes, Chloe described what she remembered of their wedding night. The next morning, the green finger.

"We couldn't remember which chapel it was. While you guys were on round two, Dante and I were frantically chasing down the paperwork to see if we could stop it. All I could think of was Mama was going to kill me."

"No wonder you were wigged out during the rehearsal dinner and the wedding," Salena said.

"I didn't notice."

Chloe patted Brooke's hand. "You were busy."

"Obviously it wasn't a complete mistake. You did end up getting naked," Salena said a little softer.

"We did."

"Then why did you run off to Bali?" Brooke asked.

Chloe played with the condensation on her glass of iced tea. "I didn't want him to feel trapped. We discussed an annulment before New Year's. Sex didn't change that."

"Technically it does."

Chloe shook her head. "Dante has a life in Italy. He only rented the condo for a short time. He was gonna leave. It was easier if I left first. Besides, if I'd stuck around, everyone would have found out about the marriage and forced him to do something he didn't want to do."

Salena was all smiles. "Then he chases you to Bali, and now it's rainbows and kittens."

Brooke and Chloe exchanged glances.

Salena's humor faded. "It's not rainbows and kittens?"

"We're seeing if we fit."

"Oh my God, you fit! You two are nuts and bolts."

"It feels that way. But it's new. And every relationship feels that way when it's new."

"New?" Salena scoffed. "There is nothing new about you and Dante. You've loved him forever."

"Loving someone and being *in love* with someone are two different things," Brooke said.

Salena sat forward. "Are you *in love* with him?"

Chloe couldn't deny the feeling for a million dollars. She looked at the two women and sighed.

"I see no problem here. Except the ones you two are making." Salena sipped her coffee.

"He still has a life in Italy."

Brooke leaned in. "What's going on with that?"

"We haven't talked about it much. He's been doing a lot of internet searches for boats. He has a couple of viewings this week."

"Do you think you'll be back and forth from Italy?" Salena asked.

"I think we need to figure out if we're going to stay married before we talk about which continent we're going to live on."

"Wow. I thought my weekend in Vegas was the crazy one. I have nothing on you." Salena signaled the waitress. "Can we get three glasses of champagne?"

Brooke shook her head. "Only two."

Chloe and Salena both snapped their attention her way.

"What? I'm driving!" Only Brooke had a different look in her eye.

Chloe put her hands together. "Oh, please tell me you're pregnant. Please, please, please . . . Mama can't stay mad if there's a baby on the way."

Brooke bit her lip. "I don't know. I see the doctor next week."

Salena waved that thought off. "C'mon. There's either an extra pink line or there isn't."

Brooke's answer was a smile.

They all squealed.

Chloe was out of her chair and hugging Brooke in a flash. "Does Luca know?"

"Of course."

She sat back down, drummed her hands on the table. "This is perfect."

"We'll tell everyone during Sunday dinner."

The waitress returned. She had three glasses, placed one in front of Brooke. "Sparkling water."

They lifted their glasses. "To babies," Chloe said.

"And brides," Brooke added.

Chloe's phone rang at her side, she answered without looking at the number. "Hello."

No one said anything. After a few seconds, she said hello again.

Giving up, she disconnected the call.

"Who was that?" Salena asked.

"Spam, I guess. I seemed to have picked up a lot of that since we returned from Bali."

Brooke shook her head. "Let it go to voice mail."

Chloe put her phone in her purse and out of her mind. "You're going to have a baby!"

~

"Do I have to duck and weave here?" Dante asked Luca as he approached.

They met on the pier at Ocean Beach. Except for a few fishermen and a homeless man sleeping on one of the benches, the pier was relatively empty. There was one restaurant midway, but outside of a beer, it was better for tourists. Plenty of local food a couple of blocks away that was actually worth eating.

Luca looked over his shoulder. "How well do you swim?"

That put a smile on Dante's face.

"Thanks for meeting me."

"Did I have a choice?"

Luca leaned against the rail, looked out over the water. "How is she doing?"

"Do you want the truth?"

Luca nodded.

"She hasn't slept well since we've been back. Tosses and turns . . . which you probably don't want to hear coming from me."

Luca gave him a sideways glance. "I'm not an idiot."

"She wants to work but is afraid to show her face."

"That's stupid."

"Is it?"

Luca shook his head. Took a breath. "How long have you had feelings for her?"

Awh, fuck, Dante wasn't expecting that question.

He leaned against the railing beside Luca. "I'm not sure how much I should say here. This is your sister."

"Keep it clean and I won't have to throw you in."

They both looked at the water. The tide was high, but the jump would hurt.

"In high school I had my share of inappropriate thoughts. Never did a thing about them. It wasn't until she started dating that I realized I was more than just attracted. I assisted you and Gio more than once in intercepting someone we didn't like when they had eyes on Chloe."

"Yeah, you did."

"I doubt her prom date did more than kiss her."

Luca laughed.

"I've stayed away a lot in the last few years."

"You saying that was her?"

"No. Not all. But each time I came home, it was harder and harder for me to see her and not pull her away and determine for myself if the snap between us was only in my head or was mutual. In Vegas she fried my last grain of willpower." He thought of that red dress and the way she looked at him when she took her coat off and revealed it. Jesus, he couldn't even hug her to say hello.

"Gio believes that the marriage was a permission slip to sleep with her."

Dante's stomach twisted. "Fuck him. That's bullshit. I didn't . . . we didn't. Yes, I kissed Chloe the night we got married, but that's it, Luca. I brought her back to the hotel and put her in her own bed. Alone. I didn't touch her until—"

Luca raised a hand in the air. "I don't need to know."

Dante turned quarter way, looked at his friend. "I get it. Gio's pissed. I broke the code. But if he thought I was such a douchebag all these years, why did he run with me?"

"He's afraid."

"Afraid of what?"

"That he lost his best friend and his sister."

Dante let the air out of his lungs slowly. "That's on him, man. I was telling Chloe today how much it sucked to have this amazing woman in my life and no one to talk about it with."

Was that a smile on Luca's face? "You better be talking about Chloe."

"Fuck you." But Dante was smiling.

"Tell me."

"Tell you what?"

"About this amazing woman." Another sideways glance. "Skipping the details."

Okay . . .

Dante leaned against the railing again. "She's beautiful, Jesus . . . I mean flawless. She's funny. Says things to me that no other woman ever has. Calls me out on my crap. She loves her family endlessly. Passionate about life. You should have seen her in Bali. The monkeys crawling on her . . . at first, she was scared shitless, then she was naming them." He paused with the memory. "Did you know that Chloe can stand on her head?"

He turned to see Luca staring at him.

"Yeah. I've seen her do it."

"Crazy, right?" He sighed, lost his grin. "And I'm not sure how to hold on to her."

Luca leaned to his side.

"People get married all the time because it's the right thing to do." Dante lifted his hand the second the words were out of his mouth. "I already told you that wasn't us. But what do I do? Jump in and fuck this up at the starting line." He pointed to his chest. "I'm perfectly aware of how bad I screwed up. I don't want Chloe to stay married to me because her family demands it. I don't want her to stay Mrs. Mancuso because of some kind of 'disgrace' that society will look down on her with if we divorce. My parents had to get married. And as soon as I graduated from high school, Dad started his extended trips. Then one day when I'm in college, poof, Dad's gone. Did his time and he was out."

Luca and Gio were both there helping Dante drink away the pain the night his mother told him that his father left for good.

Dante stared out at the waves in the opposite direction of Luca. "I have this amazing woman, and we're doing everything completely backwards, trying to make damn sure we have what it takes before we tell everyone we're all in."

"Huh."

They both turned back to look in the same direction, shoulder to shoulder.

Nearly a minute passed in silence.

Breathe in.

Let it out . . .

"Gio and I are going to back off," Luca finally said. "You're right. You and Chloe need to do this or not do this. It isn't up to the rest of us."

"Gio won't be that agreeable."

"Leave him to me." Luca cleared his throat, stood tall. "I can't speak for our mothers."

Dante moaned. "We've been summoned to church on Sunday."

Luca reached out, patted Dante on his back. "Best of luck with that."

The tension in the air had eased. "We're good?" Dante asked.

"I know you're a decent man. I know you'll never physically hurt my sister. I can't ask you not to break her heart. That would be forcing you to love someone, and no one can do that. I know. I have an ex-wife. I now have a woman who is my universe, and the difference between those women isn't comparable." Luca pushed away from the rail, placed both hands on Dante's shoulders. "Now, if you cheat on her, I'll break your legs."

Dante choked. "You had me going with the mushy stuff and had to ruin it."

"You're right." Luca started walking them off the pier. "I won't break your legs, Gio will. I'm a family man. Jail time is no example for my children."

He laughed, understanding the message. Not that he would ever do that to Chloe.

His feet stopped. "Children? As in more than Franny?"

Luca lifted his chin, puffed out his chest. "Brooke is pregnant."

Dante pulled his friend into a hug. "Oh, man. Congratulations."

"Thank you."

"I'm happy for you."

"If fire and brimstone don't take you out in church, we'll see you for dinner on Sunday. Your mother already has a standing invitation."

"I'll talk to Chloe."

CHAPTER TWENTY-SIX

Who knew going to church would be so hard to dress for? Chloe started with the white sundress she wore in Bali, with a cover-up over her shoulders. Then decided wearing white in church might set her mother off. Then she had dark slacks and a simple blouse . . . scrapped that. She needed a dress. Except she only had a couple to pick from since most of her things were still in her mother's house.

A colorful dress she'd bought in Bali, with cap sleeves, won the prize, with the same cover-up to tone down the bright colors. She wore her hair pulled back at the sides, with a slight curl around her face. Makeup . . . mascara and a soft shade of pink.

Simple.

Church approved.

So why was her heart beating so fast?

"You're beautiful," Dante said from the doorway to the bathroom.

A long-sleeved button-up shirt, jacket, and slacks. "You just stepped out of a magazine."

He moved behind her, faced the mirror, and slid his arms around her waist. "We've been to church a hundred times. This time isn't any different."

"Wanna bet money on that?" she asked.

He rubbed his stubbled cheek against hers and tapped her hip. "C'mon. We don't want to keep our mothers waiting."

They pulled into the parking lot with all the other people gathering for Sunday morning mass. Her palms were sweating. "This is worse than when I showed up here after the first time I had sex."

Dante started laughing.

"It's not funny. It's like Mama knew, too. Kept looking at me, smiling. Never said a word. Father Gomez went on about purity. I was nauseous for a week. Thought for sure I was pregnant."

"You weren't." It wasn't a question.

"No. Mama is a devoted Catholic, but not stupid. My 'period problems' needed hormones right about the time boys stopped having cooties."

"Smart mama."

"She also saw what Luca was going through and didn't want that for any of us. Even though none of us would change a thing, having Francesca in our lives." Chloe leaned forward and pointed. "That's them."

Their mothers stood together by the front door.

Chloe opened her door and found Dante by her side before she could close it.

His arm slid to a familiar spot around her waist, his lips close to her ear. "Married sex is permitted in the eyes of the church."

"Glad to know I'm all legal now," she said with a smile. "You, too."

He chuckled. "I never felt remorseful."

"Sinner," she whispered.

He didn't have time to respond before they were in front of their mothers.

"Hi, Mama."

Mari opened her arms, and although her hug was a bit stiff, it was a hug. Chloe moved to Rosa next. "Good morning, Rosa."

"You have two mamas now."

Rosa's arms circled Chloe's back.

Dante caught on, pulled Mari in. "Mama," he said loud enough for everyone to hear.

Mari smiled.

He then moved to his mother, kissed her cheek. "You'll always be my number-one mama." Rosa rolled her eyes, accepted his hug, and smiled.

They turned together and entered the church.

A quick stop at the holy water. Chloe was ever so thankful it didn't burn.

Mari and Rosa took the lead.

Dante reached for Chloe's hand and followed.

Even though they'd both just been in the church for Luca and Brooke's wedding, this time it was filled with people they didn't know. A few familiar faces, but Chloe didn't attend all that regularly. None of them did, to be honest. At times like this, when her mother insisted, they didn't argue. Mari was convincing like that. You go to church when your mother tells you to, that's just what her family did. Obviously, she hadn't asked anyone else in the family to join them today, or they'd be there.

No, this was special, just for the two people in the family who were on Mama's shit list.

Even thinking the word *shit* while walking down the center of the church had Chloe rewording her thoughts.

Poo list.

She rolled her eyes at her internal monologue to find Jesus staring at her.

A look to the left, and Mary wasn't looking all that pleased either.

"Are we going to the front to sit with Father Gomez?" Chloe whispered.

Their mothers walked straight to the front row and moved aside two jackets. They'd already been in there and saved a seat.

"Should we be worried?" Dante asked, close to her ear.

"You think?" Even the naked cherub babies were staring at her.

Mari sat first and Rosa waited for them to sit and then took her position next to Dante.

For a full minute they were silent.

Then Mari leaned forward. "Do you attend church in Italy?" she asked Dante.

"I've been known to go." His smile was pure charm.

"For more than Christmas Eve or a wedding?"

All that charm didn't respond fast enough, and Chloe's mama had her answer.

Mari looked at Rosa, and they both sat back, hands folded in their laps.

"Families go to church," Rosa pointed out. "You're a family now."

Chloe reached for Dante's hand, could have sworn she saw Jesus frown at her, and pulled it away.

Dante leaned close. "Don't let them get to you."

She placed her lips to his ear. "The cherubs are laughing at me."

His chest silently shook with laughter.

She fanned herself, sure that the air conditioner in the place must be broken. Not that they should need it in February. She tugged Dante close. "Is it hot in here?"

He was trying hard not to laugh and losing. "You're too young for hot flashes."

Meanwhile, Rosa and Mari sat like frozen pillars, staring at the pulpit, waiting for the service to begin.

Finally, the choir started to sing, and Father Gomez walked through with the altar boys and all the window dressing that surrounded mass on a Sunday.

Chloe fully expected the service to be about marriage in the eyes of the church. It wasn't. It was about loving your neighbor through your differences, which ironically, Chloe thought Gio and Luca could have stood to hear.

As Chloe saw it, she was loving her neighbor, she just married him first.

When it came time to take communion, they were first to stand and partake.

Her mother muttered something under her breath in Italian. Chloe heard the words *living in sin*, *marriage*, *eyes of God*, and then she crossed herself.

Father Gomez blessed them, as he did everyone, and they moved on.

When the service wrapped up, Mari and Rosa stayed seated.

"That was lovely," Rosa said.

"It was. We should come next week," Mari suggested.

Chloe stared at Dante. The word *NO* screamed from her retinas.

"That's a great idea," Dante told them both.

Rosa stood; Mari followed.

"You go ahead," Dante said. "I'd like to sit here for a minute with Chloe."

By now, most of the parishioners had filed out of the pews. Several stayed behind, kneeling on the board meant for just that purpose.

Chloe stood, kissed her mama and Rosa.

Dante did the same.

As they walked away, Dante knelt as he had during mass and encouraged Chloe to do the same.

A peek over her shoulder and she saw their mothers looking at them.

"Are they watching?"

She turned, looked at Jesus.

He was not happy.

"Yes."

He kept his voice low, his head close to hers. "This is going to sound terrible, especially saying it here . . . but I've learned a few things being a man."

"I already feel everything in here staring at me. Please don't say anything that will bring the walls down on us."

He nudged her, laughed.

"Our mothers don't want us to get divorced." He barely said the *D* word.

"I know that."

"And if they had it their way, we would have been married right here in front of God and everyone."

"True."

"They made us come here today to remind us that marriage might be about us, but it's about this guy, too."

"*This guy?* We're going to be struck down." Chloe looked over her head.

"I've learned that if you give a woman, even a mother, a little of what they want, they'll stop pestering you." He took her hand in his. "If we'd done this forward instead of backwards, we'd be here and talking about how we'll raise our children in the church."

Jesus stopped being so judgmental, and Chloe found herself hearing what Dante was saying. "We didn't do it forward."

"Do you want children someday?" he asked.

The question made her smile. "Yeah. Not now, I'm not ready. But someday."

"Will you raise them Catholic?"

"It didn't hurt me."

Dante looked forward. "Me either. But I wouldn't mind exposing them to other things, too. Like the temples we visited in Bali. I felt things there I wasn't expecting."

Chloe folded her hands in front of her. "Me too."

"Our mothers are only doing what they know how to do to keep us together."

"Guilt," Chloe pointed out.

"Guilt," Dante repeated with a smile.

The church was nearly empty now, and the statues no longer stared directly at her.

"Ready to go?" he asked.

"Yeah."

He offered a hand as she stood.

He stopped her before she got too far.

"Hold up."

Chloe turned.

Dante placed both hands on her face and pulled her close, his lips touching hers.

"What was that for?" she asked, smiling.

"Making sure we weren't going to be struck down. I think the big guy is okay with us."

"You're ballsy, Mancuso."

"You're going along for the ride, Mrs. Mancuso."

~

Dante felt a twinge in his jaw the second his foot stepped onto the terrace of the D'Angelo's building.

Brooke and Mari were setting the table and Giovanni was lighting one of the gas heaters to warm the space.

"There you are," Mari said the moment she saw them. "Chloe, go down and help Luca bring up the food."

"Yes, Mama."

Chloe turned, placed a hand on Dante's arm. "Talk to him."

"I will."

First, he went to Mari's side, kissed her cheek. "*Buonasera*, Mama."

She brushed him off with a smile. "Help Gio bring those lamps closer. It's chilly tonight."

"Yes, ma'am."

Dante turned to Brooke. "Don't you look radiant." He glanced at her belly and winked.

She cleared her throat. "I'm glad you're both here."

"Of course they're here." Mari nodded toward Gio.

I'm going. Dante mouthed the words.

Instead of walking straight to his friend, Dante detoured and grabbed the second heat lamp and pulled it to the other side of the table. "Gio," he called out, waited for him to turn. "Toss me the lighter."

Gio looked at the torch in his hand, then his friend.

"Toss, don't throw."

A slight smirk gave Dante a hint that his friend was still in there.

Once the lamp was lit and warming the air, he moved to Gio's side. "Can I have a minute?"

Gio looked past him, then nodded to the side of the terrace away from the others.

"I wanted to tell you," Dante started.

"I wouldn't have listened."

"I know."

"Luca seems to believe you've been living in Italy all this time to avoid her. That true?"

Dante had given that a lot of thought since he'd been back. "Part of it. I needed to grow up. I couldn't seem to do that here. People here want the party boy. No responsibilities, just have a good time. Always on vacation. No wonder you and Luca can't see me with Chloe."

"We've seen you with many others."

Dante looked Gio in the eye. "Glass houses, brother."

Gio hesitated, shoulders stiffened, and then he sighed. "But Chloe?"

"Why not Chloe? She's perfect. Her family already loves me."

Gio snapped his chin up.

"When they're not trying to rearrange my teenage dental work. Nice right hook by the way."

He lifted his left hand. "I could even it out."

"I'll pass."

Gio turned, looked over the railing of the building. The view past Little Italy and the setting sun over the bay caught both their attention. "Super fucked-up how you went about this."

"I know. I saw an opportunity and I jumped," Dante explained. "When Chloe laughed and ran along with me, I was like, 'Holy shit, this is happening.' I couldn't stop the train, Gio. I know I screwed up, but I'd be lying if I said I was completely remorseful. Hell, I half think I wanted you to find our marriage certificate. I didn't want this secret, I wanted Chloe. eHWhat is it they say? 'The road is paved with dead squirrels that couldn't make a decision.' I'm not dead. I want to do better and more. And I want to do it for her."

Gio grumbled. Yet there was a softness in his expression that wasn't there a few minutes before. "You do know how to say the right things."

"Give me an opportunity to follow it up with action. I might surprise you."

Gio offered a sideways glance. The similarity between him and Luca came in that single expression. "You better."

Dante lifted his right hand.

Gio looked at it, sighed, and then took it in his.

They followed with a man-hug, a pat on the back. Being at odds with his best friend was not a place he wanted to be ever again.

"I know you're not your father," Gio said quietly. "My fury was blind."

Dante cleared his throat from the constriction that instantly caught with Gio's words. The need to hear them was so strong he could weep. "Thank you."

Behind them, Franny's high-pitched voice was speaking rapidly in Italian.

"How does the only-speaking-Italian thing during Sunday dinners work with Brooke in the equation?" Dante asked. For as long as Franny had been in the picture, the D'Angelos only spoke Italian on Sundays. At least to Franny. Then it turned to dinners.

"Brooke is learning. But things are more lenient. Not so much for Franny. But she loves it."

Dante looked up to see Chloe watching them, a smile at the corners of her pink lips. "Makes sense if you want your children bilingual."

"Oh, boy," Gio said.

"Don't worry. We're not there."

His mother stepped out and onto the terrace as Luca was bringing in a large tray of food.

There were hugs, kisses . . . a much better greeting than the last time he and Chloe had been there.

Dante slipped away from Gio's side and moved to Chloe's.

"Better?" she asked.

"I think so."

The sound of steel hitting glass made them turn toward the table.

Luca stood beside Brooke, a bottle of champagne in his hand. "Now that everyone is here . . ." He twisted off the cork of the bubbly wine with a satisfying pop. "And before we sit down to eat—"

Franny jumped up, hands in the air. "Mama Brooke is going to have a baby!"

"Francesca!" Luca scolded with a laugh.

Mari stopped what she was doing, her excitement felt with her delighted cry.

The rooftop terrace became a buzz of joy and celebration.

"It's nice to have the spotlight off of us," Dante said to Chloe before they moved in to congratulate the happy parents.

"Amen."

CHAPTER TWENTY-SEVEN

Dante stood on the stern of the yacht, both hands on his hips. "What do you think?"

He and Chloe had just been on a tour and out in the bay with the owner. Who had taken a walk to give them time to talk.

"I know nothing about boats."

He spread his arms to the open deck. "Picture a small wedding party." He turned to the glass doors leading into the living space. "Think receptions or exclusive parties."

"Bachelorette parties?" she asked with a grin.

He draped an arm over her shoulders. "Or birthdays or corporate events. Team meetings."

"Yoga on the bay," she suggested.

"Right. Yes. I can see you recording classes on deck or offering private lessons." He walked her farther inside, took in the spacious galley. "This is a damn good size to prepare food, but I was thinking about teaming up with D'Angelo's for an exclusive, authentic menu. Something different than other charters here in San Diego." There were two bedrooms and two bathrooms on this seventy-foot beauty with an upper deck that screamed party and sunsets. "We have one like this in Positano, and two smaller vessels that offer exclusive shuttling between Capri and Positano, and when the demand for that is down, we do the sunset sail and wine thing."

"It's a bit far to shuttle to big ports from here."

"It is. The tourist and event angle is where it's at for us here. You can find plenty of budget things like that. The super high-end market already exists, but in the middle-income bracket . . . there is more demand than supply."

"You sound excited."

"I am. This is priced right. But between all the start-up costs, dock fees, business license, et cetera . . . it won't be cheap."

Chloe leaned against the island in the galley. "You need to be talking to Marco about this. Not me."

"Wife first, Marco second," he said without batting an eye. "Besides, you know San Diego. And this will affect you and me for the long haul . . . day in and day out. Not to mention we could buy a house for what this will end up costing."

Chloe picked up the flyer, waved it in the air. "A small house in East County."

"This is income."

"Without income you can't buy a home." She motioned toward the bedroom. "We'd always have a place to sleep."

Dante shook his head. "I would never do that to you."

She looked at him as if he were crazy. "I've lived above the restaurant my entire life."

"That's different."

"I'm just saying . . . we have options." She pushed away from the galley and back toward the sliding doors. "You know what I think?"

He walked up behind her, placed his arms around her body as they looked out at the other boats in the harbor.

"No."

"I think you need to make darn sure this is what you want. Positano is where you've lived all your adult life. You have a world there. Even if you eventually go back and forth, this is going to take time to build to actually pay the bills. And if there is something I've learned about a family business, you don't count on others to do that for you. If you buy this, you're going to be here for a while."

"That was the plan."

Chloe glanced over her shoulder at him. "You were supposed to have returned to Italy by now. If it wasn't for me, you would already be there."

"I was coming back. Even if seeing you every day and not being able to touch you was how it had to be, I was coming back."

Chloe lowered her eyes. "I think you need to make sure."

He placed a finger under her chin, brought her gaze to his. "What are you suggesting?"

"I think you need to go back to Italy, take a good look at that life, and ask yourself if you want to abandon it."

He felt a tiny edge of a knife at the bottom of his throat. "Do you want me to leave?"

She grasped his arms. "No. I also don't want you looking back with regret. Maybe you go and you want us there. Maybe if we're in this forever, it doesn't start here."

The edge of the knife fell away.

"You'd do that? You'd leave your family for me?"

"You *are* my family." Her words were said so quickly and with such conviction.

He lowered his lips to hers and kissed her soundly. She was soft, welcoming, and when he was done, he pulled her close.

"You're right," he whispered. "I do need to go back and fix a few things."

"I know."

"I want you to come."

She shook her head.

He pulled away. "Why?"

"When you're away, I'm going to look at my life. We haven't spent any time alone since Bali to process anything. It might be good for us.

Then we need to decide if we're making these big decisions together forever, or just pretending. I'm not trying to rush you, Dante, I'm not." She stepped back, opened her arms. "We're standing on this yacht talking about a future that I'm not sure is ours together and my head is bouncing. *Yes, no . . . what if.* That's making me crazy. This is your business and your decision unless we are *we* forever. So go back to Italy, take the long, hard look. Fix what needs fixing. Break all the hearts . . ." She offered a soft smile.

"That isn't what I need to remedy." There wasn't anyone in Positano he'd left behind.

Chloe moved close, placed a hand on his chest. "Go back. For us."

"That sounds counterproductive."

"It's not."

The owner of the yacht stood on the dock and cleared his throat.

"Let me talk to this guy. Meet you at the car."

She nodded and walked outside and took the owner's hand as she disembarked. "It really is spectacular," she told him.

Dante watched as she walked away and the owner came on board. "Well, what do you think?"

"I need to make some arrangements. Talk with my business partner. What will it take for you to hold her until I have an answer?"

"Depends on what you're offering."

Chloe disappeared from sight and Dante gave the man his price.

~

"It's good to have you back," Gio said, passing Chloe in the kitchen.

Her hands were full of plates, a smile on her face. "I missed it. Go figure."

The restaurant was stupid busy, the kind of night that left you exhausted and eating the leftovers when the doors closed. A big part of the reason was the date. Valentine's Day brought out all the couples.

Dante had surprised her with a morning breakfast, coffee, and flowers . . . and the bracelet dangling off her wrist. White gold with a simple heart with the date they eloped inscribed on the back.

She gave him a pocket watch set to San Diego time. Inside was a picture of the two of them. It was her way of saying she wanted him to come back. And she did it with a gift and not words.

He'd pressed the gift to his chest and then made love to her so sweetly she wanted to cry. Even though they weren't out like everyone else in Little Italy, dining together and drinking all the wine, they'd made their first Valentine's Day memorable.

"Chloe?" one of the other waiters yelled from across the counter. "Your people on six wanted another bottle of wine."

"On it."

Chloe walked through the restaurant and outside to the patio, dodging the foot traffic of people walking the streets. She was all smiles as she served the food and topped the pasta with even more fresh parmesan that she grated right there onto the dish. "Anything else I can get you?"

Another glass of red, another martini. *Got it.*

She tapped the table that had requested the bottle and said she'd be right out with it.

Table four signaled for their check. *Got it.*

A new table of two was on three . . .

Chloe stepped away from the patio, almost colliding with a man walking down the street. "Sorry," she apologized.

She looked up. "Oh."

"Hi." It was Eric. His gaze moved from her to the building. "I thought for sure you lied about this place, too."

"I'm sorry?"

"Nothing. I texted you. You didn't respond."

She moved to the side. "I thought I made myself clear."

His look was less than believing. "Right. And when did you find the time to meet someone and marry them between New Year's and Valentine's Day?"

"Right, well . . ." Why was she standing there talking to him? She owed him zero explanation. "Doesn't matter. I'm not interested."

She moved left.

He stepped in front of her. "Nice ring."

The hair on her neck stood up. She fisted her left hand, knowing damn well there wasn't a ring on her finger and that his statement suggested he thought she'd lied about being married.

Shoulders back, she angled to the right and pushed past him, ignoring the fact that she had to shove his shoulder to do so.

Only when she was inside the restaurant did she feel the rapid pace of her heart. Once she reached the bar, she dared a look over her shoulders.

Eric was gone.

"Hey, Chloe. You okay?" Sergio reached over the bar, tapped his hand on the space in front of her.

"Yeah." That was the strangest thing ever. "I need . . . ah . . . house cab, a vodka martini, and a bottle of chianti." She moved to the POS system to put the order in while he worked on it.

"Hey?" A deep voice behind her made her jump.

"I told you, I'm not—" She turned, stopped talking. It wasn't Eric.

"Where's the restroom?"

"I'm sorry." She pointed. "Over there, first right."

"Thanks."

It took an hour for her to get back on her game. Eric had screwed up her pace and had her looking over her shoulder most of the night. Finally, the thought of him drifted, and after the last customer was gone and the staff had cleared out, Chloe, Gio, and Luca nearly collapsed in one of the back booths with a single dish and three forks. Mainly because they didn't want to do the dishes.

"It's good to have you back." Luca winked Chloe's way.

She tapped the stack of cash at her side. "I need to replenish my account after Bali."

"Don't struggle," Luca said. "You need something, say something. I know this isn't your dream job."

"I'm okay. I've been talking to Brooke about online marketing and branding. I'm moving forward with a live online studio yoga class with on-demand encores. Free content, paid content."

"Sounds right up your alley," Gio said, then lifted a fork to his lips.

"I met two women in Bali, one lives in Spain, the other Australia . . . we're going to collaborate. Classes in Spanish and Italian. Offer something different. Dante even came up with retreats here in San Diego." She sat back, sipped the half a glass of wine she allowed with her late dinner.

Luca cleared his throat. "How are things working out with you two?"

It was too hard not to tease her older brother, so she didn't even bother trying not to. "You wanna hear about the *boom-chicka-wow-wow*?"

Gio moaned. "Are you sure Mama said we can't *ever* hit her?" he asked Luca.

Chloe chuckled. "Dante and I are great."

Luca and Gio said something to each other with the glance they exchanged.

"What?"

Gio waved at Luca, telling him to speak.

"If things are so great, then why is he leaving Friday?"

"I told him to." She took another bite, set her fork down.

"Why?"

"Because when you love someone, you let them go. If they come back, it's meant to be." She pointed her glass of wine at her brothers. "And if he stays there, you both have to promise me you'll stay out of it." Just thinking that Dante might stay made her want to cry. "It would break me. I know it would. But we promised each other we'd respect the decision if one of us wanted out."

She took a deep breath and tried to keep the moisture locked behind her eyelids. She failed.

"He'll come back," Luca said.

Chloe looked at the bracelet on her wrist. "I hope so."

~

"Shouldn't you be with your wife, celebrating the day of love?"

Dante sat at his mother's table, enjoying her lasagna, while Chloe worked a few blocks away.

"She's working. Said the money is big today and the family always worked holidays so their staff could enjoy it with their families whenever possible."

"You're newlyweds," Rosa countered.

"We newlywedded earlier. Don't worry, Mama."

His mother had the decency to blush with his words. "Things are good, then?"

"They are."

"Then why are you leaving?"

He picked up his fork. "Consider it a business trip."

"Your father had business trips."

He paused, waited for her to look up.

"I'm sorry. You're not him."

"I'm glad you realize this."

She reached out, placed a hand on his arm. "I spoke with Father Gomez last week."

"Mama . . ." Dante instantly thought the conversation was about him and Chloe. There had already been a discussion about how they were not married in the eyes of the church and living together wasn't right. The conversation quickly ended when Chloe pointed out that

Brooke and Luca were living in the same space for months up until their marriage. Technically, Brooke lived in the upstairs apartment of the D'Angelo home, but she never managed to sleep in her own bed.

Rosa shook her head. "I asked him for guidance about your father."

Dante rested his fork on his plate and gave his mother all his attention. "What kind of guidance?"

"Your father. Pretending to be something I'm not is no longer working for me. I see how you and Chloe stumble when people question you. You're married, but not. Do you accept the congratulations?" She lifted the corners of her mouth, dropped them quickly. "I'm married . . ." She shook her head. "But I'm not."

His mother stood and walked a few steps to the living room and brought him a legal folder. Her hands were shaking. "I know this is asking a lot of you, but can you see that your father gets this?"

Dante swallowed hard. He could see the fear in his mother's eyes. "Is this what I think it is?"

She nodded, tears in her eyes.

"Oh, Mama." Dante stood and pulled his mother close.

"You're right. I can't go on like this. I've been so worried about failing you and your sister."

"You're not the one who failed us."

She held him tighter.

He felt her grief and held her through it. "You're going to be fine. You have me and Chloe. Anna and Jackie. We'll see you through this."

"I will." She pulled away, wiped the tears from her eyes. "Your food is getting cold."

"You sit. I'll open some wine." He left the dining room to give her a minute and to collect himself in the process. There were so many thoughts that surfaced, things he needed to say and work through. That would wait until later, when he was with Chloe and he could rant and curse his father for forcing this choice on his mother. For causing her to cry. Again.

For now, he found a bottle of wine, a good year and decent vintage. This was a celebration, not a mourning.

He pulled two glasses from the cupboard, a wine opener . . . and returned to the dining room.

His mother had dried her tears and was sitting with her back rod-straight, a smile in place.

"I'm proud of you," he said.

"Excuse me?" Her surprise was in her wide-eyed expression.

"I know it's reversed, a son being proud of his mother, but I am. This was a hard decision. One Anna and I have been long awaiting." He set the glasses down, started on opening the wine.

"That's the good wine." She half lifted from her chair as if she were going to take the bottle away before he could open it.

"I know. Life is too short to drink bad wine."

She relaxed. "You've been talking to Giovanni."

"Yes, thankfully. It's nice he doesn't hate me anymore."

The cork came free, and he poured.

"He never hated. Confused, upset . . . never hate."

"Tell my jaw that."

His mother laughed. "Well . . ."

She took the glass he offered.

"To new beginnings."

"Yes. New beginnings."

CHAPTER TWENTY-EIGHT

"I have been at this airport more in the last three months than ever in my life," Chloe admitted as they drove into the line on the departing level of San Diego's airport.

"I can beat that. I've spent more on airfare in the past three months than I have in the past three years combined."

Chloe glanced at him from the driver's seat. "Last minute to Bali wasn't cheap, I take it."

He reached out, patted her thigh. "You're worth it, *cara*."

"At least this was half the price because of the miles," she said. He'd accumulated enough frequent flyer miles to offset the price of this ticket, which they were both happy about.

They pulled to the curb and Chloe popped the trunk.

Dante was only taking a small bag with him. Said most of what he'd need was already there.

Chloe stood back as he removed his suitcase and closed the trunk. Her throat started to constrict before he turned to face her.

Dante gave her that soft smile that melted her heart every single time and motioned with his hand. "C'mere."

She choked up as she let him fold her into his arms. "Don't cry," he whispered.

"Too late."

"I'll be back in a week."

He'd shown her the return flight, put it on their kitchen calendar and circled it.

"I know."

"Start looking for apartments. We can't stay in the Airbnb forever."

She looked up. "You're supposed to be going to Italy to soul-search."

He shook his head, lowered his lips to hers, and whispered, "I've found my soul. She's about to kiss me."

Those warm lips kissed her surprised ones.

He pulled away too soon. "Miss you already, *amore mio*."

A tear fell down her cheek. "Text me when you land."

"I will." Another kiss to her forehead and Dante turned, grabbed his suitcase, and walked toward the terminal.

She watched as he walked away.

Airport security walked by and started waving her on. "Miss, you can't stay here."

Chloe rounded the car, jumped back in, and pulled away from the curb. "He's going to come home to me," she said to herself.

She dialed Salena's number before she left the airport circle.

"Are you single and ready to mingle?" Salena asked as she answered the phone.

Chloe laughed. "I'm married but need a girls' night out."

"Even better."

They made arrangements for later that night and Chloe headed back to the condo.

Two hours later, Chloe called an Uber, anticipating a couple of drinks in her future, and headed out to the Gaslamp District to meet her best friend.

She straightened her skirt as she exited the Uber and smiled at the familiar bouncer as she walked to the door.

"I haven't seen you in a while."

"I've been busy. Have you seen Salena?"

He nodded toward the club. "Inside."

She reached for her purse for the cover charge.

He rolled his eyes and pulled back the rope. "Go on."

Yeah, he never charged her. But she always offered.

The club was loud, the music pushed her eardrums to their limits. People dancing between tables, on the dance floor. The bar was two people deep.

Chloe scanned the tops of heads to find Salena.

Sure enough, her friend was at the bar, talking with Tall, Tan, and Blond. Looked like a surfer type.

"Hey, beautiful . . ."

Chloe smiled at the man who tossed the compliment but walked on.

Salena spotted her. "Chloe!" Pushing past Surfer Boy, Salena pulled her into a hug.

"This place is crazy tonight."

"New semester . . . new blood," Salena pointed out.

San Diego was a college town, and the clubs picked up when class was in session.

Surfer Boy cleared his throat.

"Sorry, Chloe, this is Tim."

"Jim."

"Oops, Jim." Salena turned away, opened her eyes wide.

Chloe tried not to laugh. "Nice to meet you, Jim. Are you a local? Going to college here?"

"No and no. Crashing with some friends in OB. On my way to Cabo. Heard about this place."

Temporary, right up Salena's alley.

"You need a drink," Salena told Chloe.

"I do." She turned toward the bar, tried to get the attention of the bartender.

"How did it go today?" Salena asked.

"Weird. Dante left and I felt lost. The place felt empty. Stupid, right?" Chloe yelled the last part.

"You haven't left his side unless you're working since you got back."

Chloe caught the eye of the bartender, who indicated he'd get right to her.

"I know. It's good for me to get out. Him, too."

"You're not worried?"

"About what?"

The bartender asked her what she wanted; she ordered a martini.

"About him coming back."

"Who are we talking about?" Surfer Boy asked.

Salena pointed her drink at Chloe. "Her husband."

"You're married?"

"I found my soul. She's about to kiss me." Dante's words sang in her head. "I am."

"Cool."

The bartender placed her drink on the bar.

Chloe reached for her wallet.

"Women don't buy their own drinks," Surfer Boy said.

"This one does."

They moved away from the bar, found a high-top table filled with empty glasses and no people.

A song came on that Salena wanted to dance to. She tried to get Chloe on the dance floor with her and Jim, but she wasn't about to leave their drinks unattended. A rule they'd come up with the day they turned twenty-one. So far their rule had worked out.

One of the waitresses cleaned off the table, and the second she walked away, a guy walked over, leaned against the table. "Hello."

"Hi." *Oh, boy.*

"You can't possibly be here alone."

She shook her head. "Nope. My friend is right over there." Chloe pointed to the dance floor.

"No boyfriend?"

Another shake of the head.

The guy moved closer.

"My husband is out of town."

His smile fell. "Lucky guy."

Without anything else, the man walked away.

Chloe pulled her phone from her purse to text Dante. He should be landing on the East Coast in a couple of hours, and she wanted him to know she was thinking about him as he flew the final hours to Italy.

Hope your seatmate doesn't snore.

She put her phone away, saw another man walking her way.

"Wanna dance?"

She shook her head.

By the time Salena and Jim returned, Chloe was nearly done with her martini and had been hit on three times.

This wasn't the girls' night out she wanted.

How had the place she'd always gone to for a good time become a place that didn't feel fun anymore?

"Great night, right?" Salena asked.

Chloe smiled. "Yeah."

"You need another drink."

"I'm okay. Actually, I think I'm gonna go."

Salena frowned. "You just got here."

She'd been there an hour and had zero alone time with her friend. "Long day. Let's have lunch. Text me when you have time."

Salena looked up at Jim. "You sure?"

"Yeah. Have fun. I'm really tired."

A quick hug and Chloe worked her way out of the club.

On the street, a line to get into the place had formed. She stepped away from the crowd and clicked her phone for a ride.

Uber was circling and not giving her a reasonable price, so she moved on to Lyft. That ride was cheaper, but five minutes out. Which was crazy considering how many people were mingling on the streets this early in the evening.

Making note of the make, model, and license plate number on the car, Chloe stood on the corner, staring at her phone.

She should have worn a coat. The small excuse for a cover over her shoulders wasn't doing the job, and she was shivering and holding her arms to stay warm.

"Chloe."

She turned. Looked around.

No one was behind her, but she could swear she heard someone call her name.

Shaking her head, she looked at her phone, saw that her ride was a block away.

Toyota Camry . . . silver. It pulled to the curb and she opened the back door.

"Chloe." The voice was louder this time.

She looked up again.

On the opposite side of the street, someone stood there completely still.

She hesitated. When they moved, she pivoted around and folded into the back of the car. "Dalton?" she asked, confirming the name of the driver on the app.

"Chloe?"

"Yeah."

She closed the door and the driver pulled away.

"Enjoying your evening?" he asked.

Chloe turned, looked out the rear window, and could swear someone watched as the car drove away.

"I'd rather be home."

~

"I'm back in Positano," Dante said into his phone to Anna as he walked down the steps to the street where his office with Marco was located. It was early enough in the morning that the streets of Positano were still quiet.

"Oh, no, Dante—"

"No, no." He stopped Anna before she could continue. "Chloe and I are fine, great! I meant to call you before I left. I'll be back in a week and wanted to make sure you and Jackie can come for dinner with the D'Angelos when I do."

"Don't scare me like that." Anna's voice sounded just like their mother's when she was angry.

Dante stopped and watched an elderly couple walk by holding hands, and the corners of his lips lifted. That would be him and Chloe one day. "I love her, Anna."

"Duh."

He laughed.

"I'm here to wrap a few things up. There's something you should know." His voice sobered.

"I'm listening."

"Mama filed for divorce. I'm going to give our father the papers before I leave."

For a moment, Anna was silent. "I'll be damned."

"Surprised me, too."

"You ready to do that . . . be the messenger?"

"Can I deliver it with a fist?"

She scoffed. "You won't hear me telling you to stop."

Their father's abandonment had crippled both of them for quite some time. Yet together, they managed to get back on their feet, Dante with the help of the D'Angelos and Anna with the help of Jackie, her long-term girlfriend. And each other.

"Glad I have your blessing."

"I'm glad Mama is moving on."

"Me too. When he first left, I never thought I'd say that."

"I remember the fighting more than you. I kinda hoped this would happen long before he moved out. I never thought the bastard wouldn't look back, though."

"His loss, Anna. We're pretty awesome," Dante boasted.

"Yes we are, little brother. Yes we are."

He started the last block to his office. "I have to go. I'll call you when it's over."

"Love you."

"Love you, too."

He hung up, tucked the phone into his pocket, and walked through the office doors.

"Dante!" Marco welcomed him with open arms. The hug was brief, a kiss to each cheek, lots of smiles.

"I missed you."

"You've been too busy to miss me."

Not a lie.

Dante looked at the board on the wall, saw that all three boats were out. "A good day."

"Yes. We're picking up. On the weekends anyway. Still slow midweek."

"To be expected."

Marco looked beyond him. "Where is she?"

"Chloe?"

"Yes, your wife. The one you accidentally married. How do you *accidentally* marry anyway?"

Dante laughed. "Martinis and Vegas . . . and bribing the minister to call his friend at the county clerk office. Maybe *coercion* is more accurate than *accidental*."

Marco scowled.

"It worked out, don't worry."

"If it worked, where is she?"

Dante shrugged out of his coat, tossed it over a chair in their small office. "At home finding us an apartment. And I'm here to clear this one out."

His partner sat down and slowly nodded with a smile. "You love her."

Dante leaned into that thought, into the image of her smiling reflection in the mirror as they stood there in the morning, competing for space while brushing their teeth. "I've always loved her."

"Then you need to be with her."

"I know." Dante slapped his hands together, rubbed them. "I hope your wife doesn't mind hosting when we're in town."

"My home is always open to you. You know that."

"And mine to you." Dante pulled out his laptop and moved to the seat next to his partner. "Now, let me show you what I've found in San Diego and go over the plan."

It took a bit of time, but he and Marco hammered out the financials. Dante knew it was asking a lot of Marco to run the Positano end of their business virtually alone for the greater part of the year while he got San Diego up and running. But if the shutdown of 2020 had taught them anything, it was that having business in two different parts of the world was an asset that they'd wished they had then and needed to get going now.

He was on his way back to his apartment to sort and pack when his phone rang with a FaceTime call from Chloe.

His heart lit up. "Good morning, *bella*."

Her hair was up, spandex in place. Not a stitch of makeup to be seen.

Exactly how he loved her the most.

"Am I breaking the rules calling?" she asked.

"Rules? What rules?"

"Giving you time to figure things out."

He pointed at the phone with his free hand as he walked on the edge of the street, avoiding oncoming traffic. "Those are your instructions. I'm here taking care of business."

Her smile was radiant. "Where are you?"

Dante turned so she could see the ocean below. "Walking back to my apartment. If you'd called ten minutes ago, you could have met Marco."

"Another time. How was your flight?"

They talked about airplane food, and noisy seatmates, and when the signal turned spotty, Dante stopped walking and leaned against a railing and just talked.

"I went out with Salena last night," she told him.

"That's good. How is she?"

"Perfectly herself."

That made him laugh.

"It's weird."

"What do you mean?" he asked.

"The whole experience. You walk into a club, a guy hits on you . . ." She wiggled her nose.

"They'd have to be blind not to hit on you."

Chloe rolled her eyes. "I think I know why women learn to knit."

His head fell back with laughter. "I don't see you doing that."

"Maybe if Salena wasn't already zeroed in on a random guy it would have felt different. Either way, it was a one-drink night."

"Doesn't sound like you had a good time."

She shook her head. "I felt . . . I don't know, exposed."

"What do you mean?"

"Nothing." She placed a thin smile on her lips. "I miss you."

"*Cara,* I miss you, too. I'm driving out to my father's tomorrow. Hopefully he's there and I can get this part over with quickly."

"Let me know when you do. I'll go by your mother's. Bring her flowers."

Dante placed a hand under his chin, felt his throat tighten. "She'd love that."

"I'm also going to tell her she should think about dating, so don't give me that all-adoring look."

He laughed, then realized she wasn't joking.

"Aw, damn."

"Your mama's young. She deserves romance."

Dante covered his face. "I can't . . . with that thought."

Chloe started laughing.

"Not funny."

"It's hysterical."

"I think you like getting under my skin."

"Like it? I love it. Better than needling my brothers."

He sighed and touched his phone, wishing it was her. "Have you started looking for our apartment yet?"

"You left yesterday."

"What's taking you so long?" he teased.

"I'll look, but no decisions until you're home."

"Whatever you want, *bella*."

"Said like a man who has already been married for ten years."

He shrugged. "Find the peace from the beginning. Don't argue over silly things."

"No arguments here. I'll just help your mama with her Tinder account—"

"Chloe!"

All she did was laugh.

They talked about everything and nothing, and when it came time to hang up, saying goodbye was hard. Dante blew her a kiss, told her he'd call the next day.

Back in his apartment, he looked at the task he had to accomplish, and the time in which it needed to be done.

He picked up the phone and called his landlord to give his notice.

~

The next morning started early. First stop was Marco's, where Dante picked up his friend's car for the long drive to Bari.

Dante didn't put it past his father to avoid him, so he wasn't about to warn him of his arrival. Getting up long before sunrise and getting out onto the highways to cross from one coast of Italy to the other, Dante filled up on gas and headed east.

The memory of the first time he'd seen his father after he'd left California filled his head.

He'd found him in Naples. Not an easy task with a city that size. To say Joseph Mancuso was shocked to see his son standing at his doorstep would be an understatement.

Dante had dreamed of hauling off and punching the man.

Instead, he all but begged for an explanation.

Which Joseph denied him. *"I'm not leaving Italy until you come home with me."*

"I hope you like it here."

For three months Dante was a plague on his father, shadowing him throughout Naples.

Then one day he simply disappeared again.

Took Dante five months to find him. By then Dante had met Marco and had started their business in Positano. Dante followed his father, learned more about what he did for money, who he worked with . . . where he lived.

Who he slept with.

When he approached him again, he kept it brief, let him know he wasn't going anywhere.

His father moved once more, the last time to Bari, where Dante was headed now.

Unlike the last places Joseph had lived, in this town the man purchased property. Evidence in Dante's mind that he was never returning to the States.

After a stop along the way for coffee and something loaded in sugar, Dante made his way into the outskirts of the city of Bari, where his father lived.

It was still early for a Sunday morning, but some of his neighbors were already moving about the neighborhood.

His father's home was a corner flat that had a building on its east side. The car registered to his father was parked on the street, giving Dante hope the man was home.

Dante parked across the street and sat looking at the building for a long time before he opened the door of the car.

With the large envelope his mother asked him to deliver in his hand, Dante walked to the door. Before he could knock, it opened.

His father looked older, somehow. The lines on his face deeper, his hair grayer.

"I thought that was you." He stepped out the front door, closed it behind him so they were both standing outside.

"Won't even invite me in for a cup of coffee?"

His father shrugged. "If I'd known you were coming—"

"You'd have left town."

He looked behind him at the closed door. "I have company."

Dante rubbed a hand over his jaw, kept himself from saying the words he really wanted to say. "Right. Of course you do. Probably why you're speaking English."

His father tilted his head. "Why are you here, Dante? It's never a social visit."

"Did you want a social visit? I seemed to have lost the invitation. Anna as well. Remember Anna? Your daughter?"

Joseph pushed them away from the door. When he spoke, his voice was lower. "Do you think I don't know what I left behind?"

"Yes. That's exactly what I think."

"I do." He stood taller. "I think of it all the time. It's a life I didn't choose. Not where I wanted to be and not who I wanted to be with."

Dante took a step back. The sting of his father's words hit hard.

"Not you," Joseph said. "Not your sister. I loved you, you know that."

Dante shot him a look so fast his head hurt. "I don't know that. I didn't feel it then and I don't feel it now."

His father closed his lips, stood tall. "I still provide for your mother. I take care of my responsibilities."

"Your children finish high school and you're done? That's it? What do I tell my children about their grandfather? What does Anna tell hers?"

He scoffed. "Anna won't—"

"You know nothing about my sister."

"I did what I needed to do."

Dante felt his hands clench into fists. "And that's all that matters to you. Taking care of the bottom line."

"If I hadn't, Rosa would have been an unwed mother. Where would that have left her?"

Every muscle in Dante's body tensed. He knew the truth, but hearing his father say it made him want to introduce his fist to the man's face.

Dante took a step forward to threaten to do just that when the door behind his father opened.

They both turned, and a small voice came from inside.

"Papà, chi è questo?" A boy, not more than four or five, stood staring at Dante, asking who he was.

Joseph shooed the child away and closed the door.

Papa?

Jesus.

"Dante . . ."

"You didn't fuck up enough with your first family so you had to do it again?"

"It's different."

Dante was in his face, this time he spoke in Italian. "Does she know you're married?"

Joseph pushed him away from the door, lowered his voice. "Stop. Enough."

"She doesn't, does she?" Dante turned around, ran a hand through his hair. He looked at the papers in his hand. Thought about how hard his father had worked at staying away from him and his sister . . . his family. "You married her here," he said almost under his breath.

"Shhh." Joseph moved him farther from the house, his voice a hoarse whisper. "People believe we're married, but we're not."

Dante didn't trust a word his father said. It didn't matter. None of it mattered.

He thrust the envelope into his father's arms with enough force to push the man back a few feet. "You sign these papers and make everything easy for Mama. Don't miss one payment. Just because she's releasing you doesn't mean you're off the hook." Dante looked over his father's shoulder, saw the curtains inside the house fall back in place. "Don't make me come back here."

With one last look in his father's eyes, Dante turned, crossed the street, and got in the car. Without so much as a backward glance, he drove away at the same time the bells of the cathedral started to chime.

CHAPTER TWENTY-NINE

The first text happened on Sunday night.

A random text that looked like a wrong number.

I really want to meet you, call me back.

Chloe saw the text late after her shift at work and ignored it.

The next morning, the same person texted again; this time he gave his name, acted like he knew her, so she texted back. You have the wrong number.

He apologized and that was that.

Tuesday was a whole different shit show . . .

There were eight text messages from eight different numbers, all saying virtually the same thing.

Hey sexy.

Hey beautiful.

Let's meet.

They all gave their name, all acted like they knew her.

In the middle of the lunch rush, when her phone had buzzed for what felt like the hundredth time with a duplicate text, she turned off her phone and walked into the office to leave her phone there.

Luca was behind the desk, working. "You look mad."

She waved her phone in the air. "I have a feeling someone put my number on a bathroom wall with the words *for a good time call.*"

"What?"

She dropped the phone in her purse. "Nothing."

Three hours later, she handed off her last table and retrieved her purse.

Gio rounded the corner, stuck his head in the door when he noticed her. "Dante just called me, said he's trying to call you but your box is full."

Chloe dug her phone out of her purse, turned it on.

There, next to her green message app, was a red dot with twenty messages, and next to her phone app was another red dot with ten messages. "What the—"

The annoyance factor pushed a little farther back, and something else started to settle in.

Gio walked into the office and looked over her shoulder as she scowled at the messages.

"What's all that?"

Messages, some with pictures. All the same vibes. "What does it look like?"

"Looks like you're on a dating app."

"If someone's punking me, this isn't funny." Chloe opened her voice mail and pressed play on the first message.

"It's Rob. Thanks for giving me your number. Does Friday sound good? Call me."

"Who is Rob?" Gio asked.

"How the hell do I know?"

The next message, same idea, different voice, different name.

They even used her first name.

"Someone is catfishing using your name and phone number."

Chloe started deleting the calls without listening to them.

"Who would do that?"

"No idea."

The phone rang in her hand. Unknown number in San Bernardino came up. "Damn it."

Gio pulled the phone from her hand before she could send it to voice mail.

"Hello?" He answered it on speaker.

"Ah . . . Sorry, I think I have the wrong number."

Gio looked at her. "Are you calling for Chloe?"

"Yeah."

"Uhm, well. Someone is catfishing you and using my number. I've been getting calls all day."

"What the fuck?"

"I know. Dude, what app are you using?"

"Tinder."

Chloe rolled her eyes.

"Do me a favor and report the page. I've asked my friends . . . thought they were pranking me, but someone's just being a dick."

"No problem."

Gio hung up, handed her phone back. "Have you ever used Tinder?"

"Gross." Everyone knew that one was just for hookups.

"Instead of deleting all those messages, you might respond to a few, tell them your name is Bob, and ask them to report your page, get it pulled down faster."

Another text message buzzed through.

Chloe growled.

Gio grabbed her phone again, took a selfie with a stupid grin. "Send them my pic. They'll leave you alone."

"Thanks."

He pushed away from the desk, moved toward the door. "Call Dante."

Chloe waited until she was backing out of the parking space to call.

It was late in Italy, and Dante sounded tired. "Did I wake you?"

"No. I just sat down and kicked my feet up."

"How did today go?"

He told her about his efforts to sell or otherwise get rid of the furniture in his apartment and the packing of what he was having shipped to San Diego. Not a lot, according to him.

Marco agreed to hold on to his scooter, using it when needed, of course, and a handful of other things. But the rest had to go.

All of which told Chloe that Dante was in fact coming home for good.

Her phone buzzed three times on the short ride to the condo, and Dante commented.

"You're in demand today."

"It's all crap. Someone used my phone number on Tinder and my phone is blowing up."

"Holy crap."

"I know. That's why your message didn't come through. Gio intercepted a call, and I'm using his picture to try and get these guys to report the page."

"I hate those damn apps."

She pulled into the parking lot of the condo, turned off the engine. "That's reason enough to stay married right there," she teased.

He laughed. "You're right. That's it, my mind's all made up."

Chloe giggled, moved the call from the car audio to her phone, and opened the door. "How are you feeling about your dad today?" The information about the fake wife and new brother had been an all-night discussion. She wished she'd been there to comfort him. Even though Dante held himself together, seeing a parent replace you couldn't be easy.

"To tell the truth, I'm trying not to think about it."

"And I'm bringing it up. I'm sorry." She hiked her purse on her shoulder, kept her keys in her hand.

"No, *cara*. I want to talk about it with you when I'm home."

She heard a horn in the street behind her and turned toward the noise. "You still think you'll get everything done by Friday?"

"By Thursday night. Staying at Marco's. He's taking me to the airport on Friday."

Chloe turned back toward the stairs and walked the final steps to their condo.

"You really are coming back."

"You can't get rid of me."

Chloe opened the door and felt cold air on her back.

She turned.

Nothing.

"I can't wait to see you."

~

Wednesday made Tuesday look like a cakewalk.

Chloe woke up to dick pics. And not just the *Hey, baby, don't you want this?* but video shit that belonged on a porn site.

She showed up at her family home and gathered with Luca, Brooke, and Gio in Gio's rooms. She gave Gio full access to her phone, and within an hour, he determined that whoever was behind this had her number on no less than three dating apps, including Grindr and Adult Friend Finder.

"At what point does this become criminal?" Brooke asked.

Luca had a laptop open and was looking up options. "When a crime is committed."

"Harassment?" Chloe asked.

Gio, nose first in the phone, spoke up. "Nope. These guys are responding to a number given to them. Not all of them are calling you Chloe anymore."

"Which means?"

"Whoever is doing this is getting shut down and opening them back up. Whoever it is has a shit ton of time on their hands."

"I have a solution," Brooke said. "You're not going to like it."

Everyone looked at her.

"Change your number."

Chloe winced. "Or I just turn off my phone for a while. Get a temporary one until whoever is doing this gets bored."

Gio was texting into her phone. "I like that idea."

"And if it starts up again?" Luca asked.

"No brainer, then . . . new number." Chloe wasn't about to continue dodging spam for the rest of her days.

"I don't like any of this," Luca said, pushing away the laptop. "Nothing you can do other than report the profiles."

"People suck."

"They do," Brooke agreed.

"Awh, fuck," Gio exclaimed.

"What is it?"

He held her phone from his eyes, closed them, and handed it to her. "Please tell me that's not you."

Chloe snatched the phone from his hands, looked at the screen.

It was her face . . . on someone else's naked body. "I wish my boobs were that big."

Luca leaned over.

Gio yelled, "Don't." But it was too late.

"No."

"It's not me!" Chloe kept looking at the picture.

"None of this is okay." Luca stood and started to pace.

"That picture . . . of my face, I think it's from last year."

"Was it posted on Instagram?" Gio asked.

"I think so."

"I don't like the timing of this. Dante's out of town. You're by yourself. I think you need to come home until Dante's back." Luca squared his shoulders, looked directly at her.

"Are you expecting an argument? I didn't sleep last night. My phone doesn't stop buzzing and I keep looking over my shoulder."

"You think someone's watching you?" Brooke asked.

"No." Chloe handed the phone back to Gio, who wiggled his fingers, asking for it. "I'm just freaked out."

Gio dialed a number on her phone, put it on speaker.

"Cara, buongiorno," Dante's voice sang over the line.

"Awahhh, I didn't think you cared so much," Gio teased.

"Giovanni, what are you doing with Chloe's phone?" Dante laughed.

"He's being a butt. You're on speaker," Chloe told him.

"Is there a party?"

"No," Luca told him. "There's a problem that you need to know about."

"I already told him about the calls," Chloe said.

"What about the naked pictures?" Gio asked.

"Naked pictures? What are you talking about?" Dante asked.

"They're not me," Chloe clarified.

"Whoever is behind this game of catfish has photoshopped Chloe's face on explicit pictures."

Dante said a few choice words in Italian. When he started talking about arranging an earlier flight, Chloe interrupted. "Dante, back up. We've spent enough money on last-minute travel changes. I'm staying at Mama's until you're back. I'll pick you up at the airport on Friday. I'll go get a temporary phone and load it with data and see if this blows over. If not, I'll just change my number."

"And I'll hold on to Chloe's phone and try and get these sites to pull down her profiles," Gio said.

"As soon as I have my new number, I'll call you," Chloe told him.

"I don't like this."

"None of us do. But you needed to know," Luca told Dante.

"You sure you have it?" Dante asked.

Gio and Luca answered together. "Yes."

"Chloe, a word in private?" Dante asked.

She picked up the phone, took it off speaker, and walked out the sliding door and onto the rooftop terrace. "I'm fine."

"You are. I'm not."

"Other than my phone being out of commission, nothing has happened."

"I'd feel better if I was there."

"You'll be on a plane in what, forty-eight hours?" Give or take. "I didn't think I had any pissed-off exes. This whole thing is baffling."

"What about that Eric guy?"

She shrugged. "We had coffee and less than a half an hour on New Year's Eve. Besides, he is a father of two with a full-time job. We all think this is someone who is sitting at home with nothing better to do than make someone else's life miserable."

"I'm going to find out who this is and beat the shit out of them."

Part of her liked the thought of a man sticking up for her . . . the other part . . . "Great, we'll go from spending money on plane tickets to posting bail."

"Cara . . ."

"Seriously, Dante. This is a stupid prank gone too far. It will blow over in no time."

She heard him sigh. "I want to reach through this line and touch you."

"That would be a cool trick."

"Chloe . . ."

She cradled the phone, the chill in the air had her moving side to side. "Yeah?"

"I love you."

Every muscle in her body paused. "What?"

The phone buzzed.

"It's me. Put me on FaceTime."

Chloe moved farther from her brother's sliding door, pressed the FaceTime button, and saw Dante on the screen. He was standing in his apartment, his eyes stared into the phone. His lips smiling. "I love you."

She was going to cry.

"I love you, too."

He rubbed his chin. "Be extra careful until I'm home."

"Only until you're home?"

"We'll find who is behind this and make it stop."

She nodded. "Try not to worry. I'll be here and working. Surrounded by people."

"Make sure it stays that way."

"Yes, Mr. Mancuso."

"Be safe, Mrs. Mancuso."

Yeah, she was getting seriously addicted to hearing that name.

He blew her a kiss and hung up the call.

Chloe hugged the phone to her chest and walked back in the room.

Everyone was looking at her.

"What?"

"Nothing."

~

Marco walked with Dante into the terminal. After paying a small fortune for extra and overweight bags, it was time for farewells.

And they were harder than Dante expected.

Dante pulled the older man into his arms, held him tight.

"I will miss you."

"I'll be back before you know it," Dante told him.

"You will, but not to stay. Unless I can convince your bride to fall in love with Positano."

Dante pulled away from Marco's hug, kept his hands on his shoulders. "You've been a father to me. More than mine ever was."

"His loss, my gain. Go to San Diego and make us lots of money."

Marco knew it would take time for lots of anything to be made. But he pushed Dante to make the jump anyway. "If you need me, you call me."

"I will. I'm a proud man. Not stupid."

Another hug, a kiss to both cheeks.

Marco pulled away, moisture in his eyes.

Without more to say, Dante said goodbye and moved toward security.

Once he was at his gate, he texted Chloe to tell her he was on his way home.

There was closure on this lap.

Yes, he'd be back. But it would never be as it was.

Italy had always been a place he'd gone to in order to escape his reality somehow. And now, he wanted nothing more than to face it.

With his wife.

He had so much to say that started with *I love you* and ended in *forever*.

Not even his father and all of that ugly could darken the light she brought to his life.

Chloe called at the same time his section of the plane was asked to board. *"Cara."*

"You're at the airport?"

"Boarding now."

"I won't keep you, then."

"Has it gotten better?"

"Not really. We turned off my phone. This one sucks, but it makes calls."

Dante wedged the phone between his shoulder and his ear. "Hold on." He handed the attendant his passport and ticket. *"Grazie."*

"Prego."

"Listen, I have a lot of extra luggage. Maybe I should just hire an Uber to the condo. Your car won't hold it all."

"I can use . . . car . . ."

"*Cara?* What did you say?"

"Luca's car."

"You want to use Luca's car?"

The phone sounded as if it were going through a tunnel. "Are you driving?" he asked.

". . . Dante?"

The connection was awful. He wasn't sure if it was their connection or the fact that he was in a tube walking onto an airplane.

The line went dead.

Once he'd managed to stow his bag and take his seat, he texted her number and said he'd try and call from his first stop. Which was London. The next layover would be Texas, and then he'd be in San Diego.

He could hardly wait.

~

"I'll be fine. Dante will be here in a couple of hours."

"I'll come with you to pick him up," Luca said from the kitchen.

Chloe looked at the second chef, and then the interior of the restaurant. It was already packed.

"I have to buy groceries, then drop them off before picking him up."

"Chloe!"

"Did it dawn on you that I might want to surprise my husband with a special something when he gets home?" she pointed out.

Luca squeezed his eyes shut. "Why do you do that?"

Tony chuckled.

"You're busy. Man the battle station, brother. I'm all good. We'll bring your car back in the morning." She turned to leave.

"Have Dante call when you let him up for air."

She winked before walking out the back door. She'd already put her go bag in the car, the one she'd packed for the nights she'd stayed in her room at her mother's.

It was twilight, and the air was still warm from the day. Chloe was looking forward to summer.

First stop was a grocery store, where she filled up with meals for a few days, strawberries . . . she added whipped cream to the cart. She'd forgotten to grab wine from the restaurant, where they purchased it at a much better price, so she found a decent bottle and added that, too.

Dante would be tired, she knew . . .

But not too tired.

All the way home she planned the night. Or at least the welcome home.

The parking lot of the condo was quiet, as always. Luca's car, since it was larger than hers, required her to park farther away from her normal spot.

She juggled her bag and two of the grocery bags before conceding to the fact it was going to take two trips to get everything inside.

At the door, she set the bag down, put the key in the lock, and heard a click.

She twisted, glanced behind her.

Nothing.

Chloe pushed inside and kicked the door closed.

Everything was just as she'd left it two days before.

Leaving the bags on the counter, she hopped down the stairs, out to the car, and grabbed the rest of the bags.

Somewhere a dog barked, and she quickened her steps.

Once inside, she twisted the lock on the door and put everything away.

A check of the time. She had an hour.

A song she'd heard earlier in the day stuck in her head, and she hummed it as she walked into the bedroom.

Something flickered out of the corner of her eye and made her cry out.

She jumped, felt her heart in her throat.

It moved again, waving in the wind.

Chloe moved to the window and blew out a breath. Someone had put a flag on the pole outside, and a light shining up at it was casting a shadow on the bedroom wall.

"Get a grip." The second the bedroom light was on, all the monsters scattered.

After finding the outfit she wanted to surprise Dante with, she placed her hair on top of her head and slowly shed her clothing.

She took a quick shower and set a fresh towel out for her husband.

Forty minutes later, Chloe ran a hand down the front of the red dress she'd worn the night they'd gotten married in Vegas.

"The man would have to be half-dead not to react to this," she said to herself.

She put on the same long coat, the same shoes. Overkill for an airport pickup . . .

And perfect at the same time.

Yup, they'd be talking about this night for years to come.

Chloe grabbed her purse and keys and headed for the door.

With car keys in her hand, her quick strides across the lot weren't accompanied by any shadows or dogs barking.

Four yards to the car, she heard two doors open on a truck parked close to hers and saw two men get out.

Chin high, she kept walking.

"Hello!"

She hesitated but didn't look.

"You even dressed up for us. Look at you."

Two yards.

She didn't stop.

"Chloe?"

Her head snapped, feet shuffled.

Her heart was so loud and so fast she could hear it in her ears.

One was tall, a bit lanky, Caucasian, the other was shorter, bulkier; she couldn't quite make out his ethnicity.

"You have me mixed up with someone else."

They looked at each other. "Oh no we don't." The one talking was the white guy, scruffy beard.

They walked closer.

She took a step back.

"You do. I'm not who you think I am."

Beard Guy looked at his friend. "She said she likes to play the victim."

Chloe looked around. Dark parking lot. No one was out there.

"I'm not that girl. Someone is—"

Bulky Guy moved behind her, slowly.

"Stop," she said, more to herself than to them. From the look in their eyes, stopping wasn't what they wanted to do.

If she tried to get into the car, they'd stop her.

Best chance she had was to run toward the condo and scream.

She threw her purse at the man closest to her and took off running.

"Fuck yeah."

Panic hit her hard when a dozen steps in her high heels had her tumbling to the ground. She hardly felt the sting when beefy arms grabbed her waist and picked her completely off the ground and started carrying her toward the truck.

She started to scream.

A hand smashed over her mouth. "Bitch, you'll get us all in trouble."

Chloe thrashed against the man. Elbows, feet . . . fingernails.

That's when she heard someone else.

"What the fuck! Let her go."

The arms around her let loose and Chloe fell to the asphalt. Knees hit the surface a second time.

A third man, tall, took a punch to the face from the bearded guy, but came up swinging.

He took a punch in the gut before Lanky Guy pulled Beefy Guy away. "This ain't fucking worth it, man."

The two of them jumped into the truck and tore out of the parking lot.

Oh, God.

Oh, God . . .

Chloe started to shake.

"Are you okay?"

She shook her head no, then yes.

The man who saved her from God only knew what walked closer.

"We should call the . . . Eric?"

He knelt down by her side, his lip bleeding from the punch to the face.

She scurried back on the ground; fear raced up her spine.

Eric held his hands in the air. "I got a message from you."

"I didn't . . ."

"On Tinder. I matched you. You said you wanted to meet, gave me this address."

She shook her head. "It wasn't me."

"Jesus, you're scared. I'll call 911. Okay. Get the police here. Get you inside. You're freezing."

And shaking.

Eric stood and backed up several feet, pulled his phone out. He placed it to his ear. "Hi, yes. There's a woman here who was attacked. Two men, driving a truck. No, she's okay. Scraped up a bit." He covered the receiver. "Do you need an ambulance?"

She needed Dante.

Where was her purse?

"No, I think . . . okay. I'll be okay . . ."

Chloe tested out her legs, which worked, saw the blood on her knees, the scrapes on her palms where she went down the first time. One ankle didn't like the weight she put on it.

She took off her shoes and limped toward her purse.

Eric hung up his call and grabbed her purse before she could.

As he did, everything inside fell out.

The phone didn't take a liking to the asphalt any better than she did.

Eric picked it up and handed it to her. "I think the truck ran over it."

She took another step and felt that ankle again.

"Let me help you," he pleaded.

She nodded and accepted his arm.

Slowly, they walked to the condo and waited for the police.

~

Dante called Chloe's temporary number the moment the plane landed.

It went directly to voice mail.

He sent a text.

The people on the plane took their time getting off the damn thing.

Sleep deprived and in need of a shower, he was wide awake and ready for the arms of his wife.

As he descended the escalator into the baggage claim area, he searched the people waiting for passengers and came up empty.

The flight was fifteen minutes early, so maybe she didn't watch the flight and wasn't aware. He tried calling again.

Nothing.

Twenty minutes later he stood with all of his bags bundled on a rolling cart outside the terminal, his attention on his watch.

Did she think he was going to hire an Uber?

They were definitely going to get this phone thing figured out in the morning.

He waited ten more minutes before crossing the street and ordering an extra-large Uber.

~

Eric offered to carry her up the stairs, but a voice in her head screamed the word *no*.

Inside the condo, he assisted her to the sofa and helped himself to the kitchen, where he wet a couple of paper towels and handed them over.

"Do you know who those guys were?" he asked once she was settled.

"No."

He placed his fingers on her swelling right ankle.

Chloe flinched.

"Maybe some ice would help." He moved back to the kitchen.

Everything in her was still shaking.

The door to the condo was closed.

"We should keep the door open, for when the police come."

"It's cold out there."

Chloe pulled her coat closer to her frame. The dress that had been a great idea for Dante felt like she was wearing lingerie now.

He opened a few drawers until he found a plastic bag and then opened the freezer and filled it with ice.

Back in front of her, he sat on the edge of the coffee table and gently placed the ice on her ankle.

Chloe held perfectly still.

Eric's hands shook.

"Shouldn't the police be here by now?"

He shrugged. "They'll get here."

His eyes moved from her ankle to her leg, up to her knee where she was holding the paper towel.

"Let me."

"It's okay. Just a scrape."

His eyes found hers.

Eyes that had pupils so tiny it was amazing he could see out of them.

"I need to use your phone," she told him.

"Why?" He tilted his head. "You're okay."

"I need to call my husband."

Eric huffed.

Looked around and laughed.

~

"Hey, Gio."

"Are you back?"

"I am. Climbing into an Uber as we speak." Dante sat next to one of his bags, the entire back of the SUV filled with his others.

"Uber? Where is Chloe?"

"Good question. She isn't answering her phone."

"That damn thing is a piece of shit."

"I thought she was picking me up. Maybe we got our messages mixed."

"Hold on."

Dante heard Gio calling out to his brother. "It's Dante. Said he's in an Uber. Didn't Chloe take your car so she could pick him up?"

Gio came back on the line. "She has Luca's car."

"My plane landed half an hour ago."

"I'll meet you at the condo," Gio said.

Dante hung up, looked at the driver. "I think my wife might be in trouble. Can you . . . ?"

"Yeah?" The guy looked at him through the rearview mirror.

"Yeah."

Dante clicked his seat belt, and the driver took off.

~

Eric kept laughing, "Still with that?"

"I was on the way to the airport to pick him up."

Eric moved quickly. Lifted the end of her coat and flipped it open. "Dressed like that? I don't think so."

Chloe quickly covered herself. "You're scaring me."

"Why do women lie? You all fucking lie. All of you."

His eyes darted from side to side.

He was either on drugs or needed to be on drugs. Either way, something was desperately wrong with the man. The front door was a few yards away, the bedroom behind them.

"I'm not lying. If you look in the bedroom, you'll see my husband's clothing."

His beady-eyed gaze found hers again. "Why did you date me if you were married?"

"I . . . ah, uhm. We were not—"

Eric's hand moved to the ice covering her ankle.

"What? Not fucking at the time?" His hand tightened on the ice.

Her back teeth clenched but she didn't cry out.

"You need to leave," she told him.

He shook his head once. "I don't think so."

"He'll be here any minute."

Eric smiled larger than life. "Oh, good." His hand squeezed her ankle.

She winced.

"He can see us going at it and know what kind of woman you really are."

There was no time to react.

Eric pinned her to the back of the sofa, a hand covering her mouth, his knee thrust between her thighs.

Like before in the parking lot, she used every part of her body in an effort to get him off of her. Only this time she was already under him and he was pulling at her clothes, what little barriers they presented, and then started yanking at his own.

One of her arms was pinned under her, the other smashed against the side of his face, but it did nothing to stop him.

She heard a zipper.

Panic and terror threatened to take over.

Her free hand searched for something, anything . . .

A stiletto.

She pulled back and let loose.

His hand slid away, and she screamed at the top of her lungs.

~

The Uber and Gio on his motorcycle pulled into the parking lot at the same time.

Dante got out, looked around.

"That's the car, right?" Dante asked, pointing to the far end of the lot.

"Yeah."

"She has to be here, then."

The driver killed the engine, opened the back, and started pulling suitcases.

"I'll just go check—"

They heard the scream.

Dante's blood turned cold and they both bolted up the stairs.

Dante tried the door.

It was locked.

Chloe screamed again. This time, "Help!"

He put his shoulder into the door, and it gave way.

There was a man crawling on the floor, and Chloe was kicking him away.

Rage, so hot, so blinding, came out in a war cry.

Dante pulled the man to his feet; a fist went back, and he kept whaling.

They both fell to the floor; a lamp went down beside them.

The man reached for Dante's throat but never made it.

Dante couldn't tell what exactly happened, only that Gio finally pulled him off.

Dante stared at the man, dared him to get up.

Chloe's sniffle brought his rage in check.

He was on his knees and at her side in a heartbeat. "*Cara*?"

"I'm okay."

Dante pointed to Gio. "Call an ambulance."

The phone was already to his ear.

Chloe crawled into his arms. "I'm okay."

Dante folded her into his arms and rocked. "I've got you."

~

Mari held Chloe's hand on one side while Dante stood by her other.

The emergency room buzzed with activity. Someone had cleaned up the scrapes on her knees and scrubbed the asphalt from the parking lot out of the palms of her hands. They were waiting on the results from the ankle X-rays and talking to the police.

Chloe had already told them her story, starting with when she met Eric and ending with his attack. She knew, deep down, she wouldn't be able to sleep alone for weeks.

Watching the way Dante paced the room, he wouldn't either.

"There wasn't a call to 911," Officer Meyer told her. "There is a witness at your complex that has given a statement corroborating your story in the parking lot."

"That's a good thing, right?" Mari asked.

Officer Meyer nodded. "Seems cut-and-dry to me, ma'am. But since we can't get Mr. Fulton's statement right now, I won't say how this will go."

"He attacked her." Dante's voice was stone-cold.

"And the heel end of Mrs. Mancuso's stiletto landed him in surgery the minute he arrived here."

Chloe squeezed her mother's hand.

Dante's jaw tightened when Officer Meyer's cell phone rang.

"Excuse me," the officer said as he stepped away to take the call.

"I defended myself."

"They will figure that out, *cara*." Only Dante didn't look completely convinced.

The doctor walked in. "Good news. You're not broken."

Not physically, Chloe thought.

He pulled back the sheet covering her ankle and poked around, causing her to wince. "The bad news is, sprains like this can take just as long to heal sometimes. I'm going to put you in an air cast, something you can remove to shower. Crutches, because putting weight on this for the next couple of weeks is going to slow the healing process."

"I'm a yoga instructor."

The doctor smiled. "Great. Not this week. Or maybe even this month. I want you to follow up with orthopedic, especially if you aren't slowly returning to normal. Most people leave here and ignore my follow-up suggestions."

"I'll make sure she's seen by an orthopedic doctor," Dante said.

"And a counselor," he said, looking directly at Chloe. "The bruises and sprains will fade, but what happened to you tonight may take longer to go away."

Dante moved closer, placed a hand on her shoulder. "We'll find someone tomorrow."

"Thank you, Doctor."

As the doctor left, Officer Meyer returned, with a nurse following him.

The medication Chloe had been given for the pain in her leg was making her sleepy, and now that she knew she was going to be fine, all she wanted to do was crawl into bed and collapse.

"Looks like Mr. Fulton's phone was filled with dating sites and pictures of you. There are officers at his home now, another talking with his ex-wife. We will know a lot more in the next twenty-four hours."

"What do you need from us?" Dante asked.

"I have your statements. I'll need you to come into the station to sign them when you're able. The sooner, the better."

Dante stepped forward, extended a hand. "Thank you, Officer."

"Good thing you showed up when you did."

"Wish I had showed up earlier."

Officer Meyer shook his head. "Be thankful your friend pulled you off of him. He'd have been dead if it were my wife."

Chloe felt her mother patting her hand.

Officer Meyer left again and they all sighed.

Dante leaned over, kissed the top of Chloe's head. "Almost done, *amore*."

The nurse smiled as she approached. "Have you ever used crutches before?"

EPILOGUE

"I'm living with my mother again," Gio bitched.

"It's temporary," Dante said, patting him on the back.

Chloe sat on the terrace with her family just over a week after Dante returned and her life was forever changed.

As Chloe and everyone in the family guessed, it was Eric behind the crap with the dating apps. The authorities found all the messages on his phone and his computer. He hadn't even tried to hide it. Apparently, right after the New Year, his ex-wife had taken custody of his boys, and something happened with his work and he'd been laid off.

Chloe still wasn't sure how he'd known she was home the night it all happened. The running theory was that he'd followed her.

But he wasn't talking, and his lawyer wasn't either.

So here she was now, nine days later, surrounded by people who loved her, having Sunday dinner on the terrace of her family home.

She and Dante had given up the condo and were staying in the upper apartment of the building, the space Gio and Dante were discussing currently, until she was ready to face the world again.

"You can always stay with me," Rosa said from the lounge chair she reclined on.

"A bedroom next door from my mother versus an apartment two floors from Chloe's," Dante said, motioning both hands in the air, one tilted higher than the other.

Luca, her mother, and Franny arrived with the food.

Anna and Jackie had joined them, a welcome addition to their Sunday dinners.

Chloe started to get up. "I can help."

"You sit down," Dante scolded. "The doctor said three weeks."

"It's sprained, not broken."

"Let him take care of you. It won't last forever, trust me," Rosa said.

Franny ran around the table, putting napkins on the plates.

"I think we're ready," Mari announced.

Chloe scooted to the edge of her lounge chair, but before she could stand up, Dante was there helping her up. "My human crutch."

"That's me."

She hobbled to the table and he pulled out her chair.

Gio rapped a spoon to his wineglass, and everyone stopped chatting.

Chloe looked at her brother, who sat there in complete silence.

"Did you want to offer a toast, Gio?" their mother asked.

Gio shook his head. "No. Just wanted everyone to be quiet for a minute."

Chloe rolled her eyes and sat down.

Then realized that Dante was down on one knee in front of her.

"Oh my," someone said behind her.

Dante's eyes captured hers.

He held a box in one hand and reached for one of hers with the other.

Tears were already filling her eyes.

"Chloe D'Angelo Mancuso. The girl next door that I swore I would never . . . but I broke all the rules to. I have loved you my whole life. And I will love you for the rest of it. I never needed this time to figure out if we should be together. You were never a *maybe*. I knew you were an *always* from the moment I grabbed this hand and said the first 'I do.' I want to be your everything for as long as there is breath in my body. Please tell me you'll stay married to me?"

Chloe wiped the tears with the back of her hand, nodding. "I love you so much."

He leaned forward.

She reached for his kiss.

Someone started clapping.

While the family cheered, Dante pulled her close, and she whispered in his ear, "You were never a *maybe* either."

He placed a hand on her cheek. "We're going to be okay."

"Better than okay."

She thrust her left hand in front of him. "This one isn't going to turn my finger green, is it?"

He laughed and opened the box.

A square-cut solitaire, simple, elegant, and exactly her taste. "Oh, Dante, it's beautiful."

"A little birdie told me what you liked." He nodded toward the other end of the table.

Brooke smiled with a shrug.

He slid the ring on her finger and kissed her again.

"Well done, little brother," Anna said from across the table.

"Does this mean I get to be a flower girl again?" Franny asked.

Chloe said, "No."

Mari said, "Yes."

"Mama. We're already married."

Her mother stared her down. "Not in the church you're not. Not another word. Let's eat before it gets cold."

Dante took his seat.

Chloe sat staring at the ring on her finger and then up at the man who put it there.

"I think a summer wedding," Rosa said.

"Absolutely. Gives us plenty of time."

Gio leaned across the table and said, "And so it begins."

ACKNOWLEDGMENTS

As always, thank you to everyone on the Amazon Montlake team. Your dedication to all things Bybee never disappoints. Maria Gomez, thanks for always believing in my work, and Holly Ingraham for making my work sparkle just a little more than it would without you.

Thank you to my agent and friend, Jane Dystel, for over a decade of representing me and my work. We've come a long way, baby! Let's see what the next ten years bring us.

To all those ladies that one night, during that one conference in Vegas, where we all vowed to never tell. An unforgettable evening! All the names here have been changed to protect the guilty . . . I mean innocent.

Now to Kimberly:

If it wasn't for you, I wouldn't know half of what I do about the act of performing a marriage ceremony. I still can't believe you talked me into officiating your wedding. In your own words, though, "The only RN at Glendale Memorial's ER with a bigger mouth than you was me." Hon, I consider that a compliment. Your compassion and dedication to your patients and advocacy for your fellow staff always came through. I'm proud to have worked with you, and even more honored to be your friend. May you and James live a long and happy life together.

Love you, lady.
Minister Catherine

ABOUT THE AUTHOR

Photo © 2015 Julianne Gentry

New York Times, *Wall Street Journal*, and *USA Today* bestselling author Catherine Bybee has written thirty-eight books that have collectively sold more than ten million copies and have been translated into more than twenty languages. Raised in Washington State, Bybee moved to Southern California in the hope of becoming a movie star. After growing bored with waiting tables, she returned to school and became a registered nurse, spending most of her career in urban emergency rooms. She now writes full time and has penned the Not Quite series, the Weekday Brides series, the Most Likely To series, and the First Wives series.